WRITING THE RAKE

THE BLUESTOCKING SCANDALS BOOK
BOOK FIVE

ELLIE ST. CLAIR

Facebook: Ellie St. Clair

Cover by AJF Designs

Do you love historical romance? Receive access to a free ebook, as well as exclusive content such as giveaways, contests, freebies and advance notice of pre-orders through my mailing list!

Sign up here!

Also By Ellie St. Clair

The Bluestocking Scandals
Designs on a Duke
Inventing the Viscount
Discovering the Baron
The Valet Experiment
Writing the Rake
Risking the Detective
A Noble Excavation
A Gentleman of Mystery

The Bluestocking Scandals Box Set: Books 1-4
The Bluestocking Scandals Box Set: Books 5-8

For a full list of all of Ellie's books, please see
www.elliestclair.com/books.

PROLOGUE

LONDON, 1823

"Come here."

"No!" she giggled as she ran just out of his grasp, along the path of the lush gardens that backed Wyndham House, a centerpiece of Mayfair.

Alice and Benjamin had been playing this game for months — a back-and-forth that had started as a fun flirtation but was now becoming a slow smoldering fire that begged to burn something fierce.

Alice had slipped away from the dance and Benjamin had followed. A few words had led to a few touches, and now she was running away from him, a literal game of chase.

Only, she had no wish to evade him.

"Alice," he called, his voice a song, "where are you?"

She said nothing, standing as still as the tree beside her, but he was an efficient hunter, and the next thing she knew a hand clamped down upon her arm. She gave a bit of a shriek as she jumped, but before she could move, he was around the tree, pinning her back against it.

"Caught you," he said, his voice low and deep in her ear, sending shivers down her spine to her toes, which had become rooted in the ground.

"What do you propose to do with me now?" she asked, hearing the breathlessness in her voice.

"I'm going to claim you as my prize," he growled.

The next thing she knew, his lips were on hers, claiming them, caressing them, crushing them to him, an explosion of all that had been building between them.

It was fast, it was fiery, it was fierce, and Alice thought she might have lost all footing had he not been holding her tightly against him.

When he broke away from her, she could barely breathe. She looked up at him, her heart racing, her vision hazy.

Finally, she understood what it meant to be kissed with such passion, such purpose. She had always disdained a rake like Benjamin, but one thing could be said — the man knew how to kiss. Perhaps it was worth the ruination.

The only problem was that she wanted more than he could give. She wanted love, romance, marriage.

And Benjamin wasn't interested in any of those things. Of that, she was well aware.

Which was why she shouldn't be here, with him.

But she couldn't keep herself away.

Even she, a woman who always wrote a happily-ever-after, knew there was but one way this could end.

Disaster.

CHAPTER 1

"*I*sn't she beautiful?"

Alice leaned over to whisper in the ear of her sister-in-law, whose brilliant red hair tickled her nose as she did. While Celeste didn't respond, a few other heads turned her way with some consternation written upon their faces. Alice slunk back into the pew as though she could become one with it, ducking her chin as she did her very best not to look guilty.

It had been hard to keep her wonder to herself, however. Madeline was absolutely stunning in her long light-blue gown, her blond hair hanging down her back in silky curls, bilking the trends of the day, the gossamer lace veil sitting on her head like a crown while the material trailed down to grace the floor.

Alice wished she could see her friend's face as she stood before half the curious *ton* and married the charming, handsome earl who had recently appeared in society and had swept her off her feet — quite literally. It was the perfect match, as far as Alice was concerned, and she could hardly wait to write Madeline's story, for it was a love that most women would give anything for but only a few actually achieved.

"Alice," Celeste hissed into her ear, her hand on her elbow, "time to stand."

Alice collected her thoughts and twisted her head from side to side, seeing that she had, in fact, missed the cue. She stood along with the rest of the congregation, clapping as Madeline and Lord Donning turned to the crowd. Madeline beamed up at him as she linked her arm through his, and when she passed by Alice, she winked at her as she reached out and squeezed her hand.

"You're next!" she called out, but Alice just shook her head as they followed everyone else out of the church. She would love to be next — truly she would — but for now, she had to be content with *creating* love stories, for the real thing was proving far too elusive.

She was proud of herself for not looking across the church, over toward the pew where *he* sat.

Alice hadn't so much as seen him but had sensed him from across the spacious church. Anyone would, she reasoned. He had that way about him, a presence that overtook every room he entered. It was certainly not unique to her, she was sure, for she was one of many women — too many women — who had experienced much the same life-changing kiss.

Life-changing because he had ruined every other kiss that would ever come again in her future.

Damn the man.

No, she told herself decidedly as she held her head as high as her short stature allowed her to. Benjamin Luxington was not for her. He was a rake, a rascal, and she wished she had never laid on eyes on him.

But she had learned her lesson. And she would never be taken in again.

* * *

"THAT WAS LOVELY," Benjamin's sister-in-law, Fredericka Luxington, Lady Dorrington, said as they entered their carriage following the ceremony. Instead of the traditional small wedding breakfast, Madeline's father, Ezra Castleton, was holding a grand affair to celebrate the marriage of his beloved only daughter to the newly discovered and decreed Earl of Donning.

"I think *Donning* did well for himself," Benjamin opined as he sat across from Freddie, as all knew her, and his brother Miles. "The earldom was floundering when he gained the title, and Miss Castleton brings with her a vast dowry."

"Not only the dowry," Freddie added, holding up a slim, pointed finger, "but she is a businesswoman in her own right."

Benjamin nodded. Freddie was right. From what he knew, Madeline Castleton spent as much time at her family's business as her own father did, if not more.

"I'm surprised Donning is fine with it," he mused.

"How did you become acquainted with him?" Miles asked, his brows furrowed with his question as he studied Benjamin.

"Through Chesterpeak," Benjamin responded with a wince. Chesterpeak was one of his deceased father's favored friends. He was owner of The Nomad, and his home was a site of much gambling and other vices, with which Miles would be displeased.

Miles' disapproval of the connection made sense, as their father had attempted to have Miles considered a lunatic due to his deafness, and then had him nearly killed in the process.

Benjamin should have prevented it. But he had been blind to it all, and he had never forgiven himself for it.

"Was Donning acquainted with Father?" Miles asked after

reading Benjamin's lips and crossing his arms over his chest, the leather of the seat squeaking as he leaned back against the squabs.

Benjamin nodded. "Somewhat. He was better friends with Thomas Chesterpeak. Then Chesterpeak was the one who introduced me to Donning."

"I see," Miles said, but from the tight press of his lips against one another, Benjamin was rather concerned with just what he saw. Miles was likely already judging Donning before he had even met him.

"He's not a bad sort," Benjamin defended him. "Nor is Chesterpeak. He has all of the connections, it seems. I'll tell you, the people I've met through him—"

"People?" Miles interrupted. "Or women?"

Benjamin decided he was done with this conversation. Yes, Miles was right. But the way he said it, with such judgement in his tone, caused Benjamin to only want to defend himself — and for what? He had done nothing wrong, and he didn't see why he needed to argue with Miles over simply enjoying himself with women from society — women who welcomed his company.

He shrugged. "There is nothing to be concerned about, Miles."

Miles snorted. "You're too trusting, Benjamin," he said. "You have to learn to see the truth in people, and not only what you like to see in them."

"I—" Benjamin was saved from the conversation, however, as they approached the entrance of the Castleton household.

"Behave yourself, Benjamin?" Miles said with a raised eyebrow, but Benjamin said nothing in response. Once they had all departed the carriage, he allowed his brother and his wife to go ahead, while he stayed a step behind.

He would enter alone — which was always for the best.

* * *

"Oh, look!" Alice said from where they stood at the outskirts of the elaborate gilded drawing room. "There are Lord and Lady Lovelace. I heard there was some scandal involved in their marriage, but I have not determined just exactly what it is yet. And oh, there is Lord Ingersoll. He is ever so handsome, and I heard, Celeste, that he was actually interested in your friend Jemima, but of course, she married the valet. Her story has been on the tongues of many, and I think it is utterly romantic. I do hope to speak to her about it one day."

She looked hopefully at her sister-in-law, but Celeste's green eyes flashed uncertainly.

"I'm not sure that Jemima would be interested in having her story told," she said, biting her lip. "I doubt that Archie would be in favor."

Alice sighed, although she nodded in understanding. "I suppose I could change it enough so they didn't realize I was writing *their* story. What do you think?"

Celeste took a sip of her drink, cringing at what Alice determined must have been the sweet tartness of the lemonade. "I am fairly certain that most would realize just who the actual protagonists were based upon."

"Which is exactly what I would like to speak to you about," Oliver said from behind her, and Alice jumped slightly at his presence.

"Ollie," she greeted her brother, pretending they were talking about something entirely different as he was not the biggest fan of her work. "It is lovely in here, is it not? I must ask what shade of pink those flowers are."

Oliver rolled his eyes at her, although there was affection held within their depths.

"Alice," he said slowly. "I could hear you from halfway across the room. You have to be more careful."

"Why?" she questioned. "Should I not be proud of my work? You should understand."

"That's different," he said, looking at her with consternation. "We study the skies. You study other people."

"For inspiration only," she qualified, but he had that arched brow that told her that he was not pleased.

"People are beginning to suspect that you are the infamous Lady Love."

"Careful," Alice said, looking around to make sure there were no eavesdroppers nearby. "You calling me out in a crowd is not going to help matters."

"Nor is asking questions about the relationships of everyone in the room."

"Oliver," Celeste interjected, placing her hand on her husband's arm. "Alice does have much to be proud of. Her stories have been entertaining half of London since they began appearing as serials. Everyone wants to know the latest love story."

"*Fictional* love story," Alice added helpfully, but Oliver and Celeste both eyed her with suspicion, which made sense, for they were all well aware that her stories — the published ones, anyway — were all based on truth.

"Well, I have heard some rumblings," Oliver said, swirling the amber liquid in his glass. "There are some who are not entirely pleased to know that you have been asking questions."

"Which questions?" Alice said, taken aback. She had thought she was quite discreet.

"Questions regarding their connections, their business dealings, how they became acquainted, whether they are after the dowry or the woman," Oliver said, looking at her pointedly, and Alice colored somewhat at the accuracy of his words.

"It helps me tell the story," she said in defense, but Oliver only sighed.

"Please be careful?" he pleaded, but before she could answer, Celeste exclaimed, "Oh, there are Freddie and Miles!"

Alice couldn't stop her head from swiveling toward the door. She could try to tell herself she was not trying to see if *he* was there.

But then she would only be lying.

For there he was. And he was staring straight at her.

She turned her back quickly, squeezing her eyes shut for a moment in supplication. *Please don't walk over here*, she prayed. *Just Freddie and Miles. No need for Benjamin.* In fact, if he could just ignore her, that would be ideal. She was easy to ignore. She was well aware of the fact, and the only way a man would want to pay any attention to her was due to his need to conquer every female he became acquainted with. A man like Benjamin Luxington.

"Lord Essex, Lady Essex."

Damn, but he had the most beautiful, smooth voice, like fine new silk.

"And Miss Cunningham."

Could she continue staring at the back wall, not turning around, without anyone noticing?

Oliver elbowed her in the side, and she realized that she most decidedly could not. She slowly turned around and met Benjamin's beautiful blue-green eyes.

As he lifted her hand and bent over it with a bow, Alice bemoaned the fact that the man turned her entire being into liquid with just one touch. He was too handsome for his own good and far too charming. He attracted every female in the room, and she dearly wished she wasn't one of them.

But, sadly, she was one of the worst.

"How are you?" he asked, his gaze burning into her. She hoped her emotions weren't written on her face, for that would be the worst of embarrassment. She had no connection to him, no further attraction. All that had occurred between them was for research, and for research only. Or so she tried to convince herself. For she had no desire to lump herself into the grouping of women who fell for his smile and his bewitchery.

"I am well," was all she said, her words stilted, and he nodded, turning from her abruptly. She saw Celeste and Freddie looking upon the two of them with surprise as Benjamin wished them all a good afternoon and went on his way.

Which was just as well. For Alice had no need for a man like Benjamin Luxington in her life.

No need at all.

* * *

"WHAT WAS THAT ALL ABOUT?" Freddie asked as she and Miles followed Benjamin until she tugged on his elbow hard enough that he stopped.

"That seemed quite rude," Miles said with a frown.

"Miss Cunningham may not be the type of woman who would be among your usual preference, but she is quite lovely, and I thought that you were, at the very least, friends with one another. To simply drop her hand and run away like that, one would—oh." Freddie's visage fell, and Benjamin ran a hand over his face as Freddie and Miles stared at him with matching expressions of disappointment he had come to know far too well.

"Benjamin, you didn't," Freddie said, tilting her head to the side, her chocolate hair piled on top.

"I didn't!" he said, raising his eyes at the fact that the two of them would so quickly suspect him of such. "And least not… I didn't ruin her. All right?"

Freddie arched a brow, and Miles stared at him, willing him to tell the truth, and finally Benjamin relented.

"It was a chaste kiss in the gardens one night," he said, holding up his hands. "That is all. She and I are friends — or at least, we were. I never meant for anything further to happen."

"But it did," Freddie said, placing her hands on her hips. "Oh, Benjamin. Alice is young, and she likely now has fanciful notions toward you, which—"

"Which is exactly why I did not allow it to go any further than that," Benjamin said, though a bit of guilt knocked on his shoulder as he thought of the hope that had entered Alice's eyes after their kiss. It was why he had immediately left her there — alone — and hadn't pursued her since then.

"We both understand the expectations of one another," he continued. "Now, if you will excuse me, I am finished with your lectures, and I am going for a cheroot."

"Oh, I really wish you wouldn't," Freddie said, but Benjamin was striding across the marble floor before she could finish her sentence.

He had a mother already — in fact, she was on the other side of the room speaking with Alice's mother — and he had no wish for another. He was a free, independent man.

And it was going to stay that way.

CHAPTER 2

"*A*lice Cunningham?"

Alice whipped her head around when she heard her name, wondering where the small voice was coming from. She was surprised when she found that she actually had to look *down* in front of her.

"Yes?"

"A note for you, ma'am," said the young boy, who passed up a folded piece of paper. Alice looked curiously up and down the Mayfair street in front of her. She had left the wedding festivities for a moment to take in the fresh air around her, a moment outside of the same room as that of which Benjamin Luxington occupied.

She knew it was stupid, but she didn't think she could stand there for one more moment and watch him charm the whole of London society — old *and* new.

Where this street lad had come from, she couldn't say.

"How did you know who I was?" she asked with curiosity, but he just grinned impishly and winked at her, giving Alice the feeling that she wasn't going to get anything out of him unless she parted with some coin, which she didn't even have on her.

Instead, she opened the letter, her eyes quickly perusing the contents.

Find something else to write about, she read, her lips parting in shock as she did so, *and leave the rest of us alone!*

She looked down at the young lad with wide eyes.

"Where did you get this?" she demanded, but he shrugged.

"From a man."

"What did he look like?"

But the boy shook his head, refusing to impart any information. Alice ground her fists at her sides as she looked around the street, but the few people that were passing by had no interest in her.

"Will you take a message back?" she asked, leaning down so that she was on the same level as he, taking in, as she did so, the threadbare status of his hat and jacket, as well as hollowness of his cheeks, and she now wished that she *did* have something to give him, if for no other reason than to allow him to feed himself. She hoped that, at the very least, the person threatening her was paying him handsomely.

"I'm *supposed* to await your reply," he said, folding his hands behind his back and puffing his chest out.

"Tell this person that I most absolutely will not give up!" she said before sighing and straightening tall once more as the urchin nodded and then took off down the street.

Alice didn't bother to follow him — she knew better than that. All that was likely to happen was that she would end up with a torn dress and unfounded rumors about just where she had been.

Sadly, it wasn't the first time that it had been "suggested" she quit writing tales so close to the truth that no one was fooled by the names nor the settings she had concocted. It was just... her fans looked forward to each serial, and she

13

had developed such a following now, she didn't know how she could do anything different.

Besides that, no one wanted to read the stories that came out of her own imaginings. They were boring. Nonsensical. Rejected.

No, the sensational was what was in demand. And, therefore, the sensational she would give.

Besides that, she didn't see how it was hurting anyone. All ended happily. She gained permission of everyone involved. She changed names. And no one's reputation ever came into question.

Well... she bit her lip as she reflected on that. Perhaps that was not completely true. For there were the stories that named the rake as the villain, that suggested there were those who could never enter hero status due to their utter lack of respect for the majority of women.

Men like Benjamin Luxington.

Although he, unlike most of the well-known profligate rakes of London, had not yet taken a role in any of her stories.

She just couldn't bring herself to write about him.

Alice tilted her head back, the bright sun hitting her face, and she closed her eyes as she allowed the warmth to sink into her, easing her chilled bones. She should return inside sooner rather than later. She was out here without a chaperone, having managed to slip out without her mother's awareness. While her mother was not overly strict, she also had a great deal of care for her children's reputations, and after all that Ollie had done to threaten it a couple of years ago, their mother was extra diligent now when it came to Alice.

That Oliver's affair had ended in marriage didn't seem to matter. There had been scandal, which she said a baron could recover from. A baron's sister would not have such luck.

Alice finally dipped her head back to the present, determining that she would enjoy this day, and not let Oliver, nor her mother, nor this anonymous threat, and most certainly *not* Benjamin Luxington take any of her joy away from her.

She loved her work, readers loved her work, and that was all that mattered.

"Miss?"

Alice sighed. It was the boy again, and this time he was waving from the other side of the road. She really didn't want to engage in a back and forth through this poor child, but she wasn't sure what other option she had at the moment. "Can you come here a moment?"

"What is it?" she asked, lifting her skirts slightly and beginning to stride across the street. "Was my response not acceptable? I thought it was abundantly clear, but perhaps—"

Alice wasn't sure what caught her attention. It could have been the unusual sound of the horse's hooves thundering around the corner of the quiet street, or the boy's telling glance to the side, or the intuition that suddenly hit deep in her stomach. But something was most assuredly wrong, but she took a step backward, away from the boy and toward the other side of the road, intent on returning from where she had come.

It didn't seem to matter where or how quickly she went, however, for a team of two horses carrying a small phaeton careened around the corner, travelling so fast that the carriage was, for a moment, suspended on two wheels.

Alice gave out a bit of a shriek as she began to run toward the side of the road, far out of the way, but it didn't matter where she went, for the team seemed to follow after her everywhere she ran, from one side of the street to the other.

Finally, she had enough, and stopped right in the middle of the road, turning with her hands on her hips and looking up at the driver, whose hat was tipped as low as it could possibly be over his brow.

He had to stop, she reasoned, as the seconds seemed to draw out longer as the carriage approached. He wasn't going to run her down in cold blood, here in the middle of a busy neighborhood.

The carriage continued on its course.

Or was he?

* * *

BENJAMIN STEPPED out in front of the house in search of air not so stifling and scented. Here he could find a moment alone, for out back in the small gardens near the mews, he was likely to be stalked by some woman he had previously known and would prefer to forget.

If the cheroot was going to be had, it would be had out here. He struck one of the matches Jemima — Mrs. Thompkins now — had given him, pleased when it lit up immediately, allowing him to light the end of his cheroot and draw in the smoke.

He closed his eyes in silent gratefulness as he exhaled, but then suddenly he was sent into a huge coughing fit at the sight in front of him.

There was Alice Cunningham — dressed in one of her usual vibrant colors, today a gown of royal blue — stalking across the street. Her target was... a street urchin? No, it couldn't be, Benjamin reasoned, shaking his head. What would Alice have to do with such a lad?

But he had no more time to think on that, for just then a team of horses and its carriage came thundering around the corner — straight for her.

"Alice!" he called, taking a step forward, although he was sure she couldn't hear him.

Change paths, he willed the driver, but the driver only

leaned lower over the reins, apparently urging the horses on, as he turned them directly toward Alice.

She obviously came to the same realization, and she did exactly what Benjamin would have done — she attempted to run toward the closest side of the street, likely to find a place she could hide out of their path.

What she couldn't see from her vantage point was that there was a space between the stones in the wall where she could likely hide. Right now, it was her only hope as it seemed this man was determined in his pursuit of her. Benjamin willed her toward it at the same time he pushed himself into action.

He launched himself away from the wall, dropping his newly lit cheroot as he broke into a run. Time seemed to tick backwards as Alice turned and, perhaps caught by the sudden imagining of her impending end, she simply stared at the horses and driver, a hand held out in front of her.

"Alice, run!" Benjamin called out, although he was sure she couldn't hear him over the noise of the hooves and the yells of onlookers, and the shout to stop that Benjamin realized came from Alice herself.

Before she even knew he was there — before *he* even knew exactly what he was doing — he made it to her, scooped her up, crossed the road in two long strides, and, without breaking step, knelt and tossed her over his shoulder before mercifully finding the crevice in the wall.

For a moment, Benjamin didn't hear anything except for an exaggerated panting that was either his or Alice's, he couldn't be sure.

"Put me down."

Benjamin had just peered out the crevice to see if her four-legged pursuers were still after her, but they were already down the street and turning the corner — and Benjamin saw why.

The entrance to the Mayfair house where they had been celebrating was now filled with onlookers — her own brother, Lord Essex, at the very front with his hands on his hips as he stared across the road at them while his wife had her lips to his ear — perhaps she was telling him not to kill him, Benjamin thought with a wince.

He finally complied with Alice's order, except instead of simply depositing her onto her feet, he slowly slid her down over his shoulder, her delicious curves kissing his body as they left friction in their wake, until she was back on her feet, although he still held her flush against him.

"Benjamin Luxington!" she said, her entire body seemingly vibrating as she glared up at him, and Benjamin suddenly realized she was likely not about to emit a thank you for saving her life. "*You*, sir, are—"

"Very much in our debt."

Suddenly her brother was there, clapping his hands on Benjamin's shoulders, and as much as it pained him to leave Alice's delicious curves alone, Benjamin had to reluctantly step back and around to focus on her brother instead — a sorry task, for Essex's brown eyes didn't cause nearly the same stirrings within him as Alice's did.

Oliver already had Benjamin's hand in one of his, the other covering the top of it, as he pumped his entire arm up and down with more strength than Benjamin would have guessed the astronomer had within him.

"Thank you, Luxington," Oliver was saying profusely. "You saved my sister's life. Thank you very much. I'm not sure how I can ever repay you."

"I was in the right place at the right moment," Benjamin said as though there was a need to defend himself. He wasn't used to such accolades — nor did he deserve them in any way. It seemed Alice agreed, for when he turned to her, she had crossed her arms over her chest as though warding herself away from him.

"My apologies, Miss Cunningham. I shouldn't have taken the liberty to lift you as I did, but I was merely trying to remove you from harm's way as quickly as I could."

Alice opened her mouth to respond, and Benjamin found himself rather intrigued by what might next come out, for she never ceased to entertain him — even if she was being rather contrary.

"It's absolutely fine," Oliver cut in. "I'm sure my sister has no ill will whatsoever regarding your method of rescue."

He fixed a look on Alice that nearly caused Benjamin to break out in laughter, while Alice just rolled her eyes.

"You picked me up like a sack of beans," she exclaimed, and Benjamin nodded, while he was actually somewhat relieved by her indignant words, for they kept him distracted from the terror that was still swirling strong within his chest.

When he had seen those horses hurtling straight toward Alice, he had reacted too quickly to even consider what he was doing or what was happening to her. Now that she was out of harm's way and was standing here, safe in front of him, panic began to claw its way up his throat and was now causing him to nearly dissolve into tremors. He had to clasp his hands behind his back to keep anyone from noticing.

He was Benjamin Luxington — well-known rake and charmer, a man who never allowed anything to affect him. He should be celebrating the fact he had saved the life of a lovely young woman with whom his family was acquainted.

For that was all Alice was, and all she ever would be.

She was far too good for a man like him — of that, he was certain.

ALICE KNEW she was being rude. If Benjamin hadn't come along… she placed a hand over the left side of her chest in an attempt to slow the beating of her racing heart. She would have found a way to save herself, she determined. She was sure of it, actually.

She hadn't needed Benjamin — and didn't need him for anything else.

At least, that was what she continued to tell herself, for she couldn't want a man like him. Any affection she thought she had for him was simply a young girl's infatuation. She was two-and-twenty now and was much better prepared to defend herself against the charm of a rake like him.

So what if he had just saved her life in a move that was well worthy of the finest of heroes from any of her books? It was, as he had said, that he was in the right place at the right time, and nothing more than that.

Any tingles she had experienced from the touch of his body against hers were simply the resulting rush of relief at it all ending with her safety.

"What happened?" Oliver asked now, as their mother joined them on the walkway at the entrance to the house.

"Nothing," Alice said, attempting to dissuade them and their concerns, but they would not be deterred.

"Alice," Oliver said more firmly now, "what happened?"

"She was being chased down by a team of horses," Benjamin said, scratching his head in wonderment as he answered for her. "The driver was clearly targeting her. I came outside for a cheroot and saw him careening around the corner. It looked like Alice was trying to get out of the way, but he followed her in every direction she went."

Oliver turned to Alice with eyes wide.

"Is this true?"

She cast an annoyed stare at Benjamin to let him know just what she thought of his apparent helpfulness.

"Yes, most of it," she admitted.

Oliver flapped his hands out to the side.

"Why would someone have any inclination to hurt *you?*"

"Well…" Alice cocked her head, unsure of how much she should tell her brother.

"What is that?" Benjamin asked abruptly, and Alice was grateful for his interjection. Maybe he was of some use after all.

"What's what?" Celeste asked.

"That there, on the ground," Benjamin said, bending down to pick up a slip of paper, and suddenly Alice wasn't so grateful anymore.

"Nothing, I'm sure," she said, reaching to take it from his hands, but he held it too high for her to grasp.

"It's addressed to you, Miss Cunningham," he said, and Alice set the heels of her ruined kid slippers back onto the cobblestones below her. There would be no recovering the note now. Not from him — nor from Oliver, she was sure.

Drat. It must have slipped from her grasp in her race away from the horses.

As Benjamin read the note aloud, Alice ground her toe into the groove between two stones. Maybe Oliver wouldn't overreact. Maybe they wouldn't all decide that the two incidents were linked. Maybe—

"Alice!" Oliver, her typically steady, orderly, practical brother burst out. "I know you take joy in your work, but whatever you are doing to incite such threats, it must stop. Immediately. My God, but you have made someone far too angry."

"Oliver." Alice placed her hands on her hips as she regarded her brother. "Do you really think that threatening me should cause me to stop? People enjoy my writing, and the thought that someone wishes to stifle me only makes me want to continue. Someone obviously has something to hide.

I will do all I can to uncover the truth to make sure it isn't something that will hurt another."

Oliver rubbed his forehead. "Maybe you can write something else, Alice. Something less scandalous. But that, we can discuss later — when we are not standing in the middle of the street outside of a wedding celebration. What is clear, however, is that you need to be protected."

"Oh, Oliver," she said, shaking her head. "This was a one-time, silly incident. There is no need—"

"There *is* a need," he said firmly, and Alice's mother pushed forward toward her, a worried expression on her face.

"Oliver is right, my dear," she said, tears swimming within her eyes. "What would we have done if those horses had trampled you? If Lord Benjamin had not come along when he did? Oh, Alice, I can hardly bear to think of it."

It was her mother's fear that cut through her defiance, slicing deeply into Alice, causing her own worry to escalate ever so slightly.

She reached out and took her mother's hand in hers.

"All is fine," she said softly. "I'm sorry, Mother, I didn't mean for you to worry so."

"I just…" her mother shook her head, her gaze locked on the ground. "I need you to take what Oliver is saying with a great deal of seriousness. Until we determine where this is coming from, we must ensure you are safe. Perhaps you should stay home until then."

"Stay home?" Alice looked up, her mouth agape.

"I know you enjoy your outings," her mother began with a wince, for that was an understatement, as Alice lived off the opportunity to socialize with other people, "but just for a while—"

"I will be careful," Alice said, trying to assure them all while at the same time refusing to look at Benjamin. What must he think of this family squabbling? He likely assumed her to be incapable of making her own decisions or looking after herself, which was far from the truth. While she appreciated all that both Oliver and her mother did for her, she was also proud of her ability to make her own life.

Oliver sighed.

"I know better than to *insist* that you remain at home, but I certainly cannot watch you every hour of the day," he said, rubbing his temples. "We shall have to hire a man to look out for you, to follow you when you go out and keep you safe."

"Oh, Oliver," Alice said, already shaking her head. "I cannot ask you to hire someone to do such a thing."

"Of course I will," he said firmly with a do-not-argue-with-me-right-now look at her. "I—"

"If I may," Benjamin interrupted, lifting a finger up in between them, "I have a suggestion."

"Of course," Oliver said graciously, and Alice steeled herself at just what he might enter for consideration into this conversation.

"I hope I have proven myself capable of looking out for Miss Cunningham," he said, glancing over toward her, "perhaps—perhaps I... I could look out for her."

Alice nearly laughed. He couldn't even finish the sentence without stumbling over his words.

"I assure you," she said before her brother could get a word in, "that is absolutely not necessary."

"No, really," he said, his face quite serious.

All of a sudden, a knot of nerves began to form in Alice's stomach, for if she knew her brother — and she did, very well — he would latch onto this idea like a title-seeking young lady on a single duke. She didn't think she would be able to survive it.

"It would be my honor," finished Benjamin.

Oliver beamed, and Alice nearly groaned. Benjamin

couldn't have chosen a word that her brother would understand better than "honor."

"Very good," Oliver said. "Now that we have settled everything, we should all be returning to the festivities before people begin to think there is a scandal brewing out here."

But wasn't there?

"Why don't you come to call tomorrow, Luxington, and we will determine all of the details?"

"Very good," Benjamin said, nodding, and when the two of them shook hands, Alice swallowed hard, suddenly feeling as though her future had just been decided, and she had no say in it whatsoever.

CHAPTER 3

*B*enjamin pushed back the long lock of hair from his forehead as he climbed the stairs of the dark stucco townhouse at the end of the palace-front terrace.

As he crossed the green, he saw something peculiar around a copse of trees and couldn't help from taking a quick detour to inspect it, finding that it was a huge telescope, the likes of which he had never seen before. He recalled that both Oliver and Celeste Cunningham were astronomers, and he reflected on what was required to create a good marriage — did one have to share hobbies and interests?

Not that it mattered. For he wasn't marrying. Now that his brother had children of his own, Benjamin was no longer even the spare. His life meant nothing. He was merely an uncle, and that was all that was required for him to be — which was exactly how he wanted it, for he wasn't fit to take care of another human being. He could barely look after himself.

So what had he been thinking in volunteering to look after Alice? One moment all was well — he had done his duty, saving Alice Cunningham's life, and had been thanked for it, even if she hadn't been the one to do so. Then the next thing he knew, he was offering to turn that one heroic effort into a full-time affair.

It was, he realized afterward, the thought of another man taking on the responsibility that had led him to make the inane suggestion, even though he had no reason to have any claim whatsoever toward Alice Cunningham.

He had made a mistake with her once, and it had cost him her friendship. He had promised himself never again.

For Alice was not a woman with whom to dally. She was a woman who deserved respect and a lasting relationship. She deserved a man who would dote on every ounce of her generous curves, who would ensure that the twinkle was ever-present in her eye, the mischievous smile always on her red bow lips, the romance radiating from her tender soul always plentiful.

He was a philanderer. A rake. A Lothario.

He was just like his father.

With a heavy heart, he knocked on the door of number 12, which was opened by a wizened old butler.

"Lord Benjamin Luxington, I presume?" he said, one of his grey eyebrows arched.

"Guilty as charged," Benjamin said, but sobered when the butler didn't laugh, but merely held the door open and led him down a corridor and into a drawing room.

"Lord Essex will be with you momentarily," he said as Benjamin helped himself to a seat on the caned mahogany lounge chair before the butler departed.

He glanced around the room, wondering which of the Cunningham females had decorated the creamy white drawing room with its splashes of vibrancy. He wondered if Alice had a hand in the current color palette, and then shook his head, reminding himself it didn't matter. He would never know the touch of Alice's hand on the walls of his house or another he took in the future.

"Benjamin?"

He came quickly to his feet, surprised when it was Alice who slipped through the drawing room door, as if he had summoned her from his thoughts and into being.

He was only convinced she was real because he had never seen this gown on her before, a simple white muslin with royal blue embroidery.

"Miss Cunningham," he said with a bow, and she waved her hand in the air toward him.

"That is quite enough of that," she said smartly. "You and I have come to know one another well enough for us to be Benjamin and Alice, and even if it had not been so previous to now, I believe yesterday determined that to be the case going forward."

He nodded, hoping that her dismissal of formalities meant that she had somehow forgiven him for his past indiscretion.

"Now, Benjamin, we have but a moment or two before my brother arrives to speak with you — Celeste assured me that she would keep him occupied for a few moments. I have not been able to talk any sense into him, but I am hoping that I can do so with you."

"Oh?" he arched a brow. Perhaps she wasn't so keen on forgiveness after all.

"You and I both know that this silly idea can never come into being."

Despite the fact that he had arrived with this very thought in mind, he found his defenses awoken.

"Why ever not?"

She tilted her beautiful head of dark hair to the side as her warm brown eyes searched deeper into his soul than he figured another had ever looked.

"*Because,*" she said, placing so much emphasis on the word that he knew he was supposed to know exactly what she meant by it. He knew most women would have been embarrassed by such a discussion if they could even bring themselves to put it into being, but not Alice. No, she held her head high, not even a stain of red on her cheeks, although he noted the censure in her eyes. "Because there is the opportunity that one of us might relapse into our previous romantic entanglement, and we cannot have that."

Benjamin swallowed hard at her frankness. No, they certainly could not have that.

"I assure you, Alice, that I can hold myself in all manner of control."

She eyed him. "I have no doubts that is the case, Benjamin. While I am aware that you frequently find yourself in the arms of one woman or another, you made it quite clear after our one brief liaison — which I'm sure barely registered in your memory compared to your usual romantic escapades — that it was not an encounter you wished to repeat."

Benjamin stood rooted to the spot on the floor in front of the chair, knowing his mouth was likely hanging agape and his eyebrows near his hairline.

She stared at him defiantly, the vision of patience as she awaited his response — one he had no idea how to formulate.

"Alice, I— that is, I wasn't aware that you thought, that I, that... oh, bollocks."

He rubbed his fist against his forehead.

"You do not have the right of it whatsoever," he finally mumbled.

"No?" she asked, tilting her head to the side, causing a lock of hair to fall off her forehead and hang suspended in the air. "Then, pray, enlighten me."

"Alice, when I kissed you… it was because I was no longer able to hold myself away from you. However, even in doing so, I knew that it was wrong."

"Because I would not fall into bed with you?"

"Yes," he said, pleased that she understood, but then when her face twisted in anger, he realized that he was going about this all wrong. "No," he amended. "Not in the way you think. You are a woman who should only be courted by a man who will do right by you. I am not that man."

"I didn't think so," she intoned, and he sighed.

"It's not you, Alice," he tried again, but just then the door opened and in walked Lord Essex.

"Lord Benjamin," Alice's brother said smartly, "thank you for calling today. I wish there was more I could do to express my gratitude."

"None needed," he said as Lord Essex eyed his sister.

"Alice, what are you doing in here alone?"

"I required a moment to speak with Lord Benjamin," she said, holding her hands behind her back, "to tell him that I do not require his services."

"Well, you may very well feel that way, but I certainly do not agree," Essex said. "Will the two of you sit?" He waved his hand to the furniture that was placed around the marble-top table, just as a maid entered with a tea tray. Benjamin was tempted to take a seat on the wide white-diamond patterned sofa with the hope that Alice would sit next to him, but decided that he shouldn't push it.

"I had thought we could have a drink, but Alice insisted on joining us, so tea it is," Lord Essex said with a bit of a resigned sigh.

"We *are* discussing my life," Alice interjected, and Essex nodded.

"So we are. As I was saying, we greatly appreciate your offer, Luxington—"

"However, Lord Benjamin was just telling me that, unfortunately, he hadn't realized that his other commitments would keep him from the promise he made yesterday," Alice interjected, casting an imploring look upon him.

She was right. It was exactly what he had come to tell Alice and her brother. Except now that he was here, and well aware of Alice's misconceptions regarding his intentions toward her, he found that he could no longer bring himself to deny the request. He wanted to prove to her that he wasn't the man she thought he was.

"Actually," he said, leaning forward in his chair and forcing a smile upon his face, "I am especially devoid of responsibilities at this point in time and I would enjoy having somewhere to focus my efforts."

"I am sure you have some gambling and whoring to do," Alice said smartly, to which Oliver exclaimed, "Alice!" and she quickly mumbled out an apology.

"My only question," Benjamin said, looking to Oliver now, "is how we will explain my presence in Alice's life?"

"Well," Oliver said slowly, "I do have one idea."

They looked to him expectantly.

"You could be courting her."

"Absolutely not!" Alice exclaimed, while Benjamin's heart raced, although whether with excitement or horror, he couldn't rightly say.

Oliver dipped his head.

"I agree that the excuse has its downside. When the engagement is broken, it will negatively affect Alice's reputation, but perhaps it can be done in such a way that both parties can emerge with their reputations intact. Besides that…" he stole a glance at his sister somewhat warily, "Alice has clearly built for herself a reputation that some take issue with, so this could, actually, help her regain some respect."

"Oliver, may I have a word?" Alice asked, but Lord Essex

ignored her and her fisted hands and looked to Benjamin instead.

"Well, Luxington," he said, his hands out in front of him. "What do you say?"

* * *

ALICE WAS GOING to kill her brother.

Not literally, of course. But perhaps he could become a character in one of her latest stories and she could kill him off within the pages.

She supposed it wasn't quite fair to blame him as she did, for he had no idea of why she had her reservations. But she did wish that he would, at the very least, allow her a moment to come up with a reason for why she had no wish for Benjamin's continued presence — particularly as her apparent beau.

She had but one hope now. She stole a glance toward Benjamin, whose face showed no sign of what he was thinking. She could hardly believe she had opened herself up and shared everything she was feeling with him, but she hadn't seen any other way to convince him of her way of thinking than to tell him the truth.

She didn't particularly care for his suggestion that she was too pure and innocent for him to touch, for she had heard a number of stories about him from all manner of other women who were far more innocent than she could claim to be.

It didn't help that he was as handsome as he had ever been. His hair was the perfect shade of chestnut brown tinted with the slightest bit of red when the light brushed upon it the right way. His eyes were a mischievous blue-green that seemed to understand exactly what she was thinking, and that jawline... she nearly sighed aloud. If only she could simply enjoy looking at him, without his very presence causing her to tingle in all of the ways that she knew were wrong yet would be so deliciously, wickedly right were he to come closer.

She gazed at him imploringly, hoping that he would understand exactly what she was trying to say.

Tell him no. Tell him that this is a ridiculous idea. Tell him that this would destroy your reputation and you could never engage in such an idea.

Suddenly a wide smile lit Benjamin's face, showcasing each beautiful, perfect, white tooth. Or so it seemed.

"I love the idea," he said, turning knowing eyes on Alice. "I think it will work just fine."

"I don't think—" Alice began, standing, trying to make the two men pay her some mind, but she was quickly interrupted by her brother, who strode across the room to shake Benjamin's hand.

"Thank you, Luxington," he said. "We are happy to make it worth your time."

"Oh, no," Benjamin quickly said. "I couldn't take anything."

"I insist," Oliver reassured him, and Alice rolled her eyes, although it didn't matter as neither of them was paying her the least bit of attention. "With our recent discovery, Celeste and I have been most fortunate to gain the favor of the king and have been rewarded rather handsomely. I cannot see how some of our rewards could go to any greater purpose than Alice."

"Well, I never," Alice said, placing her hands on her hips.

"It's true," Oliver said, finally looking over at her. "In fact, I wasn't going to tell you this, Alice, but we have put aside a substantial amount for your dowry."

"My dowry?" She knew she sounded like a parrot, gaping at him as she did, but she was astounded that her brother would choose now — in front of Benjamin — to share all this with her.

"Why, yes," he said with a warm smile. "Are you not pleased?"

"Not really," she said, attempting to couch her words in softness so they wouldn't sound so harsh. "I would prefer to attract a man who wants me because of who I am and not what money he will receive for taking me off your hands."

"Perhaps now you can have both," Oliver suggested, "for some men have no choice but to marry a woman with wealth. Wouldn't you agree, Lord Benjamin?"

"I think that is enough discussion for today," Alice cut in, walking over to the door and holding it open for Benjamin, despite Oliver's frown of disapproval.

"Thank you, Luxington, for your very *kind* offer," Oliver said with a look of reproach at his sister. "We shall be in touch."

"My schedule is quite open," Benjamin said. "Send around a note whenever you please."

Alice had a feeling she might be staying home much more frequently than usual.

CHAPTER 4

"*O*liver, this is ridiculous," Alice said, following her brother across his study toward his desk a couple of days later. She had tried to stay home to prevent any reason for Benjamin's assistance, but she had found herself pacing up and down the corridors of the townhouse, searching for something to do.

She had tried to sit and write her stories, but, having always been inspired by conversations with her friends and her observations of others, she had found that the words refused to flow.

So she had finally decided that she would go speak with a woman who now knew more about love than Alice ever would. "I am only going to visit Madeline. Mother is not even accompanying me — just Ingrid. If Benjamin must come, then Mother will insist on joining to ensure all is proper, and then instead of a wonderful visit with my newly married friend, it will turn into an entire circus."

"Trust me, Alice, such a grouping is nothing near a circus."

Alice paused to pet Perseus, one of Celeste's dogs, who

blocked her exit from the room with his body, nuzzling his head against her leg until she submitted to his insistence that she show him some affection.

She absently rubbed the top of his furry head just as Andromeda, their second dog and his mate, came in to receive her share.

"Oliver," she said with exasperation from her crouched position. "There is something else that you haven't thought of."

"Oh?" he murmured, without looking up from the star map draped across his desk.

"No one is going to believe that Lord Benjamin is courting *me*."

That caught his attention.

"Why would you think such a thing?"

"Because," she explained patiently, "if it were not for the fact that he doesn't have a title, every woman of the *ton* would be after him — to wed. As it is, they all want a share of him, and only some are interested in marriage. Everyone knows that he has no intentions of settling down with one woman — and even if he did, it most certainly would not be me."

"Why ever not?" He still seemed genuinely perplexed, and Alice was touched by his loyalty, if slightly perplexed by his ignorance.

"If a man had his choice of any woman, would he choose one who was of less-than-average height, more-than-average roundness, and just barely-over-average attractiveness?"

Oliver frowned, dropping his quill pen. "You can't really think that of yourself."

"I am a realist, Oliver," she said, dipping her head to the side as she studied her brother. "And I am well aware of what my areas of strength are, and conversely where a man might find me lacking."

"I think you are wrong," he insisted.

"You are my brother."

"Even so," he said, shaking his head, "every man finds different women attractive. I wouldn't be so hard on yourself, Alice."

"Well—

"I am here to call court!"

His rich baritone sent shivers down her spine, and Alice stood as she whirled around, pleased that she had chosen a particularly beautiful white day gown with purple trimming to wear to visit Madeline. It was not at all because she knew that Benjamin might be accompanying her, she began to tell herself, but then quickly realized that was a lie. She sighed. She had dressed for him.

"Don't tell me you are that disappointed to see me." Benjamin said with a wink as the dogs jumped up on him to say hello. Alice realized he thought that her chagrin was for altogether different reasons.

"My brother may have been slightly mistaken," she began, "for I do not require an escort to walk a few streets to visit a friend."

"It's a beautiful day for a walk," he said easily. "Not to worry, I will allow you to visit in peace. In fact," he brightened, "I can spend some time visiting with Lord Donning while we are there."

"Oh, that's right," Alice murmured, "I forgot that you were friends."

"How is it you know him?" Oliver asked, seemingly genuinely curious, which Alice was as well.

She was puzzled when an uneasy look covered Benjamin's face.

"We had mutual acquaintances," he said.

"Had?" Alice questioned, picking up on the word, and Benjamin nodded slightly.

"Yes, my… well, my father introduced me to another friend, a man with whom I made some investments," he explained, and Alice stole a glance over at Oliver, wondering if he also found Benjamin's explanation slightly suspicious, but he mostly seemed politely intrigued. "Donning and I met at an establishment where he operates his business."

"I see," Alice said curiously. "Did you know him before he became the earl? It was rather intriguing, how it was so difficult to determine the heir for so long."

"It was," Benjamin acknowledged. "My understanding is that there were many other pretenders who came forward before he understood his lineage."

"How fortunate, then, that they were able to prove his claim," Alice said, before deciding that she had no choice but to continue on with her visit. It seemed Benjamin would accompany her, whether she liked it or not.

"Come along, then," she said to Benjamin. "Let's go, before my mother hears of where we are off to."

The last she heard was Oliver chuckling behind them as she found her reticule, summoned her maid, and made for the door.

BENJAMIN ATTEMPTED to study Alice without her realizing exactly what he was doing, although it was difficult from his vantage point as he walked beside her toward the home where Donning and his new wife had taken up residence.

The butler — Woodward, he had learned was his name — had been showing him into Lord Essex's study when he overheard Alice and her brother speaking on the other side of the door. She had been very critical of her own shortcomings — or how she saw them, at any rate.

It was true she was not the *most* striking woman he had

ever met. But there was more to her that most other women did not possess. She had wit and charm, made even better by the fact that it was not practiced, but rather naturally refreshing.

While she didn't seem to be particularly kind to herself in terms of her looks, he thought she was beautiful, in her own way. Benjamin appreciated the fact that every woman held her beauty in a different sort of way, but Alice drew him more than most — which was exactly the problem.

She looked at him suspiciously out of the corner of her brown eyes — *warm, laughing* brown eyes, to everyone but him.

"What are you doing?"

"Accompanying you to your friend's house," he said, deliberately misunderstanding her.

"No, I mean why are you looking at me like that?"

"Like what?" he asked, feigning innocence.

"Like you are trying to solve a puzzle."

"Perhaps I am," he said with a practiced, charming grin that worked on most women.

But not this one.

Not today.

"I am not a puzzle," she said with a frown. "In fact, I am more open than, I'm sure, nearly every other woman with whom you are acquainted."

She was right about that.

"Perhaps I am simply intrigued by you."

She snorted.

"There is no need to charm me, Benjamin. You have already done so quite successfully."

"Then why do you treat me as though I am the enemy?"

She sighed. "I explained that to you already. Please, do not make me live through that embarrassment again. Ah, here we are. I believe this is the address."

"It is."

"Have you been here before?" she looked at him curiously as he rapped on the door.

"I have, a couple of times," he said. "Lord Donning hosted... parties, before he was married."

"I see," she murmured, and he worried that she actually did understand exactly what he spoke of. It was not that Donning's parties were particularly scandalous. It was just that many of the men and women who attended did so in order to engage in some activities that might be frowned upon by others in polite society, such as drinking too much, gambling too much, and engaging in too much... open affection with one another.

"Lord Donning is quite devoted to your friend," Benjamin reassured her, although the truth was, he had no idea what Donning's affections were regarding his wife. He *did* know that the new Lady Donning had quite the dowry, but he thought — at least he *hoped* — that it hadn't factored into a reason as to why Donning had married her.

The door swung open, revealing a rather dark entryway and a butler who didn't seem particularly skilled in social niceties.

"Come in," was all he said, before leading them just a few steps through the door and into a dark, empty parlor.

Alice's maid followed them in, and she stepped forward a bit closer to Alice and Benjamin as though slightly spooked by the entire situation. Benjamin had to admit that he felt like shivering himself at the dark curtain that covered any hint of sunlight, the rich purple brocade sofas, and the navy papered walls that were nearly devoid of any decoration.

"Is this how you recall the house?" Alice whispered to Benjamin, who had to admit that he didn't remember it quite like this.

"We only saw the dining room and the drawing room," he

said, "although it was night and there were quite a few candles lit."

"Alice?"

All three of them jumped, startled at the intrusion.

"Madeline!" Alice exclaimed, recovering quicker than Benjamin did. "How lovely to see you."

But even Benjamin noticed the hesitancy in her step as she approached her friend, and he could see why. At her wedding less than a week ago, Lady Donning had seemed vivacious and full of love. Now she looked... pale and sickly, far from the bright and happy newlywed.

"Are you all right?" Alice asked, not mincing words, to which Lady Donning gave a little laugh.

"Of course."

"How was your honeymoon?"

"Oh, wonderful. I hadn't been to Bath in some time. It was unfortunate that we had to leave so early," Lady Donning said with a soft smile before finding him across the room. "Lord Benjamin. How are you?"

"Just fine," he said, watching her look back and forth between him and Alice. "I hope you do not mind that I accompanied Miss Cunningham. I haven't spoken to your husband since the wedding and when I heard she was coming, I thought I would join in."

"Of course," she said graciously, "Stephen is in his study."

"Thank you," he said, and then couldn't help but add with a wink toward Alice, "please do take good care of my Miss Cunningham."

He hoped they couldn't hear his chuckle as he exited the room.

* * *

ALICE SLOWLY TURNED TOWARD MADELINE, knowing exactly what she would be greeted with.

"*His* Miss Cunningham?" she repeated Benjamin's words, her blue eyes wide.

Alice cringed. "It's a long story," she said, biting her lip, and Madeline sat down less than gracefully on the dark sofa.

"Do tell," she said.

"It's a… temporary arrangement," Alice hedged. "It seems that there is someone who is not particularly pleased by all that I am writing about."

"Oh?"

"I had a near-miss, outside of your wedding, actually," Alice said before describing to Madeline all that had happened. By the end of the story, Madeline was leaning forward in her chair, her mouth agape.

"Alice!" she gasped. "That's terrible. And far too frightening. What are you going to do?"

"Keep writing."

Madeline smiled and nodded, sitting back into the sofa. "That's the spirit. While I cannot help but be worried about you, I do applaud you for it."

This was why Alice was friends with Madeline. If there was anyone in this world who would understand precisely how she felt, it was she.

"Ben— *Lord* Benjamin graciously volunteered to look out for me, despite the fact that I don't feel it is necessary whatsoever," Alice said, rolling her eyes. "Which explains his presence today. Oliver, of course, is convinced that I am in imminent danger."

"As much as I understand your commitment to continue with your craft, I don't think it is a bad idea myself," Madeline said, biting her lip. "I do feel better knowing that you are protected."

"But by Lord Benjamin?" Alice said, raising her eyebrows.

"What has he ever done that provides him with the proper credentials to look after a woman?"

"Well," Madeline said slowly, obviously attempting to hide her smile, "I would say that most women seem to be quite pleased by his attentions."

Alice tossed a throw pillow at her friend's jest before throwing herself back against the sofa. It was dark and ugly, but soft, at least.

"What am I going to do?" she asked, and Madeline looked at her sympathetically.

"Do you still have feelings for him?"

"I don't have any *feelings*," Alice said, wrinkling her nose, "besides annoyance, aggravation, and attraction."

Madeline dipped her head to the side as she studied her. "Attraction can be controlled. If you actually have an emotional attachment to him, however—"

"I most certainly do not."

"Well, then, there is nothing to worry about," Madeline said with a nod of her head.

"Madeline, I have been far too selfish, making this conversation entirely about me," Alice said, coming to attention, peering across the dark of the room. "You *must* tell me all about your honeymoon. And your marriage."

"Why… are you still going to write the story?" Madeline asked, not meeting her gaze but instead staring down at her intertwined fingers. Alice paused when she noted that Madeline seemed more frightened by the thought than excited, as she had been when they had spoken of it before the wedding, when Alice first started writing the story.

"Do you not want me to?" Alice asked with a frown. "It will of course be a work of fiction… with a great deal of emphasis on what makes your love story so lovely and true."

"Of course I do," Madeline said quickly. "I just thought… that perhaps it might be a bit boring."

"Boring?" Alice asked incredulously. "How can you say that? Why, Stephen came out of nowhere, a rags-to-riches story, providing proof beyond reasonable doubt that he was the true heir to the earldom. Not only that, but he then swept you off your feet when he asked you to dance. You swooned in his arms! You said he was the most charming, humorous, sweet man you had ever met and you could not wait to marry him."

"All very true," Madeline said, but Alice didn't miss the way she twisted her hands together.

"Has he done something?" Alice asked suspiciously, but Madeline quickly shook her head.

"No, of course not," she said with a small smile. "We had a lovely time on our honeymoon. He has just been a bit... absent since our return, that is all. I am sure he is just catching up with everything he missed while we were away."

"I'm sure," Alice said, but she moved closer across the sofa so that she could better study Madeline. She seemed much paler than usual, her deep-blue eyes appearing sunken into her face. "Well, tell me what you thought of your wedding. Was it as beautiful as you could have ever imagined it to be?"

Madeline's eyes brightened at that, and she began to describe in detail all that Alice had missed. She briefly glossed over the wedding night, her cheeks turning a bright pink, and Alice didn't pry. It wasn't as though she could write of that anyway, although she was quite intrigued by what lay in wait for her — were she ever to marry herself.

She closed her eyes for a moment, wishing that Benjamin's face didn't appear as the man approaching her and the wedding bed. Damn him and that glorious, chiseled jawline. Oh, and the dimple. She couldn't forget that.

She sighed and refocused on Madeline, making sure not to miss a thing she said.

For she had a story to write.

CHAPTER 5

*B*enjamin considered Alice out of the corner of his eye, his hands in his pockets as he shortened his long stride to match hers as they returned to Essex's townhouse.

She was rather quiet, which he had come to realize was not at all typical of her. He looked behind him to make sure that her maid was a good enough distance away so as not to hear them.

"Is there anything amiss?" he asked as casually as possible.

"No," she said, but then paused for a moment, "well, perhaps."

"Is it Lady Donning?" he asked, assuming it to be so after seeing the lady himself.

Alice looked up at him with question in her gaze. "She didn't seem well, did she?" she said, wrinkling her button of a nose and he had to resist the urge to reach out and tap it. "I had thought perhaps I was seeing things, but if you think the same, then there could very well be something wrong."

"I confess that I do not know her well," Benjamin said, fighting the strange rising need now to reach out and take

Alice's hand within his as they walked. "But she did strike me as a woman who was somewhat sickly."

"Which is not the case whatsoever." Alice frowned. "How did Lord Donning seem to you?"

"As well as ever," Benjamin said with a shrug. It was the truth. Donning had been his usual self. Somewhat secretive, not revealing many details of his honeymoon, but seemingly pleased with his new bride — and her dowry, although Benjamin was not about to tell Alice that for it would only cause suspicion.

"I am writing their story," Alice confessed, and he looked over at her.

"Does Donning know?"

"I'm not sure," Alice said, biting her lip. "I asked Madeline if I could talk to him, to gain his perspective, and she seemed somewhat hesitant. She said she would speak with him." She turned, lifting her face up to Benjamin. "Would *you* ask him for me?"

"Me?" he asked, raising his eyebrows. "I'm not sure that I should become involved in your meddling."

He hadn't realized that she had stopped walking until a few seconds went by and he didn't hear her response. He turned around to see that she was stopped on the cobblestones, arms folded across her chest.

"What are you doing?" he asked, refusing to walk back to collect her. She was a grown woman. She could come to him.

"What did you just say?"

"I asked what you were doing."

"Before that."

He sighed. "Could we not stand here in the middle of the road shouting at one another?"

"Did you or did you not call my work 'meddling'?"

"Oh." He ran a hand through his hair, "what would you have me call it, then?"

"Writing? Entertaining? Creating? Storytelling?"

"Very well," he said, not missing the curious stares of onlookers as they passed by. "I'm not sure that I would like to become involved with your storytelling."

"Why not?"

"Because…" he searched his mind for a plausible reason, "because that is women's work."

He didn't think her eyebrows could have risen any higher. He was wrong.

"*Women's* work? Most people believe that the best writers are men! In fact, many women *pose* as men so that their writing is respected."

"Not writing in particular," he tried again, becoming exasperated by her inability to see reason and understand just what he was trying to say. "Writing romantic love stories. No respectable man would involve himself in such a thing."

That got her moving, at least. Except, instead of joining him once more, she stormed past him in a flurry of skirts.

"Alice?" he said, looking at her maid with some desperation, hoping she would provide him with an idea of what had gotten into her mistress, but she just barely concealed her smirk as she strode by him, following along behind her mistress.

"Alice!" he called, attempting to keep his stride controlled so that no one could accuse him of chasing her around like a faithful puppy. He finally caught up to her. It was amazing how fast she could travel despite all of the material around her much shorter legs. "Did I say something wrong?"

"You are unbelievable," she said, continuing her fast clip. "You obviously have no respect for what I do — none whatsoever."

"I do," he argued. "Tell me this. Who reads most of your stories?"

"People."

"Women," he countered. "They are your audience. So it only makes sense that a woman is telling the story. I meant nothing by it."

"Very well," she said, but he could tell that she was only trying to rush through the conversation.

"Fine," he muttered. "I will speak with Donning." Then he sighed inwardly. He had no idea where that came from, but for whatever reason, he had a great desire to return to her good graces.

She stopped walking again, but this time she was looking up at him with a smile on her face, causing her dimple to appear. "You will?"

"Yes." *No.* Damnit, why had he said that? Donning would think him a fool. "He said he would be visiting Chesterpeak's club tonight. I'll see him there and will ask him."

"Oh." She didn't seem thrilled with the thought anymore, though why, he had no idea. The woman was a mystery. Pleased with him one moment, vexed with him the next. "Well... thank you."

"You're welcome. Are you happy now?"

She certainly didn't look happy, but a forced smile crossed her face. "Yes, of course. Here we are. You have safely seen me home with no mishaps along the way. Enjoy your... time tonight."

And with that she was in the house, shutting the door on his face, leaving him utterly perplexed.

AND SO IT was that Benjamin entered The Nomad with an incomprehensible degree of trepidation. He felt as though he was doing something wrong, which made no sense whatso-ever. He was a single man, regardless of the agreement he had made, and he should have no qualms about enjoying himself.

He couldn't explain, however, the fact that he didn't even notice the women who sat in the back of the main room until one of them — Jenny, her name was — called out to him with a wink and a smile. When he said "hello" and continued walking, he didn't miss the shock on her face as she gaped at him.

When he had looked over at her, all he could see was Alice. Instead of Jenny's blond hair, it was Alice's dark, sleek head of chestnut strands that he wanted to touch. Instead of Jenny's light-blue eyes, it was Alice's warm chocolate ones that he wanted to gaze into. And instead of Jenny's — or any of these women's — voluptuous curves, it was Alice's lush body he longed to take into his hands.

But besides all of that, he wasn't here for women. He was here to speak with Donning — and Chesterpeak — as it was past time that he was updated on the investment he had made with the establishment's owner.

"Luxington!"

There was the man himself, exiting from one of the back rooms to greet him.

"It's been some time since you've been here. I was beginning to worry," said Chesterpeak with a laugh, although as he rubbed his mustache he gazed at Benjamin with more seriousness, causing Benjamin to realize just how much time he had been spending here prior to this past week — since he had begun seeing Alice more frequently.

"Nothing to worry about," Benjamin said with forced cheerfulness. "I was just occupied by a few other things."

"Good to hear it," Chesterpeak said, clapping him on the shoulder. "What can I do for you tonight? Cards? Dice? Women?"

"No, actually, a conversation."

"With…?" Chesterpeak said, glancing over toward the women who were just beginning to circulate the room. It was quite early in the evening, Benjamin realized. Usually he didn't find himself here until the later hours, but he had been unsettled following his walk with Alice.

"With you," he said, causing Chesterpeak to snap his head back slightly in surprise.

"Oh?"

"Could we go into your office?"

"Of course," Chesterpeak said smoothly, although Benjamin didn't miss the hint of annoyance that flashed across his face before he hid it well.

Benjamin followed him, surprised to find that Donning was within.

"I hope you don't mind if Donning participates," Chesterpeak said, waving to one of the wooden chairs in front of his desk, and Benjamin shrugged. He actually kind of did, but he didn't see any way to politely say that with Donning sitting here in front of him.

"Good to see you again, Luxington," Donning said, although he seemed more interested in the amber contents of his glass than in Benjamin, but Benjamin nodded his greeting. When he had seen him at his townhouse that afternoon, Donning had been all smiles and gaiety. Tonight, he seemed more subdued, and Benjamin wondered why the fluctuating moods.

"Now, what is it you wished to speak to me about?" Chesterpeak said, leaning back in his chair, which squeaked as he did. He crossed his ankle over the other knee. "I feel as though I have been summoned to see the headmaster."

He laughed at that, to which Donning snorted with a smirk, and now it was Benjamin's turn to feel the slight of the other schoolboys.

"It's about my investment," Benjamin began, and Chesterpeak and Donning exchanged a look.

"What of it?" Chesterpeak said.

"I'd like to know what is happening with it," Benjamin set out, not understanding why there should be an issue with it. "Is the return still expected within a fortnight?"

"I was just speaking with Donning about that," Chesterpeak said. "It could be about a month or so. Perhaps a bit longer until everything is straightened away."

"I don't understand," Benjamin said with a frown. "I thought it was a simple loan."

"It is," Chesterpeak said hastily. "However, I promise that it will see *significant* returns. Won't it, Donning?"

"It will," Donning said with a nod. "There was a slight hiccup in the whole thing."

"Which was..." Benjamin steepled his fingers together in front of his nose, looking back and forth between the two of them.

"There was a... clause that I was not aware of, and I need to straighten it all out before we will be repaid in full."

"Could you elaborate on what exactly this investment was for?" Benjamin asked, as he began to feel slightly ill from the clandestine conversation between the two men.

"Perhaps in time," Chesterpeak said smoothly. "We have to ensure that we can trust you, first."

Benjamin was beginning to realize that he should have ensured that he could trust *them* before he had entered into this scheme. But his father had vouched for Chesterpeak, and so he hadn't seen an issue — until he had realized the full extent of his father's own crimes.

Now, he questioned everything his father had suggested to him.

"I'd like to see repayment — or an explanation — by the end of the month," Benjamin said. "Is that possible?"

"Of course," Chesterpeak said with a smile that seemed far too practiced and easy. "Now, do you have more business to discuss or can we get onto some fun?"

"That would be all," Benjamin said, rising and following the two other men to the door of the study. "Oh, Donning, I do have one favor to ask of you."

"Oh?" he said, stopping outside of the door as Chesterpeak continued on.

"As you know, I have been spending some time with Miss Cunningham. She would like to write a bit of a tale of your love story, and was wondering if she could speak to you of it."

Donning stared at him without a change in expression, and Benjamin thought for a moment that he would rage against the very thought. But instead, he laughed, a loud, long guffaw that Benjamin hardly knew how to respond to.

"You're doing the bidding of a woman, now, Luxington? How quaint."

Benjamin gritted his teeth and held his tongue, instead adopting his usual, easy smile.

"You know what it's like when you're trying to court a woman, don't you, Donning? You go to extremes."

"I suppose I know that better than most," Donning said, reaching into his pocket and pulling out a couple of cheroots, one of which Benjamin accepted. "I do hear that Miss Cunningham has a rather fine dowry."

"Oh?" Benjamin said nonchalantly, feigning no prior knowledge of the fact. "Is that so? I thought her brother a closer to middle-class baron."

"He is," Donning said, lighting the cheroots, "but he and his wife have recently gained favor of royalty with all of their stargazing and such."

"So I hear." That, Benjamin could not deny.

"I imagine it has provided them with a substantial

income, and it seems they are favoring Miss Cunningham with some of it. Must want her out of the house!"

"Perhaps," Benjamin said noncommittedly.

"Well, if you're serious about the woman — which, I have to admit, Luxington, I never thought you would be — then this would be a good one. She could set you up for some time. If you need help winning her, ask Chesterpeak. He can be… surprisingly helpful." Donning laughed and a trickle of something akin to dread began to creep down Benjamin's spine. "Speaking of which, there's a game of faro beginning. Care to join?"

"Perhaps later," Benjamin said, feeling rather ill. "I think I need to get some air. You'll agree to speak to Miss Cunningham?"

"If it helps you get into her money — or her bed — of course," Donning said with a wink, a smile, and a wave as he continued into the main room. "Talk to you soon, my friend."

Benjamin waved back, but he couldn't bring himself to respond. Somehow he had the sense that he had been wrong about Donning.

Very wrong indeed.

CHAPTER 6

*A*lice sat at her writing table, looking out at the green beyond, tapping the feather of her pen against her temple as she searched for the correct words. Some days the words flowed so effortlessly it was as though she didn't even have to think, but simply allow her characters to speak the words they longed to say to one another.

Other days, she could barely scribble a word down on the parchment in front of her.

Today was one of those days.

It was maddening.

Perhaps it was because she had a deadline to meet and no particular direction for her story. Or perhaps it was because she would much rather be writing the story of her own heart and mind. Or, she had to begrudgingly admit, perhaps it was because she couldn't stop thinking about Benjamin Luxington.

He was as equally maddening as her lack of focus. For he was everything that was wrong with a young man, and yet everything right as well. Handsome, charming, but so much so that every woman who laid on eyes on him was drawn in by his winning smile and laughing eyes.

He had this way about him that made one feel as though she was the only woman in not just the room, but the entire world as well. It was dangerous, for it was so easy to forget that he would move on and do the same for the very next woman he spoke to.

She sighed, resting her head in her hands, wishing the greenery dancing in front of her out the window would tell her what to write next — or what to do about the very handsome man who was suspiciously now courting her.

"Is something amiss?"

Alice whirled around at his voice, so unfairly nonchalant, especially when he laughed as she nearly fell off her chair, just managing to catch herself. There he was, framed in the doorway, his clothes perfectly draped on his perfectly muscled body, his perfect dimples indented around his perfect smile.

She had never so admired another while so greatly hating herself in the same moment.

"What are you doing here?" she asked, and he snorted.

"How lovely to see you too, Alice," he said, mocking her. "I hope you are having the most wonderful day."

She dipped her head to the floor as she realized how ungrateful she must sound.

"My apologies," she said, pushing back her chair and rising to face him, twirling her pen between her fingers as she did so, noting that her hands and arms, free of gloves as she wrote, were covered in ink stains, and she hid her hands behind her back, hoping he wouldn't see them. "I am most vexed by my work and I am taking it out on you."

"What's wrong?" he asked, gesturing toward the pages on the desk as he took a seat on the off-white loveseat with its high scrolled arms, sprawling almost lazily upon it.

"The ideas are not flowing as they should," she said, retaking her seat after turning her chair to face him instead of the desk.

"What are you writing?"

Alice tilted her head as she studied him. "Do you really want to know?"

"I asked, didn't I?"

"I suppose you did," she said, smiling at the thought, "therefore you must feign interest, whether you are entertained or bored beyond belief. I am currently writing Madeline's story. The first bit was published this week, and now I must finish the second part in order for it to be printed within a month."

"You do not write it all at once?" he asked, lifting his brows.

Alice arched an eyebrow.

"You do not read any serials in newspapers or magazines?"

"Some of them," he said, sounding awfully defensive, but Alice kept herself from teasing him, for he seemed quite perturbed by her accusation.

"When I tried to publish my first work — a novel — I could not find a publisher who was interested in printing it," she explained, the ache in her chest returning when she thought of it. She had put her entire soul into that book, that work of fiction, and no one would take a chance on her. "However, there was one publisher who also owned a magazine. He was desperate for new content, and was searching for something that ladies might be interested in reading. When he found out my brother was a baron, he asked me if I would write a column for him."

"A gossip column?" Benjamin asked, to which Alice shook her head, though she knew there were a few too many similarities between the work of a gossip columnist and what she did.

"I told him that I would write fiction, and proposed the idea of a serial — a piece of a novel in each publication, continuing month to month. He agreed, but suggested a hybrid of the two. I can make up names and embellish or change characters and personalities, but they must all be based on true stories in order to draw interest. I agreed, but on one condition — instead of stories of scandal, I would write tales of love."

Benjamin was nodding as she spoke, and when she stopped, he looked at her with a bemused expression.

"I receive permission for every story I write," she insisted, now feeling it was her turn to defend herself. "And I allow Madeline to read her own story. It's only fair."

"Except that you have obviously written something someone is not particularly pleased about," he pointed out, and now she discarded her pen completely, sticking it into the loose chignon at the back of her head.

"Which I do not understand," she said, tapping her chin. "I am always so careful."

"Well," Benjamin began, clasping his hands around one knee as he looked up at her expectantly, "Donning has agreed to speak with you."

"Really?" Alice exclaimed, rising from her chair once more, which caused Benjamin to stand himself, as graceful as ever. "About him and Madeline?"

When Benjamin nodded, Alice couldn't help herself. She was so pleased — and relieved — that she threw herself into his arms and planted a kiss on his cheek before she even realized what she was doing.

"Thank you," she said before stepping back smartly after her over-the-top display. "Thank you very much."

"Of course," he murmured, turning away from her, and

shame washed over Alice at her overenthusiastic reaction. He had simply been answering the petition of a friend, whereas she had acted as though he had given her the world — or a new storyline, at the very least.

"When should I meet with him?" she asked after clearing her throat, trying to cover up her embarrassment.

"I will arrange it," he said, and Alice wondered why he now wore such a frown. "In fact," he continued. "I think I should be present during your interview.

"Why?" Alice asked.

"It would be most proper," he said, seemingly somewhat ill at ease now.

"I would like to go visit Madeline again sometime this week to see how she is doing," Alice said. "Perhaps then?"

"Perhaps," he agreed, and then continued asking questions about how the serial worked.

"So you are telling me," he said, "that in order to read your works, I need to find all of the magazines they have been published in?"

"Correct," she said, but then considered the question. "I am told that they have proven successful enough that the publisher is considering printing them as novels as well."

"Is there one available?" he asked. "I'd like to read one."

Alice's head snapped up at that and she studied him with surprise, finding his greenish blue eyes clear with undisguised curiosity. She wondered what was motivating him — did he actually want to read her work or was he simply interested in assessing whether or not she wrote anything that was worth reading? "Are you serious?"

"Of course," he said, nodding smartly. "I wouldn't jest about something that means so much to you."

"Well… thank you then," she managed, trying not to read anything into his words. He was probably like everyone else — interested in how she managed to swing the gossip of the day into something that was worth reading.

She hesitated, having one other thought. She shouldn't do it, and yet…

She walked over to the bookshelf beside her, rummaging through until she found what was she looking for.

"Here," she said, grunting as she lifted out stacks of papers, holding them out to him before she lost her nerve.

"What are these?" His fingers brushed against hers as he took them from her and set them down on the desk, the touch sending a wickedly delicious thrill down her spine.

"My manuscripts," she said. "The first drafts, so they might prove somewhat difficult to read as I have marked them up with edits and cross outs and various additions. But then you don't have to go searching for anything else. I've written but a few short tales so far. Madeline's is to be my longest work yet."

"What about your first story — the work of fiction?"

"It's in there…" she said with some hesitation. She hadn't revisited it in some time, and she was hesitant about showing it to anyone again, least of all Benjamin. Especially when it hadn't been good enough to publish. "It's at the bottom."

He beamed at her. "Then that is what I shall read."

"Are you sure?" she asked, unwilling to have him doubt her abilities as a writer. "It was the first thing I wrote, so I don't know—"

"But it is entirely from your own imagination."

"It is."

"Then I look forward to it," he said, his regular, charismatic self, and Alice took a deep breath, telling herself that if the book was ever published, as she dreamed it would be, then anyone could read it. Anyone, including Benjamin himself.

"Do you ever…?" he began, but then trailed off, as though unwilling to ask her.

"Do I ever what?"

"Writing other people's stories, do you ever think it might be somewhat… intrusive?" he asked, looking up at her from beneath his hooded eyelids with those lashes that were nearly sinful for a man to possess.

Alice bit her lip, for he came awfully close to the truth.

"Sometimes," she said, "although I make all attempts to do so in a way that honors their love story and that they are more than happy to agree to. I would never write it in a way that would hurt anyone or make for gossip that they are not happy about."

He nodded, but Alice didn't want to speak of it anymore, for she didn't like the idea that he might think less of her.

She looked up at him now, not wanting to insult him but hoping that he would understand.

"I suppose it's like… well, like when you are with all of your women. Some may see it as taking advantage, but I am sure that all is consensual and that they are more than happy to take part in your… activity."

He blinked at her words, before looking down at his hands, folded in his lap. Deep within her, she was hoping that he would deny what she said, that he would tell her that he hadn't been with nearly as many women as she supposed, that he had thought of no one but her since he had met her.

But she was to be denied that.

"I, ah… yes, I suppose you are right," he said, nearly stuttering over the words. "But Alice, when you say all of my women, I would like you to know, I am not nearly the, ah, *prolific* rake it may seem I am."

"No?" she questioned, unable to believe she had pushed the conversation so far, but now that she had, she was unable to stop. It was in her nature, she supposed, to probe when she shouldn't, to go too far. "It seems to me that there are a great deal of women who are quite proud to boast of their times with you."

Benjamin scratched his head, his lips twisted into a discomforted smile.

"I suppose that could be said, especially of my past, but I assure you, Alice, that it has not been that way, since... since..."

She looked at him expectantly, needing to know what he was going to say, wondering if it was possible that he might say *since he had met her.*

"Since everything that happened to my brother. I've been more... careful about who I spend my time with."

"Oh," Alice said, disappointment stirring in her chest. "I see. Well, that is... that is good, I suppose."

"Yes," he said, much more eager now. "And now that I see how happy my brother and Freddie are, I want to make sure that I don't destroy that opportunity for any other young woman. Which has made single young ladies completely off limits."

"So you prefer married older women?" she asked, raising her eyebrows, not enjoying this turn in the conversation, although she knew it was thoroughly her own fault.

"No!" he exclaimed. "Well, not always." He winced. "There have been some widows who enjoy a casual relationship, and then there are other women who don't expect anything in return, for it is more of a... profession to them, I suppose."

"Prostitutes, then," she said, suddenly feeling as though she was going to be sick.

"Not prostitutes, no," he said, shaking his head. "More in the line of... mistresses."

Now he was the one who looked ill.

"Why are we even speaking of this?" he asked.

"Because it is important to me to know the intentions of

the man who is courting me… even if it is no more than a guise."

"If it helps at all, I have not seen any other women since we began our pretense of a courtship. In fact, none at all since the Donning wedding."

Alice wished she didn't experience a thrill at the thought. She was an idiot for allowing it to matter. This conversation should only be further proof for why she should stay as far from Benjamin Luxington as possible. Instead, she only wanted him more, enjoying the way he lazily swung a leg back and forth over the arm of that loveseat.

"None?"

"No."

"Not even—"

"No."

"Oh," she managed. "Well, thank you for considering my-my reputation, I suppose."

"Of course," he said, standing again. "I'll arrange to speak to Donning tomorrow, if that suits you."

"Of course," she echoed him, standing as he made to leave.

"And in the meantime," he said, lifting the papers in his hand. "I have some reading to do."

At that statement, her heart skipped a beat.

"Enjoy," she said, forcing a smile, and followed him to the door. He looked back at her, waved, and then continued down the corridor.

Any chance Alice had of concentrating on Madeline's story went with him.

Instead she sat down to begin writing a new story, although it took some time for she couldn't find her pen. She looked underneath everything on her writing table, on the floor, around all the surfaces of the room. How could someone lose a quill pen?

Oh yes. She fished it out of her chignon and dipped in the

ink to begin the new story. One of a man, a woman, and a fabricated romance.

She knew she and Benjamin would never see their own happy ending together.

But that didn't mean she couldn't create her own on the page.

CHAPTER 7

*B*enjamin was so engrossed in the story before him that he wouldn't have remembered his appointment had his valet not reminded him that Miss Cunningham was expecting him.

He dressed much more hurriedly than usual, chagrined to find himself late in arriving to meet her. He found her — with her maid — awaiting him outside on the front steps.

"Alice!" he said in greeting her. "You look lovely today."

"Thank you," she said graciously. Benjamin was being entirely serious — her blue dress, a slight hue darker than most of the lighter colored frocks favored by most women — brought out the chestnut of her hair and the dewiness of her cheeks. She held a reticule larger than most in one hand, and he imagined it included a tablet and pencil for notes. "And thank you for arranging this."

"Of course," he said, just as her mother appeared on the front step.

"Lord Benjamin," she greeted him, and he bowed his head in greeting. Alice looked very much like her mother, which promised that Alice would age just as gracefully. "I find myself otherwise engaged this afternoon, or else I would have been more than pleased to accompany the two of you. As you are visiting the home of a married couple and will be walking, if it is not inconvenient for you, I hope that it is proper enough for you and Ingrid to accompany Alice."

"That will be just fine," Benjamin said, secretly pleased that they would be alone, although he steeled his features into a neutral expression. "I promise all will be proper and respectful."

"Very well, then," Lady Susan said. "Enjoy your visit."

Benjamin held his elbow out to Alice, pleased when she both easily and comfortably looped her arm through his. He wasn't sure why he, a man who was accustomed to the touch of more women than he would care to admit to, should be so affected by a simple, respectable gesture, but he was none-theless when it was with her.

"How was your morning?" she asked, and he looked down at her with a smile on his face.

"Enlightening."

"Oh?" That pretty, pink mouth rounded. "How so?"

"I was reading the most titillating story," he said, teasing her. "It was *quite* romantic."

"You began reading my book, then." Suddenly, it didn't seem like she could hold his gaze any longer, as she stared rigidly in front of them.

"I found myself quite curious last night," he said, "and I stayed awake nearly half the night, more than enthralled. I've never read anything like it before."

She looked up at him suspiciously. "You're just saying that."

"I am not!" he defended himself. "It's the truth. I finally fell asleep on my sofa, and when I woke in the morning I began reading once more. In fact, I would have stayed there and finished it had my valet not reminded me that I had a very important engagement with a very important lady."

She snorted. "That charm doesn't work on me, Benjamin."

"No?" He had a sudden, inexplicable urge to prove that it did very much.

"Well... not anymore," she amended.

"Tell me, Alice, do you feel nothing when I am around?"

"Friendship," she said primly, but he noticed a flicker of amusement in her eyes.

"What about when I touch you?"

He lifted one of his hands to tuck a stray tendril of hair into her bonnet, and she started in surprise, looking around to see if any other passersby had noticed.

"I appreciate the gesture, but no," she said, although he saw the working of her throat and recognized the lie.

"Or," he said with a quick glance to each side, noting that there was no one about who was paying them close attention besides her maid. He leaned down close to her as he began to surreptitiously steer her toward one of the buildings, "what about when I whisper in your ear?" He allowed his breath to caress her and could sense her leaning in close to his side as she took a swift inhale.

"It... it tickles," she said, but her eyes closed for a moment, as though she was enjoying the sensation far more than she let on.

In one swift motion, he pulled her into a space between the nearby buildings and gently pushed her up against the brick behind them.

"How about when I kiss you?"

"Oh, so you do remember?" she said, narrowing her eyes at him, surprising him with her cheekiness.

"Do you honestly think I could forget something like that?" he asked huskily, before he leaned down and without any further contemplation or flirtation, devoured her lips with his, as though they were meant to press against one another, to fit each other like nothing else had ever done so before.

They hadn't just been words. When he had kissed her that evening, in the gardens outside of the ballroom, he had been overcome by just how much she had affected him. It had shocked him enough to cause him to pull away and to allow reason to invade.

Reason that he had obviously lost again. How else could he describe what was currently happening — what had caused him to forget his vow of protecting others for a change — people like Alice, *good* people, who had done nothing that should cause them to have to suffer from the misery he seemed to bring to everyone who was close to him.

But then her lush body molded into his, and he groaned, bemoaning the fact that he wasn't a better man, but a man who allowed his base urges to overcome his best intentions and drive his actions instead.

Despite her protestations earlier, Alice seemed as eager as he, twisting her fingers in his hair and matching the movement of his lips, caressing his with both a sweet innocence and yet a hidden carnal longing that he could sense was buried deep within.

Oh, what would it be like to bring that out, he wondered as his arms encircled her waist, drawing her closer still as he held her just an inch away from the rough wall behind her.

He could stand here kissing her all day, he reasoned, and he likely would have, had a gasp not invaded his consciousness from just behind him.

He lifted his head from Alice, turning to see her maid flitting back around the corner. He looked down at Alice with a grin.

"It seems we've been caught," he said. "How loyal to you is she?"

Alice nibbled her lip, already rosy with his kiss, and he longed to replace her teeth with his own, but knew that now that he had returned to reason, it wasn't the time to dissolve back into it.

"I'll speak with her," she said. "Perhaps I can make it worth her while not to say anything. Although..." she eyed him as she pointed her index finger into his chest before trailing it downward, "it would serve my brother right to know what all of his machinations have led to."

"Oh, love, this all began long before the agreement was made with your brother."

"Is that so?" she asked, challenging him with her brown-eyed stare beneath eyelids that had become heavy with her own growing desire.

"It is," he said, stretching one arm above her head and leaning in close, "and I think I have proven my point."

"Which is?"

"That you are not, in any way, immune to my charms."

She didn't reply, but tossed her head, ducking under his arm as she began to return to the street beyond, and Benjamin paused for a moment, enjoying the view of her walking away.

It took just a few strides to catch up with her, and her maid quickly began to follow them again, though the girl's cheeks were flushed as she looked back and forth between the pair of them.

"Alice?" he said gaily.

"Yes?" she responded, although she didn't turn to look at him.

"We're going the wrong way."

She stopped, looked up, beside them, and behind her, and

then turned and began marching in the other direction, toward the Donning residence once more.

It took great effort for Benjamin to keep from laughing.

"One more thing," he said when he had caught up to her once more.

"What else could there possibly be?" she asked with exasperation.

"I told you that I quite enjoyed your work."

"You did."

"But there was something missing."

She looked at him sideways. "What do you mean?"

"The story was interesting, but I didn't quite believe in the romance."

"Pardon me?" she asked, both insult and intrigue captured in her voice.

"You told me — the reader — all that your hero and heroine thought of one another, but I didn't feel it. That depth of passion, the love they apparently couldn't do without, somehow fell flat."

He expected her to become angry, or perhaps defensive at his words. But she surprised him once more. She tilted her head, looking up at him from underneath the brim of her bonnet.

"You're right."

"I am?" he asked, somewhat incredulously.

She nodded.

"I didn't know how to write it because I had never felt it myself. That's why I have been writing about the experiences of others — because they can tell me what it is like."

He picked up her arm and tucked it into the crook of his elbow again — where he felt it belonged.

"Well, then," he said, just as Donning's house came into view. "We'll just have to see about providing you with your own knowledge, then, won't we?"

He didn't give her a chance to reply as he rapped on the door and the butler let them in.

* * *

It took Alice some time to regain her composure.

Well, the truth was, she didn't know if she would ever regain her composure after *that kiss*.

Damn, but Benjamin Luxington knew how to use his lips. She was well aware that she should never have allowed him to take such liberties in the middle of the day, in the middle of the street, in the middle of Mayfair, even if they had been shielded by the house.

But he was right. She was far too susceptible to his charm, and there didn't seem to be anything she could do about it but give in.

She would just ensure that she only allowed him to tempt her physically, she reasoned. It would be good for her — for her writing, that is. She just had to keep her heart protected, for she knew for certain that if there was ever a man who could break it, it was Benjamin Luxington.

The butler led them past the parlor where they had met Madeline before and into what must be Lord Donning's study. It was as dark as the parlor had been, the one window covered with deep green curtains. She nearly didn't see Lord Donning until he rose from the chair behind his desk.

"Miss Cunningham," he said, bowing low over her hand, smiling at her. His hair was coiffed, his dark eyes glinting at her. "How lovely to see you. Thank you for your visit."

She nodded in greeting. "It is I who must thank you, Lord Donning, for agreeing to speak with me. Will Madeline be joining us?"

He shook his head. "Sadly, no. Madeline had another engagement planned for today."

"Oh, I am sorry to hear it," Alice said, although she was rather surprised. She had thought Madeline would be interested in being a part of this discussion. Perhaps her friend hadn't been aware she was coming.

"Next time," Lord Donning said smoothly before waving his hand out toward the chairs beyond the desk. "Please, have a seat, and tell me just what it is I can do for you."

Alice did as he asked, although she was grateful that Benjamin was with her. There was something about Lord Donning, although she couldn't determine exactly what it was that bothered her about him. He seemed too smooth, too polished, a man who might say one thing in front of her but quite another when her back was turned.

"Has Madeline told you about the serial I am writing?" she asked, and he inclined his head.

"She has, but perhaps you best explain it to me as well."

And so she did.

She thought that Lord Donning's eyes might have darkened as she did so, but it was difficult to tell in the dim light.

She finished by asking that he tell her about the first time he met Madeline and what he thought of her.

"Did you love her the moment you saw her?" she asked, to which he smiled thinly.

"She's a beautiful woman."

"She is," Alice agreed, "is that what first attracted you to her?"

"Yes," he inclined his head, and Alice was surprised, for most men told pretty lies about the grace and charm of a woman drawing them in. "Isn't that what attraction is?" he asked, and Alice shrugged.

"I wouldn't know."

"No," Lord Donning said, drawing out the word, "and yet you have attracted our Lord Benjamin here, so you must have *some* idea of how to do so. Although it doesn't take much for you, does it Luxington?"

He laughed, a long guffaw, and Alice felt rather than saw Benjamin grow tense and lean forward in his chair.

"That's enough, Donning," he said tersely, surprising Alice, for the only mood she had ever seen from Benjamin was the teasing, jovial side. His brow was furrowed in anger now, his lips pressed tightly together.

"My apologies," Lord Donning said, waving a hand in the air, and Alice looked down at the still-empty page in front of her. Lord Donning may have agreed to speak to her, but he certainly didn't have anything helpful to impart. Which was odd, for Madeline had always spoken so highly of how romantic he was. "I'm sure the young lady knows your reputation well enough, however, for she writes about every liaison within the *ton*. There must be many tales on her pages about you!"

Alice held her breath for a moment, hoping that Benjamin wouldn't think much about the statement, for she had no wish to speak to him about it any further.

"Lord Donning," she attempted once more. "When did you decide that you wanted to court Madeline?"

He leaned back in his chair, stretching his arms high overhead with his fingers interlaced before he rested his head back into his hands once more.

"Let me see... when I danced with her," he said, then dropped his hands and just stared at her.

Alice sighed. This was going to be a long interview.

CHAPTER 8

*B*enjamin was beginning to wish that he had never offered to assist Alice with this conservation with Donning, even if it had pushed him into her good graces. As Donning evaded another one of her questions, she rubbed her forehead, smearing pencil over her eye in the process.

As tedious as it all was, at the very least, he appreciated the time he was afforded to sit and study Alice at work. She was tenacious, that was for certain. Benjamin was well aware that Donning was simply being an ass, but for all Alice knew, this was his usual personality. He gave her one-word answers, laughed when all in the room were aware that Alice was not telling a joke, and began to respond to her questions with ones of his own.

"And just why are you so interested?" he asked now, and Alice sighed.

"We've been over this, I believe," she said, repeating exactly what she was doing and why she was speaking with him. "Perhaps it is best that we speak another day — a day when Madeline is available as well. The two of you together might have more to say."

"I don't think that is a good idea," Donning said, steepling his fingers together, looking at Alice over the tips of his index fingers, which were now pressed together.

"Why not?" she asked, and Benjamin found her rather brave as she held herself up tall and matched his stare.

"Because I think, Miss Cunningham, that this is a rather ridiculous way to pass your time. Perhaps you would be better to focus on your own life and finding your own husband. Why, you're practically boring Luxington here out of his mind. I have some advice for you, Miss Cunningham. Act like a lady and you will attract a gentleman."

Alice didn't break her stare, but she also didn't move. She seemed rooted to the spot, her mouth opening and closing a couple of times as though she was searching for the proper response.

Before he could even think about what he was doing, Benjamin found himself rising from his chair and leaning over Donning's desk.

"Now, see here, that is quite enough," he said, surprised at the surge of protectiveness that had encompassed him at Donning's remarks. "Alice is a highly skilled writer, and a great many people enjoy reading her stories. If you do not have the inclination to offer your own story, then we will find someone who will. Good day, Donning."

He was already halfway to the door before he realized that Alice wasn't following him, and he stood and began to motion to her to join him, but it seemed that she was not quite finished.

She stood, placed her notebook and pencil into her reticule, and walked slowly toward the desk, where she placed her hands nearly exactly where Benjamin's had been moments before.

"I am sorry if I have inconvenienced you," she said softly. "I obviously never should have come. All I ask is that you continue to treat my friend with the respect and affection she described to me upon first meeting you. For she deserves nothing but the very best."

Donning leaned forward, obviously attempting to intimidate Alice and scare her away, but Benjamin was impressed that she held her ground. He was tempted to go place himself between the two of them, but he was also aware that Alice enjoyed fighting her own battles.

"Madeline is my wife now, and I will treat her however I would like."

It seemed after the entire interview, there was finally something that shook Alice, for her face clouded over like a storm and she straightened and joined Benjamin at the door without even a glance behind her.

Benjamin shot Donning a look over his shoulder, slightly perturbed by the wink and self-satisfied smile that crossed the face of the man he had considered a friend.

"Luxington," Donning called after them down the corridor, and he and Alice exchanged a look of question. She waved him back, likely just as curious as Benjamin about what further the man would have to say.

Benjamin stepped around Alice's maid and into the doorway, waiting for Donning's words.

"I've got her primed for you now," Donning murmured. "Go comfort her now and close this with her."

Benjamin didn't even know how to respond, so he simply shut the door behind him as he continued down the corridor and rejoined Alice.

"What did he have to say?" Alice asked immediately once they left the shuttered house. The sun was a huge beacon of light, the fresh breeze filling Benjamin with cleansing he didn't even know that he needed.

"Nothing," he said bitterly, "nothing of importance."

"I didn't know he was anything like that," she said,

looking up at him imploringly. "I thought he was a good man. Madeline seemed to be so infatuated with him, and she's a smart woman, a good judge of character. Her father is a businessman, and had always hoped that she would one day take over his company despite being a woman. If Lord Donning doesn't even approve of me writing a serial, I can hardly imagine that he would be interested in Madeline continuing to work."

Benjamin shook his head slowly. "I would agree with that."

"What do I do?" she asked somewhat helplessly, and he looked down at her with some question.

"In terms of…"

"Of the serial. Of Madeline. Of her husband."

"Well," he said, cocking his head. "I suppose you should start by speaking with your friend. As for the serial, well… maybe it's time to write some of your own work, instead."

"Pure fiction?"

He nodded. "Your work is good, Alice. You just need some confidence. And a little romance yourself."

He winked at her, attempting some levity as he stroked the underside of her wrist, tracing the ink stains that covered them, ink stains that were as much a part of her as the fingertips themselves. She had removed her gloves in order to make notes and she hadn't replaced them, having left them in her reticule — a matter of which he intended to take full opportunity.

She gave him what seemed to be an attempted glare as she shook her head at him, but he knew from the way she leaned into him that she wasn't immune to his caresses. Oh, he was a sinner. For an innocent young lady was exactly the sort of woman he should be staying far away from, and yet perhaps it was exactly that forbiddance that was enticing him.

Or... he looked down at her, a strange warmth filling him at the sight of the dark tendrils of hair peeking out from her bonnet. Was it more than that? Was it Alice herself? He couldn't remember the last time — or *any* time, come to think of it — that he had felt the need to protect a woman, or to claim her as his own. The fact was, he enjoyed that others saw him and Alice together, and he didn't want to think of what would happen when this was all over.

He was so caught up in his thoughts that he didn't notice the threat until it was too late. The sharp, deadly blade whizzed through the air, flying right between his shoulder and Alice's head. It fell to the ground with a clatter in front of them, and he and Alice stopped short, staring at it and then one another.

"Is that—" she began, but that was all she got out as he grabbed her and took her to the ground, covering her body with his in case there were more weapons being sent their way. He looked around them, trying to determine from where they could have been thrown, but he saw nothing but Ingrid, who was whimpering behind a nearby bush, and a passing wagon, continuing in the other direction. He thought he caught the blanket over the back of it billowing, but he couldn't say whether or not it had been moved by a human hand or the wind.

Finally, once a few moments had passed with no additional threats, he stood, holding out a hand to help Alice up. Her bag had fallen to the ground, its contents spilled out around them. She bent to replace everything, but he held up a hand to stop her and began to do so himself as Alice comforted Ingrid.

"Are you all right?" he asked when she returned, and she nodded, although her face had turned quite pale. Her eyes, however, were narrowed, and he finally realized that she was angry.

"I just wish whoever is doing this would stop being such a coward."

"A coward?"

"Yes," she said, nodding her head emphatically. "Just step up and confront me like a real man or woman, instead of hiring people to run me over or throw daggers at my head. All just because I am telling love stories!"

"There must be more to it than that," Benjamin said, shaking his head as he passed her bag back and looked around ruefully at all of the people on the street who were staring at them with unabashed curiosity. "A little gossip never led to an attempt on one's life... did it?"

"Not the way I write it," she said, straightening her bonnet, and he leaned in to rub the smudged pencil off her forehead, every nerve on edge as he stepped close to her. How was it that a fully clothed, innocent young lady could ignite a fire in him hotter than a half-dressed woman throwing herself at him?

It was a quandary he wanted to further explore, but one he knew he never could.

Which tore at him in more ways than he wanted to admit.

"I have to ask you something."

"Oh?" she said, raising her eyes to him.

"Was Donning right? Have you written stories about me?"

Her eyes shuttered at that, and she began walking again.

"No, I haven't," she said, so softly that he nearly didn't hear her.

"Why not?" he asked, jogging to catch up.

"I just... haven't. Besides, I would never do so without your permission. I would guess that half of them aren't even true. The relationships you do have... well, they don't exactly make for *love* stories."

Her words were so accurate it was like that very dagger had plunged into him, and yet he couldn't fault her for saying them, for she was right. He had always been proud of himself for his ability to attract all manner of women — until he had realized that he had been basing his life upon his father's approval, the approval of a man who knew nothing of what it meant to build relationships of any kind based on love or any real affection.

But he could change it all, could he not?

"I do apologize it did not go better with Donning," he said. "I didn't realize that he could be such an ass."

"It's not your fault," she said, biting her lip as she looked off to the side. "The story doesn't really matter much. So it doesn't work out — there will be a few disappointed readers, perhaps, but if Madeline agrees, I can still write the rest as pure fiction. It is Madeline I am concerned about now."

"Have you seen her lately?"

"I haven't."

"Where does she like to frequent? Perhaps you can catch her without Donning at some point."

Alice brightened considerably. "That is a good idea, actually. I know exactly where she might be."

"Good." He nodded brusquely. "Well, then, I hope to see you very soon, Miss Cunningham."

He tipped a finger on her nose, wanting more than anything to kiss her, but knowing that was the last thing he could do here, in full view of the window of her brother's townhouse.

She laughed at him before nearly skipping up the steps, and Benjamin found himself walking away with a much jauntier step.

Since he was in the neighborhood, he decided it was long past time he visit his brother and his wife. He had to admit he somewhat missed living with them, although now that they had children running about, he had felt that the house had become much too crowded with his presence.

Besides, living there had always been a reminder of his failures.

Perhaps he should have ridden today, he reflected once he made it to his brother's house. But, then, it was a fine day, and it wasn't as though he had much else to do but traipse around London.

It was Miles' wife, Freddie, who greeted him in the drawing room, telling him that Miles would be down in a moment.

"How are you, Benjamin?" she asked, and when she studied him, Benjamin received the same impression that he always did — that Freddie really wanted to know the answer, and wasn't just asking to be polite.

"I'm well," he said decisively. "I've been... occupied as of late, and it's been good for me."

"So I hear," she said, settling back into the Georgian Chippendale camelback sofa just as Miles walked into the room.

"Benjamin," he greeted him, and Benjamin nodded back.

"Good to see you, Miles."

The brothers didn't need to say much more. Miles never said much, anyway. He had been nearly deaf his entire life, and had grown up hiding it by letting most think he was standoffish.

The truth was, however, he often missed much of what was being said around him, despite his incredible ability to read lips. Of course, conversation had improved considerably for him since their father had passed and he had met Freddie, for with her in his life he had come to the conclusion that it no longer mattered if others were aware of his disability.

Today he also wore the ear trumpet headband Freddie, an inventor at heart, had fashioned for him.

"My apologies," Benjamin said, "I had forgotten that you would be at the House of Lords today."

"There is no issue," Miles said with a wave of his hand. "What brings you to this part of Mayfair today?"

"I was actually escorting Miss Cunningham to a meeting of sorts with Donning."

A slight uptick of his eyebrows was the single indication that the information surprised Miles.

"Would this have something to do with the serial she has been writing?"

"You know of it?"

Miles motioned to his wife. "Freddie enjoys it and has spoken of it. Can't say that gossipy romances are much to my taste."

"They're not gossip," Benjamin found himself defending Alice's work. "She writes only what others tell her about, and ensures they are happy with her storytelling."

Miles sat back in his flamestitch wing chair with a satisfied smile.

"You are quick to defend Miss Cunningham."

"I am only speaking the truth."

"Miles," Freddie admonished, though she wore a smile as she did so, "leave Benjamin alone, darling."

"I am merely pointing out an observation," Miles said, running a hand though his hair, slightly lighter and redder than Benjamin's own. "I think it's a good thing, actually. Miss Cunningham seems to be a pleasant young woman, and it is time that you found someone to share your life with."

Benjamin sat up straight at his brother's words. "You are right, Miles, in that she is... pleasant. I have agreed to look out for her for a time, 'tis true, but I most certainly will not be marrying her."

"Why ever not?" Freddie cut in, her gaze troubled. "You *are* courting her, aren't you?"

"Because I will never marry," Benjamin said determinedly,

ignoring her second question. "I wouldn't want to shackle someone to the likes of me for the rest of her life."

"Benjamin—" Freddie began, but he interrupted her.

"Don't say it, Freddie," he said, shaking his head. His brother's wife was a kind soul, but he didn't want to hear her make excuses for him. "What you think is not the truth. I just bring trouble, wherever I go, and Alice doesn't need that in her life. Even yesterday, I arranged for her to see Donning, and the man berated her the entire time we were there."

"Donning is a knobhead," Miles said dryly. "I've always told you that and I have no idea why you have remained friends with him — or Chesterpeak, for that matter. They both enjoyed friendships with our father. That should tell you something."

"He's always been fine before," Benjamin said with a shrug, "but we all know that I am not the best judge of character."

"Oh, Benjamin," Freddie said with a sigh, but his restlessness had already forced him up out of his chair, one that matched Miles', and he wandered the room, looking at everything but also nothing at all.

He heard a rustle of skirts that told him Freddie had stood as well, although she didn't cross over to him, for which he was grateful. "I have an idea," she said, and Benjamin looked across the room at her. She was short and slim, yet carried a strength within her that he had always admired. "Why don't we host a dinner party with our family and Alice's? Then perhaps we can all get to know one another a bit better."

"I'm not sure—" he began, but Miles had rejoined the conversation, clapping his hands together.

"Two days' time? We'll send a message to Oliver and Celeste," he said, nodding to his wife, who smiled broadly.

"Perfect," she said with a curt nod.

"But—"

"Thank you for calling, Benjamin," she said, before he could argue any further. "We shall see you and Miss Cunningham very soon. Now, come say hello to the children, will you?"

Benjamin climbed the stairs in a daze, aware that he had been properly handled, but not entirely sure just how or what he was supposed to do about it now.

CHAPTER 9

"*H*ello, there," Alice said to the clerk sitting behind the front desk of Castleton Stone. Benjamin was trailing behind her, as usual, but she had asked him to allow her to run this errand herself. Her mother had also accompanied her today, noting that she was interested in seeing Madeline again as it had been some time.

"Hello," the young man greeted her. "How can I help you today?"

"I am actually here to see Lady Donning," she said, smiling at him, eager to see Madeline. "We have an appointment."

The clerk nodded, leaving his post for a moment. When he returned, however, he had a look of apology on his face.

"It seems that Lady Donning sent round a note just a few minutes ago," he said. "I hadn't yet seen it. Lady Donning is unable to join you today, and she sends her regrets."

Alice's stomach sank, and she glanced back, exchanging a look with Benjamin, who seemed equally as troubled at the news.

"Is her father in?" she asked, and the man seemed a bit unsure.

"He is, but I'm not sure that he is seeing anyone at the moment."

"Will you please check for us?" she asked before softening her voice and tilting her head to plead with him. "It's important."

He looked up at her, meeting her gaze before he finally relented.

"Very well," he said. "Excuse me once more."

And so it was that a few minutes later, the three of them found themselves escorted into the office of Mr. Ezra Castleton, who stood when they entered. Pleasantries exchanged, they seated themselves around a small table at the outskirts of the room.

"Thank you for seeing us, Mr. Castleton," Alice began. "I know you are a busy man."

"It's no problem at all," he said, looking around at the three of them, although his gaze settled on Alice's mother. Alice didn't dwell on the thought, however, for she knew she didn't have a lot of time and she had to address what had brought them here.

"It's about Madeline," she burst out, knowing she should likely have brokered the subject more delicately, but was unable to keep from doing so out of concern for her friend.

"Oh?" he said, furrowing his generous brows.

"Have you seen much of her as of late?" Alice asked, to which Mr. Castleton slowly shook his head.

"No, but then she is newly married," he said, his words slow and measured. "They were visiting Bath, of course, and then she has been setting up her house here in London. I didn't expect her to return to the office as much as she had previously."

"I suppose that is true," Alice said, although she couldn't

shake the feeling that there was more to it. "It's just… not like her, to not be here, at work with you."

Mr. Castleton sighed, placing his hands over his stomach as he leaned back.

"It's no secret that I had hoped Madeline would take over the business one day," he said, "but she married an earl, and I know that a great many responsibilities come with the role of countess. I am beginning to come to terms with the fact that I will have to look to another succession plan."

He was quiet for a moment before staring off into a corner of the room. "I was a fool, anyway," he mumbled, "to think that a woman would have any interest in business."

"I don't believe that was the case at all," Alice said, leaning forward. "It was my understanding that Madeline very much had an interest in the business."

Her mother surprised Alice by placing her hand on Mr. Castleton's sleeve.

"I'm sure she is just becoming used to her changing position," she said with a gentle smile. "You will likely be seeing much more of her again soon."

Alice frowned. She appreciated that her mother was attempting to placate Mr. Castleton, but she just wasn't sure that she agreed.

She opened her mouth to say so when the door opened abruptly, and in stepped the subject of their conversation.

Alice's mouth dropped open in horror. Madeline looked awful. Her hair seemed thin and brittle, closer to straw than gold as it fell out of its pins to sag around her face. It appeared she was even paler than before, if that was possible, and her eyes were sunken in to her face, surrounded by dark circles.

Seeing the lot of them, she forced a smile.

"I am so sorry I am late," she said, closing the door behind her. "It is lovely to see you all."

"What about the note?" Alice asked, to which Madeline widened her eyes.

"The note?"

"Yes," Alice said slowly. "The one saying that you would be unable to join us today. The one your clerk said he had received."

"Oh, yes, that note," Madeline said, her laugh a pitch too high, a bit too giddy. "I had thought that I would be held up, but circumstances changed."

Her gaze flitted between all of them so wildly that Alice gave in to the urge to stand and draw Madeline's hands together.

"Why don't you come sit?" she asked, pushing her own chair toward her before finding another. "We were just speaking with your father about the business."

"Right," she said, placing her hand over her father's, squeezing it before pulling it back. "There is always much to be done here at Castleton Stone."

"It's good to see you," Mr. Castleton said gruffly, and Madeline looked up with note at his tone, likely because Mr. Castleton was not a man prone to much emotion.

Alice looked back and forth between Madeline and her father.

"Are you still working here much?" she asked Madeline, who she felt more distant from than she ever had before.

"Not much since my marriage," Madeline said softly, her eyes in front of her.

"Well, Miss Cunningham came here to see you, Madeline," Mr. Castleton said. "Why don't the two of you go for a walk around the building, find a place to sit down? I'll entertain Lady Susan here."

Alice started at the warmth in his tone as well as the fondness in his gaze when he looked down at her mother. The truth was, she hadn't particularly thought much of her mother in terms of romance, but she supposed that with her father passed, there was no reason her mother *wouldn't* be interested in a man, and she was still certainly a most attractive woman.

She was so caught up in her musings that she didn't even move until she heard Benjamin clear his throat from his seat against the wall, and when she looked up, she saw the laughter in his eyes and realized that he had accurately guessed exactly what she was thinking.

"That sounds lovely," she finally managed, turning to Madeline, who nodded, although when she stood, she seemed to sway slightly. "Are you all right?" Alice asked, to which Madeline nodded brightly.

"Of course!" she said. "I know just the place where we can speak. There's a little window seat down the corridor that is quite lovely."

Alice saw Benjamin follow them down the corridor, and she leaned into Madeline and whispered in her ear, "Who do you think is going to chaperone our parents?"

Madeline laughed a bit, showing signs of her old self.

"I only just realized my father's interest in your mother myself," she said, leading Alice over to the bench and lowering her voice. "Now, what was so important that you arranged to meet me here?"

Her eyes, the color of blue violets, were somewhat cloudy, but they looked at Alice with intent, and Alice squirmed for a moment, unsure of exactly how to ask Madeline about her marriage without overstepping.

"Did Lord Donning tell you that I came to see him the other day?"

Madeline sat back in some surprise.

"No, he didn't actually."

"Benjamin arranged for him to see me to speak further

about the story that I'd like to write." She hesitated for a moment. "Your husband was not... pleased about it all."

Madeline looked down at her fingers, which she was twisting together.

"No, I do not believe he is happy about the whole thing. In fact," she looked up at Alice imploringly, "would it be possible for you to halt it?"

"The story?"

"Yes." Madeline bit her lip as she nodded. "Stephen had assured me that it wasn't an issue, but he has become rather perturbed by it all. It seems he feels that it will mean too many people becoming privy to our personal lives, especially with him only recently becoming a member of the nobility."

"I understand," Alice said gently, never wanting to push her own agenda on someone else, although she questioned the quick change in direction and worried about whether or not her friend had any say in this decision. "I am sorry to hear it."

"I know that your publication was based around this," Madeline said, hanging her head slightly, tendrils of her blond hair brushing against the side of her face. "I'm ever so sorry."

"Don't be," Alice said brightly. She reached out and patted Madeline's hand. "I only thought that it was quite lovely, is all. Perhaps I could write a fictionalized ending for it, if you agree."

"I suppose that would be fine," Madeline said slowly, although her countenance dropped once more.

"Now," Alice said, attempting levity, "tell me what you have been up to recently."

Their conversation was nothing else much out of the ordinary, and soon enough Alice found herself returning to the carriage with her mother and Benjamin.

She glanced over at her mother, who wore a perpetual small smile the entire journey home.

"I never knew you were so well acquainted with Mr. Castleton," Alice said slyly, and her mother started.

"I don't know him that well," she said softly. "Mostly through your friendship with Madeline."

Alice nodded. She and Madeline had come to know one another in their youth through their shared love of museums and libraries — places that most young women their age had no particular care for. Madeline always had a head for figures, however, while Alice was much more suited to deal in words.

"Well, I have to say I approve," Alice said, and her mother gasped somewhat at Alice's revelation that she knew of what her mother was thinking and feeling — perhaps because she was suffering from the same malady.

She heard Benjamin chuckle from behind them, as he was following closely enough that he could assist if there were any dangers, although Alice and Oliver had made light of the possibility so as not to worry their mother.

As it happened, Alice hadn't shared the knife incident with Oliver yet, but she told herself it was because there just hadn't been an opportunity — certainly not because she didn't want to give him additional reason to insist that she stop her work nor stay inside.

Benjamin helped them into the carriage before settling on the seat across from them, and, as much as she loved her mother, Alice wished that, for a moment, she was here alone with him. Oh, the fun they could have, she thought wickedly. But then her eye caught Benjamin's, and by his spreading grin she realized that he had either correctly read her thoughts once more, or else he was having the same thoughts as she. Heat rushed through her at the knowledge.

"Lord Benjamin," her mother said, "how is your mother doing? I have not seen her in an age."

Benjamin's face completely changed to the picture of charming innocence as he responded to Alice's mother. "She is quite well. Lovely of you to ask."

"I am looking forward to seeing her again," Alice's mother said, and from the innocent smile that she cast first upon Alice and then Benjamin, Alice knew that her mother had something in mind. "I hear we are to have a dinner one of these nights."

"We are?" Alice asked, and Benjamin nodded.

"That's right," he said, holding a finger in the air. "I had forgotten."

Alice felt that this was information that was not fit for forgetting, but she was well aware that her mother wouldn't approve of her saying such a thing.

"When is this?" she asked, her heart suddenly beating rather hard. It was one thing to pretend a courtship when Benjamin was basically following her around from one engagement to the next, but something entirely different when she would be trapped in a room for the evening with both of their families.

"Freddie said something about tomorrow," Benjamin said nonchalantly, and Alice hoped her gaze accurately portrayed just how much this was not a trivial matter.

"Yes, that sounds wonderful," her mother beamed, and Alice looked at her in horror. How had no one thought to tell her of such an event? "We are looking forward to it, are we not, Alice?"

"Yes," Alice said weakly, "we most certainly are."

CHAPTER 10

"*I*'m not sure whether I feel sick from excitement or dread," Alice said the next evening, joining Celeste at the bottom of the stairs where they were to meet before departing.

Her sister-in-law tilted her head to regard her with pity.

"It is always that way when you are beginning to fall in love."

"In love?" Alice repeated, her eyes wide as she shook her head emphatically. "Oh, no, I most certainly am not falling in love with anyone. I am simply speaking of tonight's dinner."

"Yes — with the man who is courting you."

"*Pretending* to court me."

"Yes, Oliver shared as much."

Alice knew that Oliver would never keep such a thing from his wife. She wondered if she would ever find a love like that, in which she and her husband trusted each other so implicitly that there was never a doubt that they would know everything about one another.

Celeste waved a hand in the air.

"He seems more interested in spending time with you than a man who is simply pretending."

"He has nothing better to do, I suppose," Alice said dryly, and Celeste laughed.

"A man like Benjamin Luxington can always find something to do," she said, to which Alice sighed, for she was well aware that it was the truth.

She just didn't want to think about what else he might be doing in his spare time.

"You look lovely," Celeste said, scanning Alice up and down, and Alice nodded, knowing she should smile and say thank you, but she was unable to due to the nerves in her belly — which was ridiculous. She had seen Benjamin many a time lately. Why should tonight be any different?

Because his family would be there, as would hers. Because this felt like something people would do if they were *actually* courting, and it made it all too real.

Alice smoothed her hands over the blue silk she had carefully selected, then patted her hair, which her maid had fashioned into a chignon of the latest style.

"You are beautiful," Celeste insisted, her own gown floating down over her protruding stomach. "Now, Oliver is waiting at the door to escort us to the carriage."

"It seems rather silly, considering that they live so close," Alice noted, which Oliver and her mother overheard from the doorway.

"We are not walking for a dinner engagement," Oliver said, rolling his eyes at his sister as he escorted the three women to the waiting carriage. "It might be a short ride, but it will be a ride nonetheless. Alice, can I speak with you for a moment?"

She nodded, wondering what her brother would have to say that he wouldn't want to discuss in front of their mother and Celeste. She took a few steps with him away from the carriage.

"Tonight is all well and good, but Alice, we both know the reality of this arrangement." He paused, rubbing his temple, and Alice knew he was trying to put into words something he didn't actually want to say. She could help him and put him out of his misery, but she rather enjoyed watching Oliver squirm. "I just... I don't want you to get any romantic, fanciful notions," he said, his expression pained. "I had thought that this was a good idea, but now I'm not so sure. There haven't been any additional attempts on your life, so maybe the runaway horses were an accident. Perhaps I am putting you at risk of harm of another sort."

"You mean from Benjamin?"

He nodded stiffly. "A man like that... well, I'm not sure if he is the type that will ever choose to settle with one woman. I don't want you to get your heart broken. I also don't want to see you ruined."

Alice straightened. She would never tell her brother this, but his words were actually exactly what she needed to hear. They were a reminder of the truth — a truth that she had best remember.

"Not to worry, Ollie," she said. "My heart is most definitely intact, and I am more than aware of the consequences of losing it to a rake like Benjamin Luxington. I will be careful, and I will keep my distance."

He nodded, seemingly relieved.

"Oh, and Ollie?"

"Yes?"

"Remind me to tell you about the knife."

Before he could ask her anything further, however, she had lifted herself up and into the carriage, with Oliver squawking behind her.

* * *

BENJAMIN FOUND himself pacing the front parlor, nervously looking out the window at the street beyond. It was just a dinner, he reminded himself. He had had plenty of dinners before, with all of these guests who would be present this evening. Except Alice. Had he ever had a dinner party with Alice before? He couldn't be certain.

"Benjamin?" He looked to the door to see his mother framed within it. "Is everything all right?"

"Of course," he said gruffly, straightening his cravat for what felt like the tenth time that evening. "I was waiting for you."

She smiled, seeing through his lie, as she walked across the room and perfected his cravat for him. When she finished, she placed a hand on his shoulder as she looked up at him, her stare so eerily like Miles'.

"Oh, Benjamin," she said softly, surprising him when a sheen of water covered her eyes. "I feel as though I have never properly apologized to you."

"Apologized for what?" he asked, furrowing his brow. His mother was one of the kindest souls he had ever known. How she had managed to survive marriage to his father nearly unscathed, he would never know.

"I spent so much of your life protecting Miles that I never realized the extent to which I was neglecting you," she murmured. "Your father was so insistent that you follow his every move, that you learn from him, that I often just let him do as he pleased. Which I shouldn't have. I should have been there for you."

"I'm perfectly fine," he said, smiling down at her as he attempted to ease her concerns. "There is nothing to apologize for."

"I'm not so sure about that," she said, frowning. "You deserved more from me."

"Well, you are here for me now," he said, attempting levity. He was never one who was much for showing true thoughts and emotions. It was much easier to keep everything light and easy. That way no one got hurt — most especially himself.

"Alice Cunningham… are you serious about her?" his mother asked, taking her cue from him and leaving their previous conversation behind.

Benjamin paused, unsure of how much to tell her. He didn't want her to raise her hopes when nothing was ever going to come of this, but he also knew she wouldn't entirely approve of the fact that he was pretending a courtship — even if he had good reason to.

"She and I have an understanding," he hedged, and she tilted her head as she considered him.

"Oh, Benjamin," she said with a sigh. "Have you not thought that perhaps it is time for you to become serious with a woman? She seems a lovely girl. Maybe it's time you settled down and started a family."

He was already shaking his head.

"I don't think that life is for me, Mother."

"That life?" She looked as though any option besides marrying and having children was a foreign one.

"Yes," he said, turning from her to look out the window. "I don't think I would make much of a husband. Or a father."

"Miles didn't think so either," she said softly, stepping up behind him. "And he is a wonderful father to those two children."

"But what if…" he muttered. "What if I am just like him?"

They both knew he was no longer talking about Miles.

His father had been a bastard of the worst sort, but what truly bothered Benjamin was the fact that he'd wholeheartedly approved of Benjamin; had raised him to be the man he was today.

"You are not like your father," his mother said, but Benjamin could hear the lack of conviction in her words.

"I am."

"Not in the way that matters most," she said. "Think of what you did for your brother — you saved his life."

"Only because Freddie ensured that I did so," he said, rubbing his brow with his thumb. "I was almost too late."

"Because you didn't want to believe that your father would do something so dastardly," she said, bringing a cool hand to his cheek. "You have such goodness in you, Benjamin, and you were hoping he had the same. You look for the best in people, and that is a trait that many lack."

He saw motion out the window, and took a step closer, pushing aside the curtain to see there was a carriage coming down the street, pulled by four horses who, while not all matching, were clearly the set of an owner of some means.

"The Cunninghams are here," he said with relief at being saved from this conversation. He turned around and bent down, kissing his mother on the cheek. "You look lovely tonight — as you always do."

She patted his face, but when Benjamin saw the concern that radiated from her as she stared at him with sadness, he couldn't help but turn away, although he did hold out an elbow to escort her. He had no wish to be pitied — especially by his own mother.

But the knowledge that Alice was now here brightened his outlook considerably, though he tried to temper his face into his usual pleasant smile. He couldn't have anyone realizing just how much he cared.

For he barely wanted to acknowledge the fact himself.

* * *

ALICE HAD BEEN to Freddie and Miles Luxington's townhouse once before, but it seemed that everything had changed now that she faced the possibility of a future with a member of their family — even if that future was only in her own imaginings.

For Benjamin Luxington had been more than clear that he had no intentions toward her beyond this arrangement. Any advances or tension that might have been between them were the same as he held for any other woman he became acquainted with. The man was loved by all, she reminded herself. She was no different from any other.

But all of the rational thought cleared from her mind when she was shown into the drawing room. Her gaze flew to him, and warmth rushed through her when she saw that he had met her stare with his usual grin.

"How lovely you are all here," said his mother, stepping away from Benjamin's side as she came over to Alice and placed a hand upon her arm. "I am so pleased we could get together. Hello, Susan," she said to Alice's mother.

"Delilah," she greeted her. "It has been far too long."

Why did the thought that their mothers enjoyed one another's company matter? Alice had no idea.

She took a deep breath as she looked around the room and greeted Freddie and her husband, Miles. Everyone here was friend or family, and yet Alice still felt somewhat on edge by the thought that all eyes were on the two of them. For that was why they were all here, were they not?

While she had known it all along, she was suddenly overcome with the realization of how many people this was going to affect once it came out that it was all a hoax. She took one deep breath, and then another, as she tried to calm the anxiety.

"Are you all right?"

Benjamin was instantly at her elbow, as though he could

sense that there was something wrong without even being told.

"I just… I think I need some air for a moment."

"Allow me to take you for a tour of the house," he said, leading her out the door, and she nodded gratefully.

"Are you going to tell me what has you so anxious?" he asked, his voice light in her ear as they escaped through the door to the parlor beyond. While this was not exactly proper, somehow she had the feeling that the remaining people in the room who might have noticed would ignore the slight indiscretion.

"It's just…" she began, but wasn't sure how to tell him.

"It's all right," he said, leading her toward the sofa. "You can trust me."

She looked up at him, into those chasms of his sea-green eyes, and seemed to drown within their very depths.

"I suppose I am feeling rather guilty, is all," she said with a self-conscious smile. "Besides Oliver — and likely Celeste — everyone else is under the impression that we are courting with the potential to be married. When the truth is revealed, what is that going to do? Our mothers will be so terribly disappointed."

He reached out, cupped her chin in his warm hands, and stroked her cheeks with his thumbs. "If your mother is anything like mine, then I'm sure what she truly wants is for you to be happy," he said. "She might be disappointed, true, but ultimately all will be fine. And you will be safe — for I promise that I will not let any harm come to you."

Alice wrapped herself up in those words. She may only have him for a time, but he was so fiercely protective that it was difficult not to lose herself in them.

It only seemed natural that she tilted her head up toward him, and when she circled a hand around the back of his neck, he moved into her kiss as naturally as could ever possibly be.

Oh, but the man had skills. He teased her lips with his tongue before languidly delving in and tangling with hers with such passion that she found she was already molding her body into his, craving his closeness. He lit such a fire within her, and Alice was becoming very aware of just what was missing in all that she had written before. She was missing this connection between two people, one that was so very primal in need, a hint of desperation on the edge of passion.

She found herself nearly clutching him in her desire for more, her need to go further than this kiss which, as devastating as it was, was also only a tease of what else awaited her — if she was ever lucky enough.

But when he stepped back and away from her, the harsh emptiness of the air between them reminded her that as much as the kiss meant absolutely everything to her, it was just another day for him.

She turned away so that he wouldn't see how much it hurt her.

"Alice," he breathed, his voice husky. "You're killing me."

"I'm what?" she whirled around at that, studying his face. The sun was just beginning to set, casting a golden glow throughout the room that highlighted his prominent cheekbones before sliding down his perfect jawline.

"I know I have no right to be kissing you against the sides of houses or in my mother's parlor," he said, gazing at her with such intensity that she nearly had to step backward. "But I find I can't keep myself away from you. When you aren't with me, I think of you. When I'm in your presence, I can't help but imagine you in my arms. And whenever I have you alone, I cannot stop myself from pulling you close and showing you all that has been running through my mind since I saw you last."

Those words, said in that husky baritone voice of his, had her pulse hammering through her veins so hard that she could practically hear it in her ears.

He took a step closer to her again, and while he wasn't quite touching her, Alice could have sworn that she could feel waves radiating off him.

"I have no complaints," she said, pleased with herself for a half-intellectual response even when her brain seemed to have turned to mush. His eyes flashed as he smiled at her wickedly.

"I've noticed."

She gasped, but then he laughed, throwing his head back with such unabashed joy and she wished she could give herself over to it just as easily.

When their eyes met once more, however, he sobered suddenly.

"Just what am I going to do with you?" he asked, his voice just above a whisper.

She had some ideas.

"Well," she said, closing the small gap that remained between their bodies. "You could kiss me again. And then, next time, when we are not in your mother's parlor, maybe we could explore a little more."

Alice was well aware that she was not saying anything that a self-respecting woman should. And yet, somehow, it didn't feel sinful at all. In fact, it was actually freeing to say what she thought, to put what she wanted out there in the world. When his eyes only darkened and he actually seemed interested in what she was requesting, she tested her suggestion a bit further.

"I don't suppose..." all right, perhaps her heart did beat a little harder, "that you might be open to the possibility of this being more than a ploy? That this courtship… well, that it could have the potential to turn into something altogether true?"

He stared at her for a moment, his expression guarded, and suddenly Alice was aware that she had very likely said the wrong thing. How many times had he possibly been thusly propositioned? How many other women had fallen in love with him in the past?

"You know what? Forget I said anything," she said, her words coming out in a rush of breath. "It was just an idea, but obviously not a very well thought-out one. I had just considered the fact that you and I obviously get along well, and both will need to marry one day… well, I will anyway, but—"

Her words were cut off when he kissed her again, and even though Alice was aware that he did so only in order to force her to stop talking, she didn't really mind his methods.

She wasn't sure how long they would have stayed fused together, nor how far the two of them would have gone in this delicate parlor overlooking the street, had they not both finally noticed the steps from outside the door.

Benjamin quickly released her, and she had but a moment to compose herself before the door swung fully open.

"I hope you are not compromising my sister, Luxington."

Oliver stood at the doorframe, his body held somewhat tensely.

"Of course not," Benjamin said, the words sliding so easily off his tongue that Alice couldn't help but wonder how many times he had said them before.

"We were just discussing matters pertaining to Alice's protection."

"Such as ducking knives?" Oliver said dryly, and Alice glowered at her brother.

"All was fine, Oliver," Alice insisted.

He shook his head at her, clearly in disagreement, but she

knew he wouldn't be inclined to discuss it with Benjamin. "It is time for supper," he said. "If the two of you are ready."

"Of course," Benjamin said, leading her out the door by placing his hand at the small of her back, and she shivered at the contact.

Oh, this man was no good, she thought. Yet so good at the same time.

It was a dilemma — and one she had no idea how to solve.

CHAPTER 11

*D*inner actually went surprisingly well. Benjamin had been more nervous for this than he had been for any event in some time, which had shocked him. He had no idea why — it wasn't as though this was actually leading to anything, even though apparently Alice hoped it would.

Bloody hell, he wished she hadn't asked it of him. When she had looked up at him with those warm, hopeful, innocent brown eyes, he had nearly given in. It was becoming more and more impossible to deny her anything she requested. How was he supposed to hold himself back when he wanted nothing more than to give her everything she could ever want?

She just could not have *him*. Not in the way she wanted. No one could. For he would only bring pain and misery, as he did everyone else who ever came close. He wouldn't make an ideal husband for Alice or for any other woman, which she needed to understand, just as much as he had to keep himself away from her. For any more episodes like the one they had just entered into and he might find himself in the position of having compromised her.

Oliver was forgiving, but not that forgiving.

"Freddie tells me that you are the author of the delightful stories I have been reading," Lady Delilah said, to which Alice nodded.

"I am," she said.

"Tell me," Benjamin's mother leaned across the table toward Alice as though she was asking her to share a secret between the two of them, "who is this new story regarding? The rumor is that it is the romance of the new Earl and Countess of Donning!"

"Well," Alice began slowly, "that was the original plan. However, Madeline, that is, Lady Donning, is a dear friend of mine, and she has recently informed me that they are no longer interested in having their story told."

"Oh, that is too bad," Lady Delilah said, setting down her fork as she sincerely seemed quite dismayed by the news. "I was so looking forward to it. The intrigue of the new earl, the unlikely romance, the beautiful wedding..." she sighed, and Benjamin realized just how much his mother truly was disappointed.

"Alice has another serial in the works, however." He entered into the conversation, although when Alice shot him a look that was normally reserved for her brother, he wondered just how much his contribution was welcomed.

"Oh?" He couldn't have said who asked the question, for it seemed the entire table turned as one to look at him.

"Yes...?" he said, unsure if it was the right thing to say, but forging on ahead anyway. "It's a novel of complete fiction. I've just finished reading it myself."

"You have?" Alice asked, wide-eyed, and he nodded, satisfied with himself.

"I don't believe I have even read it yet!" Celeste said, and Alice smiled apologetically at her sister-in-law, who rubbed her belly as though it would comfort herself.

"Actually," Alice said slowly, and Benjamin realized she was about to reveal something of consequence, "I am also working on a new story. Another work of fiction. Rather than a serial, however, I would like to have it published."

"And have you read this new book as well, Benjamin?" Celeste asked, clearly still not pleased that he had been given access to Alice's work before her.

"I haven't," he said, staring at Alice, intrigued by what she had written. He knew he shouldn't ask in front of their families, but found he couldn't help himself. "Are there any familiar characters?" he asked.

He saw Alice swallow quickly, two little pink patches appearing on the cheeks of her heart-shaped face. "No," she said, shaking her head so hard that a tendril of hair fell out and graced her temple. "This is true fiction. Meaning, fabricated. Not real. No likeness to—"

"I know what fiction is," he said gently. "I was just teasing."

"I say, Benjamin, what are you doing to the poor girl?" Miles asked, and Benjamin realized suddenly and shamefully that he had so enjoyed bantering with Alice that he had forgotten his brother likely hadn't been able to follow the entire conversation.

"Just jesting," he said, allowing Freddie to inform her husband of what had been exchanged. Benjamin sat back somewhat grumpily. He lost his mind when Alice was around. That was the problem.

"If it is anything like your other stories, I'm sure it will be delightful," Benjamin's mother said with a smile, and Alice nodded shyly. Why she had no confidence in her own work, Benjamin had no idea, but he wished she would realize how talented she was — whether she was writing her own stories or that of others.

"I saw Lady Donning the other day," Freddie said as she lifted a glass of red wine to her lips. "Has she been ill?"

"Not that I am aware of," Alice said, although Benjamin could tell that she was choosing her words carefully. "We visited with her a few days ago and she did seem to have some of her spirits returned, so perhaps she has just been a touch overwhelmed."

"Perhaps," Freddie said, although she inclined her head as though she didn't entirely believe it. "She just seemed so wan, so fragile. She was at the seamstress, but when she stopped to talk to me outside of the shop, her husband immediately summoned her from the carriage."

"You know the man, don't you, Benjamin?" Miles asked now, his green-eyed stare piercing into him.

"Somewhat," Benjamin said rather uncomfortably, beginning to wish that everyone would stop pairing him and Donning together as the man was seeming to have increasingly ill-advised behaviors. "I met him through an... acquaintance.'"

"Ah, that's right," Miles said bitterly. "Chesterpeak. Father's old friend."

"Miles," Freddie said softly, placing a hand on his. "I'm sure not every acquaintance of your father's was of the same ilk that he was."

Miles tilted his head. "Most of them were."

He was right. Which made Benjamin feel all the worse about his association with them — an association that, he decided, he would end. He had no wish to return to his clubs and Chesterpeak's establishment and his mansion of mayhem, so thinly disguised as a home, anyway, although what he would do with his time — and his heart — after Alice no longer needed him, he had no idea.

All he wanted now was to be in her company — alone,

preferably — and to revel in the comfort she always seemed to know exactly how to provide.

He didn't get his wish until hours later, after the gentlemen rejoined the women following the supper hour. He asked her for a turn about the room, to which she nodded, although of course she would be the one to come right out and comment on it.

"No more straying into deserted parlors?" she asked, raising an eyebrow, to which he shook his head.

"That, I have realized, is a rather poor idea indeed."

She laughed just under her breath, and he wanted more of the sound.

"Tell me more about this new story you were discussing at supper. How is it coming along?"

She sighed.

"Not particularly well," she said with a quick look at him out of the corner of her eye. "I didn't want to focus on Madeline's plight, and this was the first thing that came to mind."

"I have an idea," he said with enthusiasm as they came to a stop at the far end of the room. "What are you doing tomorrow?"

"Nothing out of the ordinary," she answered with some question in her eyes, which danced between his as she studied him. "What did you have in mind?"

"A surprise," he said, grinning at his sudden idea.

"All right…" she said warily, lowering her brows at him, and he wondered just what he had done to cause her such caution.

"Nothing untoward," he said, holding his hands, palms up, in front of him. "I promise."

"Very well," she said, and he didn't miss the flash of interest in her gaze. "I look forward to it."

"Be ready in the early evening," he said, to which she nodded.

"I can't wait."

Neither could he.

* * *

ALICE WOULD HAVE LIKED to say that her time with Benjamin inspired her to sit down the next morning and write romantic scenes that were filled with love and passion and all of the tingles and vibrations she had felt from being in Benjamin's presence — and his *arms* — last night. But, alas, she could hardly sit down for more than a moment. She was too much on edge to do anything that required more than a few minutes of her attention.

Instead, she found herself wandering through the house in search of things to do. She went outside on the green with Perseus and Andromeda, their energy matching her own. She returned to the house and looked through Celeste's window telescope for a while — although she, of course, was not looking up at the sky which was currently bright with sunshine. Instead, she studied the passersby. She didn't like to think that she was being intrusive. Rather, it was a study, she told herself. A study of people that would assist her in her writing. For the more she came to know people, the more she could write people.

She wondered if that couple walking by was courting or married, trying to discern by the way they walked together. And was the governess with the brood of children longing for her employer, or had she decided to spend her life alone?

Bored of her musings, she wandered downstairs and began to organize her writing desk, which was usually rather haphazard. There were quills in one area, inkwells in another, spilled ink covering the surface, and pieces of parchment every which where. As she did so, she came across the manuscript that Benjamin had returned to her last night, and began to make a few notes of changes.

"Is everything all right?"

"Gah!" Alice jumped and whirled around, finding Celeste standing in the doorway, a hand on her belly, which was becoming more prominent every day. "You scared me."

"I'm sorry," Celeste said, walking into the room, laughter on her lips. "I didn't mean to."

She sat down with a sigh, and Alice took pity on her, walking over to take the chair across from her.

"How are you feeling?" she asked, having no idea what it must be like to suddenly heft around so much additional weight.

"I feel quite large," Celeste said with a laugh. "I know it's my stomach that looks the largest, but even my ankles seemed to have ballooned in size."

"Do you think you will have a boy or a girl?" Alice asked, placing her chin on one fist.

"Some days I am convinced there is a boy in there," Celeste said, shrugging. "Other days I just know the baby is a girl."

She laughed, and Alice smiled warmly at her. She had loved Celeste ever since she had begun working for her brother, and she thanked God every day that he hadn't married the nasty Lady Venetia he had previously been engaged to. But that was a story for another day — one that Alice had not yet written but had every plan to do so, as soon as she convinced her brother of the idea.

"Well, I can hardly wait," Alice said. "Anything you need, you know I will help with."

"Oh, I can see this baby needing plenty of time with his aunt," Celeste said, before furrowing her brow. "Or her aunt."

"I'm convinced you will have a boy," Alice said. "With hair as red as yours and an attitude just as fiery."

"We can only hope," Celeste said with a wink. "Now, tell me, what has you so restless? Woodward said that you have been in every room of the house at least three times already, and the dogs are tired out from following you around after their play in the yard." She paused, studying Alice knowingly. "If I was to hazard a guess, I would suppose it has something to do with the very handsome man who is supposedly courting you."

Alice leaned forward in her seat, cupping her face in her hands.

"Except you know that he is not, in actuality, courting me."

"That doesn't mean that nothing is there between you," Celeste answered and Alice swallowed hard, dropping her arms and looking down at her hands, where her fingers began tapping a beat on her knees.

"We are friends," she said cautiously, "and I cannot deny that I do feel an intense attraction toward him. How could I not? Look at the man. And he knows exactly how charming he can be, too."

She scowled, and Celeste only laughed lightly.

"I saw the way he was regarding you last night," she said. "There is an intensity behind his eyes that I don't think anyone could deny. I wouldn't be so sure that he doesn't have any designs on you."

"He does not," Alice said morosely. "I only wish that he did. Is that so bad?"

"Does he know how you feel?" Celeste asked.

"That's the worst of it," Alice said, humiliation washing over her anew at the remembrance of what she had told him last night — and the fact that he had cleverly kissed her instead of actually responding. "I did tell him, and he didn't seem interested. Not in anything beyond... whatever this is."

Celeste tilted her head to the side as she studied Alice.

"I'm not sure what to think. Freddie has said that Benjamin has been a different man since everything that happened with his brother and when his father died."

"Maybe so," Alice said quietly, "but he still says that he does not want to marry."

"Are you going to be seeing him again soon?"

"I am, actually," Alice said, brightening at the thought, even with all that she had shared with Celeste. "He has a surprise for me this evening."

"Oh, how intriguing," Celeste said with a smile. "I wish I could be your chaperone. But alas, I am not good for much at the moment."

"You are growing a human," Alice said, standing and patting Celeste on the hand as she made her way to the door. "Mother is going to accompany us. I have to go get ready, but not to worry, Celeste, I am prepared for whatever might come." She grinned. "And I just might have a bit of fun along the way."

Would it be so bad? Alice wondered later as Ingrid helped her dress. She chose a gown that was flattering and yet versatile, as she had no idea where they were going tonight. She longed for Benjamin in a way that she could hardly explain, and she was ready to say to hell with it and explore this heated tension between them.

And yet if he would never marry... she could be ruined. Unless they kept it between them. Maybe that was the question she had to consider.

Could she trust him?

CHAPTER 12

*B*enjamin didn't know why he had thought this would be a good idea. All he was doing was opening himself up to the very temptation he was doing all he could to avoid. It was as though there was an angel on one of his shoulders and a devil on the other, each pulling him from one side to the other.

He knew he should be doing all he could to protect Alice from a distance and keep himself from getting too close. But he couldn't help that his very nature wanted nothing more than to sweep her into his arms and show her passion unlike anything she could ever put onto a page.

They were in just the place for him to do so.

The familiar dark greenery with its soaring pavilions soon came into view. Just through the trees, he could see the lights and glimpses of people already milling about.

Alice leaned forward in her seat to look out the window.

"The Vauxhall Gardens?" she said, gasping as she did so.

"The very same," he said from his seat a very respectable distance away from her. "Have you been?"

"Not in some time," she said. "Oliver was never much

interested. He was always working in the evening, when the gardens become *interesting.*"

She flashed a smile toward him, and Benjamin cringed, for she was obviously remembering their kisses and suggesting that perhaps this would be the place to share more of them.

The problem was, he was not the only one to pick up on the hint.

He risked a glance across the carriage, seeing the two women exchange a look.

"Mother," he said. "Are you sure that you and Lady Susan are up for such a visit?"

"Of course," his mother said, waving her hand as she looked at him knowingly. "We are both quite interested in seeing all that the gardens might hold this evening."

Lady Susan looked from her daughter to Benjamin, and he had a feeling that she was well aware of the risks of her daughter entering the dark of the gardens.

"Is there entertainment this evening?" she asked, likely hoping there would be much to distract them so that they wouldn't be tempted to sneak away.

Benjamin's hope was that Alice would have some fun, and, at the very least, have the opportunity to view some romance that might inspire her.

"There is," Benjamin said in answer to her question. "There are musicians playing tonight, although, I must confess that I do not know much about them." He looked at Alice ruefully. "I am not much of a connoisseur of the fine arts, I'm afraid."

"You are now a reader of one of the most popular serials in London," she said with a grin, her eyes crinkling delightfully at the corners as she did so. "That must count for something."

He laughed at that, long and loud, and she saw their

mothers exchange a glance of satisfaction. He sobered. He was raising everyone's hopes again — just as he told himself not to do.

He sighed.

But then he saw Alice's thrilled smile, and it was suddenly worth it again.

As Benjamin reached out a hand to help her alight from the carriage, a thrill raced through him at their touch, even through the gloves they both wore. He tried to catch her gaze to determine just what she was thinking, but she was too busy craning her neck to take in the extravagance around them.

He led the ladies through the entrance as Alice began to describe everything around them. He could see it all for himself, of course, but he actually enjoyed listening to her view of it all.

"I've never seen such a blaze of light in the evening before," she said, nearly breathless. "There must be thousands of lamps stretching out below us. How do you suppose they light them all? Oh, and look, Benjamin, there in the middle of the gardens, that must be the orchestra box. It looks like a large temple. I can hardly believe that we cannot see it all the way from Mayfair, it's so brightly lit. And what's that over there?"

He followed her finger as they continued to walk, smiling at her enthusiasm.

"That's the Turkish band," he said. "And on the other side are saloons that hold the Pandean band and the Scottish band."

"I can hear the music already," she said, quickening her pace once they reached the rocky path. "We *must* go see the orchestra."

He looked to their chaperones, who nodded, and then he

led them through the middle of the pleasure gardens, which were already beginning to fill with people.

"You know what is wonderful about a place like this?" she asked, and he cocked his head toward her.

"I suppose there are many wonderful things about it, but I am curious to learn what you think."

She smiled shyly at him. "All of the *people*," she said, waving her hands around to the gathering crowd. "Unlike many of the social events we attend, it is not just the *ton* nor the wealthy merchants. Here, there is everyone who can afford entrance."

He nodded. "It is not only the rich who like to get out of London and enjoy some fresh air now and again."

"Now tell me," she said, leaning in close to him so that their mothers couldn't hear. "Why did you suppose a place like this would spark inspiration for my stories?"

He looked down at her with surprise.

"No one has told you of what can happen in these gardens?"

She quirked an eyebrow, and the upturn of one corner of her lips told him that her words were teasing.

"No."

"Ah, well let me educate you, my lady," he said with a conspiratorial smile. "These gardens are a place of magic. There are many well-lit paths which lead to places unknown, where you can find all sorts of amusements — some that are offered by the gardens themselves, and others that are of your own making."

"I assume that you have a map of these paths memorized," she said wryly, and he pulled her arm tighter against his side.

"One doesn't need a map," he whispered. "We'll just follow our intuition."

She looked up at him with hooded eyes, and he couldn't help the thrill of anticipation that coursed through him at the thought of what the two of them could get up to in one of the very dark corners.

Benjamin tried to smile at her, but it seemed that one corner of his lips wouldn't even turn, for he was suddenly so overcome by his need for her. Benjamin had never been one to be jealous. He appreciated that he could enjoy some time with a woman and then both of them could move on to whatever — or whoever — came next.

But with Alice, he had this unexpected need to possess her, to ensure that everyone knew that she was his and his alone.

The thought scared him, and yet also sent a thrill of anticipation through him at what that would mean.

A throat cleared behind him, and as he tore his gaze from Alice's to see his mother's pointed glare, he realized that he had been wearing his thoughts on his face without regard for what others around them might think. Alice's mother, thankfully, was as overcome as her daughter had been with all of the festivities around them, and wasn't even looking at them at the moment.

"The orchestra's beginning," Benjamin said gruffly, as the overture began to resound through the air, and he led them through to find the best vantage point of the musicians.

He stood next to Alice with their mothers beside them, and he allowed his hand to brush against hers. He pretended it was an accident at first, but then he left it where it was. He saw her gaze flicker over toward him, and the corner of her lip curled up slightly as she didn't pull away.

He saw the orchestra through her eyes, and as its majesty struck him anew, he realized how much he had been taking for granted.

The entire edifice above them was made of wood, painted white and the color of a symphony of blooms, ornamented by various painted objects and lights. At the upper extremity a fine organ had been erected, while at the foot, the musicians were seated in a semi-circular shape around the vocal performers.

One of the women singing caught his eye and smiled suggestively, but Benjamin found himself completely unaffected. It seemed that only one woman could currently stir anything within him.

"Well, well, fancy seeing you here."

Benjamin closed his eyes before turning to see who had found him. Unfortunately, his guess was correct.

Chesterpeak.

"And who have we here?" Chesterpeak leaned forward around Benjamin to take in Alice, and Benjamin sighed, for he saw no way around introducing them.

"Mother, Lady Susan, Miss Cunningham, this is Mr. Thomas Chesterpeak," he said, before looking a bit more intently at his mother. "He was an associate of Father's."

"I see," his mother said, her gaze hard, revealing nothing to anyone who didn't know her, but Benjamin was well aware of what that hardened stare meant. She didn't trust anyone who had anything to do with her late husband — Benjamin excluded.

"A pleasure," Chesterpeak said, sweeping off his hat and bowing low before the women. Alice was eyeing him with a look of distaste, however, telling Benjamin that the man's charm was obviously contrived in her eyes as well.

"How are you acquainted?" she asked rather bluntly, and Benjamin noted her mother fixed a disapproving stare on her.

"I met Mr. Chesterpeak through my father," Benjamin answered truthfully. "It is actually through Mr. Chesterpeak that I also came to know Lord Donning."

"Oh," Alice said, her eyebrows winging up, saying more than her words did. Suddenly her distrust of Donning apparently also grew — all because of the connection to his father. "I see."

To Chesterpeak she said, "one of my good friends recently became Lady Donning."

"Ah yes," Chesterpeak said, perhaps a bit too knowingly. "I am well aware. I introduced them."

That was news to Benjamin. However, Chesterpeak had always been quite helpful in introducing Benjamin to many different women, so it wasn't a surprise. He seemed to have strange connections to members of the nobility. Benjamin had never thought much of it before, but now he was beginning to wonder how it had come to be that way. Chesterpeak took money as investments, but how did he have such a hold on them all, as he'd had on Benjamin's father?

"Well, I best be going," Chesterpeak said. "It was lovely to meet you all."

As he turned away from Benjamin, he winked at him, sending a chill down Benjamin's spine. What was he on about? He had always believed him somewhat harmless, but he was beginning to think otherwise.

Alice watched him walk away before tilting her head up to Benjamin. "There's something off about that man," she said, frowning after him, and Benjamin nodded slightly. He agreed wholeheartedly, but he wasn't sure how to tell Alice. For he had far too much invested with Chesterpeak. His stomach hurt as he began to realize what a mistake he had likely made.

With a large cacophony, the orchestra began in earnest and it was difficult for Benjamin to hear any further conversation, as much as he was interested in Alice's thoughts.

She was still brushing up against him, and he was twitching to reach out and touch her, to see what was underneath the long silk navy dress she wore. While it was loose and free-flowing, every time she moved it hugged her curves and he wished that he could feel them for himself.

He swallowed hard as imaginings of what was underneath floated through his mind. He thought of her passionate kisses, and knew without question that if he ever had her bare in his arms, she would be just as willing, just as supple—

"Do you think we could go for a walk?" Alice asked in his ear and he found that his throat was too constricted to say anything, although he did manage a nod.

He stepped over to his mother, explaining to the two women that they were going to further explore the gardens, and would they like to come along?

They were about to most likely agree— for he highly doubted that Lady Susan would be pleased with her daughter walking the gardens with a known rake, even if she was approving of their match — when Ezra Castleton approached with a wide smile on his bearded face.

"Lady Susan!" he said with aplomb before greeting the rest of them.

"Is everyone at the gardens tonight?" Alice asked in disbelief, and Benjamin leaned in and explained that it was one of the opening nights — the first in which the weather had been agreeable enough for the orchestra to play, and she nodded in understanding.

"I have a supper box if you like to accompany me?" Mr. Castleton asked, to which Alice seemed somewhat crestfallen. Her mother looked over at her and then back at Mr. Castleton as though attempting to decide whether she would prefer to chaperone her daughter or accompany the man she was obviously interested in.

Benjamin stepped over. "I promise we will stay to the lit paths," he said solemnly, and finally, she relented.

"Very well," she said.,"but do take care to stay within sight of all passersby."

"We will," Alice said, her face breaking into a smile, and Benjamin suddenly had every wish to ensure that smile stayed on her face for a very, very long time.

He lifted his elbow, took her arm, and led her off into the night.

CHAPTER 13

*a*lice was absolutely thrilled. While she was still somewhat thrown about her mother's potential interest in Madeline's father — and he in her — he could not have come at a more opportune time.

For a stroll through the dark garden paths with Benjamin was exactly what she had been craving.

Well, that, and his kisses. Or more.

Alice had heard her fair share of stories of what could happen in the paths of Vauxhall Gardens. Benjamin had brought her here to inspire some romance in her writing. Well, what better way than to experience it for herself?

It was all a physical attraction, she reminded herself. It couldn't be more than that. She knew Benjamin wasn't interested in marriage, and she wasn't naïve enough to think that she could change his mind. She had known far too many women who were convinced that they could make a man into something he was not. She had asked once. He had declined. So be it. She would enjoy Benjamin for who he was, and then when he moved on, well, she would too.

But first, she would write their story.

With a few adjustments. Her stories always finished with a happily ever after.

She pressed herself closer to him, pleased when he responded by dropping his arm to around her shoulders. He toyed with a curl at the back of her neck, which sent shivers down her spine and she tilted her head back to look up at him.

"The gardens are beautiful," she mused. "Celeste and Oliver would enjoy it here — why, the lights themselves look like constellations."

"They're supposed to," he said, "although I don't think they can actually rival the stars themselves."

"Well, that is quite romantic, Lord Benjamin," she said with a laugh.

"I promised you romance, did I not?"

"That you did," she said with a nod before biting her lip in thought. "What do you make of my mother and Mr. Castleton?"

"I think that your mother is a beautiful woman and Mr. Castleton is a distinguished gentleman, so it rather makes sense."

"It just seems... odd, to think of her with anyone other than my father."

"Understandable," Benjamin said, then squeezed her shoulder. "I spent my life wishing my mother was with anyone *but* my father."

Alice nodded, dipping her head. She knew he held anger deep within him toward his father, although he was always quick to cover it with a ready smile and a flirtatious comment. It seemed, however, that whatever had happened with them in the past had left deep scars upon his soul.

Would he ever be inclined to talk about it?

Benjamin elbowed her lightly before pointing off into the trees, where she saw a couple disappear, and she looked up at him with wide eyes before they both started laughing, although there was a strange underlying tension to their humor. Tension laced with anticipation. Alice had a sense she knew where this walk was going, and she could hardly wait until this particular story reached its climax.

"Was your father really so bad?" she asked hesitantly, and Benjamin turned to her so swiftly, his eyes filled with such horror, that she wished she had never asked.

"He wasn't bad. He was horrible. He was the worst man I have ever known," he said. "If it wasn't for my mother, Miles would have spent his life locked away, far from society — all because he is deaf. If that wasn't bad enough, he nearly had him killed after he and Freddie married."

Alice stared up at him in horror. She knew that Benjamin's father had attempted to have his brother declared insane, but she hadn't known the extent of it. It was appalling, and she was beginning to better understand why Benjamin did all he could to distance himself from his father and his past.

"Would you like to know the worst of it?"

There was more? *Did* she want to know? She supposed she was the one who had sent them down this path so now she had to join Benjamin until the finish.

Benjamin continued despite her silence.

"He approved of me. Thought I would be the better son to follow in his footsteps than Miles. Apparently being a philanderer and a gambler and a drinker was exactly the man made in his image."

Alice stopped on the path, turning so that they were facing one another. She took Benjamin's hands in hers and looked deeply into his eyes, which were swimming with trouble as they searched hers as though he was trying to find a lifeline to save him from drowning.

"You are a good man," she said urgently. "You have done

everything you could to be there for your brother, to save him and support him. You are building a life for yourself outside of your father's image. You spend time with your mother, you look after everyone who needs you. And you have done nothing but protect me and make me feel safe and secure."

He looked down, breaking their locked gaze before returning his eyes to her, his mouth twisted in a wry smile.

"I'm not worthy of praise from a woman like you," he said, the lanterns swaying around them causing the light to dance across his face, "for the truth is, I am far from having the best of intentions."

"What does that mean?" she asked, not understanding.

"It means…" He took a step closer, his words growing harsher and more guttural as he spoke, "that I am not protecting you out of the goodness of my heart. I am protecting you because I cannot stand the thought of another man watching over you from day to day. Because I like the fact that others might think you and I are actually together. And because I want you with every fibre of my being, while nothing and no one can tempt me otherwise."

Shock and a responding desire flared up within Alice, and her body tilted toward him of its own accord.

She stepped forward, closing the gap between them, and lifted her face to his.

"Then take me."

"I can't," he said with a groan.

"I'm asking you to."

"Alice… I can't offer you anything," he said, his mouth twisted in apparent pain. "I don't want to marry."

"I know," she said, not hiding the resignation in her voice. "I am aware that one day this pretend courtship will be finished and I will move on and marry a man who will provide for me and who will fill all of the credentials one looks for in a husband. But he won't draw me like you do. There won't be this intense passion, for I don't see how it could ever be possible with another the way it is with you. The problem, Benjamin, is that I don't think I can ever move on to consider another until I am able to fulfill this longing that you have stirred within me."

She knew the moment her words broke through his resistance, for he lost the tension that had held his shoulders up tight to his head and the wrinkles in his forehead smoothed.

His eyes were no longer troubled, but instead they turned dark and stormy. Before Alice had time to say anything else, he had taken her hand and was practically dragging her into the thick brush of the gardens. Alice's heart beat fast, as though she had run miles over the pathways instead of taken a leisurely walk on the arm of a man so handsome he could be nothing but sinful.

A fact which she was now completely embracing.

As soon as they reached the outside of a small gazebo, Alice was swept up into his arms so quickly and completely that she gasped in surprise. Then Benjamin's mouth was upon hers, and the storm that had been building between them was no longer just a threat but imminent.

Benjamin's hands were everywhere at once, it seemed, creating a marvelous friction as they slid down her dress, skimming over her breasts, her waist, her hips.

"Benjamin," she said between breathless kisses, "have you ever done this with any other woman within these gardens?"

She didn't know what had possessed her to ask the question. She had been the one who had so desperately wanted this. Why was she potentially putting an end to it?

Because she wanted to be the only one in something — *anything* — with him. A fact which would likely never come to be, but somehow it bothered her greatly to think of him with any other woman, even if it had been in the past.

He tilted his head to look down deeply into her eyes, as though he needed her to understand the sincerity of each and every word.

"Alice," he said, with more solemnity than she had ever heard from him before, "I know I am no virginal, honorable man. But you must understand that ever since you and I began spending time with one another I haven't even looked at another woman, let alone felt any stirring for one. You are the only woman who has occupied my mind, let alone touched my body... or my heart. In fact, you are the only woman who has ever come so close to reaching me here before." He tapped on the left side of his chest.

They were the words she needed to hear, that sent all thoughts out of her head, the heat spiraling down to the very core of her that longed for him so desperately.

Alice met his eyes, read the sincerity in them that told her, without question, he was not saying this in order to convince her to do anything she didn't want to do.

She wanted this as badly as she could tell he did — if not more.

"Kiss me, Alice," he whispered, and she stared up at him for but a moment. A moment in which she questioned if she should. A moment in which she wondered if she would fall too deep. A moment in which she remembered her vow to never allow him this close again.

"I told myself I wouldn't," she whispered.

"As did I," he said, pressing his forehead against her. "Can I admit something to you?"

"Of course."

"I'm scared."

That jolted her back, and she stared up at him.

"You're what?"

"Scared," he said, but then laughed. "I'm scared that by

crossing this line with you, I might fall too deep to climb out the other side. But I can't seem to keep myself away."

With the vulnerability of his words, the moment of hesitation was gone, forgotten, and she was reaching up, pulling him close and kissing him with all of the passion that had been building deep within her. Benjamin's hands slid up her sides until they cupped her ribs, and he left her lips for a moment to nip at her neck. She tilted her head to the side, inviting him in, as gooseflesh bumped along her arms, although she couldn't say whether it was from the cooling night air or all of the wondrous sensations Benjamin was causing along her skin.

He kissed the corner of her lips, one side, then the other, before his mouth descended, demanding, devouring her, and the moment Alice opened to him, his tongue invaded, replacing all of her thought, her breath, her stubborn resistance.

She had thought their first kiss was one that could never be replaced; that had ruined her for all others. She was wrong.

This was the kiss she could never come back from. A kiss that now included knowledge of each other, of who they were and what they meant to one another. Alice had never felt more attuned to her body, yet at the same time she also felt as though she was floating, watching all that was happening to her, with her, from afar.

"Alice," he whispered gruffly against her mouth. "Let me show you romance. Let me show you love. Let me make you feel all you've ever wanted to feel."

"Please," she practically moaned, and soon his hands slid around to cup her breasts, her nipples hardening under the touch of his thumbs.

Alice couldn't help but respond in turn, attacking his cravat until it finally came loose and floated to the ground.

What she was going to do with him now, she had no idea, but she enjoyed the feeling of his taut, warm skin against her fingers as she slid them around his bared neck.

Benjamin tugged down the bodice of her gown, baring one breast, before bending his head and sucking one bud into his mouth.

Alice gasped in surprise as he seemed to pull right from her very center. She found herself moving against him, and he stepped her back until she was up against the wall of the gazebo.

"Inside," he growled, and soon she found herself lying on a hard, cold, stone bench.

But she didn't care.

For above her was the most warm, supple man she had ever met.

He interlaced the fingers of her right hand in his left, stretching them high above her head. The other hand slid down, until he was toying with her skirts, finding the hem, before beginning to slowly, carefully, inch it up, his fingers gliding along her skin. Alice felt every inch, as her hips began to rock against him.

Finally, his hand disappeared under her skirts completely, capturing her thigh in its grip. She gasped as he began to inch closer to where she was yearning for him with everything within her, and when he began to place pressure on the most tender of places, she lost sense so completely that she knew if he hadn't been holding her there, she would have fallen off the bench.

He circled, he stroked, and then his fingers slipped inside of her and began a wondrous back and forth. Alice nearly cried, but he caught her moan in his mouth, his tongue matching the thrusts of his fingers, the cadence only increasing in time with her desperation, until finally, blessedly, the mounting pressure exploded around her with such force that she screamed into his mouth.

He gave her a moment to recover, until she lay there, limp, sated, satisfied.

"Benjamin," she said as he squeezed their hands which were still joined. "That was…"

When she didn't continue, his laugh was part-jovial, part-growl. "Is my writer lost for words?"

"Yes," she said, incredulously. "I am. Benjamin… what about you?"

"What about me?"

"Don't you want, ah—"

"No," he said, kissing her on the lips. "I've done enough to ruin you. Far more than I should. Besides, we should be getting back," he said gruffly, and Alice was still in somewhat of a daze as she stared at him, to return to reality.

"Must we?" she asked with such despair that he laughed.

"There is nothing I would like more than to stay out here with you throughout the night," he said, his eyes warming at the thought. "But we have already disappeared for far longer than is proper, and it is getting chilly."

Alice looked down to her arms, now broken out in goose-flesh, and he skimmed his hands over top of them, noticing the same.

"Here," he said, wrapping his jacket around her shoulders. "Wear this until we come close to the crowd once more."

Alice tugged it tightly around her, reveling in the sense that she was still wrapped in his arms. His scent wafted up from the fabric, and she closed her eyes as she took his arm once more, leaning her head against his shoulder.

"Thank you," she said softly, and he leaned in and kissed her tenderly on the top of her head.

"You have nothing to thank me for," he responded in a

low tone. "I am the lucky one — to be spending time with you."

She closed her eyes again, and allowed herself this one moment.

One moment, to wish for more.

CHAPTER 14

*B*enjamin would never think of the Vauxhall Gardens in the same light ever again.

It was the place where he had discovered treasure so valuable, so precious, and he was the last man who should have been privileged enough to have had the opportunity to explore, let alone plunder.

At least he had stopped himself before taking her innocence. That, he could not do with a clear conscience, knowing that she would be wed to another one day. The thought caused a ball of undisguised jealousy so close to rage to begin forming deep in his stomach, but he supposed that was the price for caring for someone as he did Alice.

It was why he had always vowed he would never allow himself to develop such feelings for another.

Saying goodbye to her once they reached her townhome was a nearly impossible task, but he considered his efforts herculean as he had done so with a smile on his face. His mother had looked at him somewhat oddly and when she asked just how he had enjoyed their lengthy tour of the gardens, she donned a wry look of some disbelief at his neutral answer. He hoped he hadn't given anything away. At least, nothing that would implicate Alice.

She was still innocent, he reminded himself when the guilt began to creep in again. He had made sure of that, even as he had broken the solemn vow he had made to himself to never dally with a young lady who should be married to a respectable gentleman.

He was now torn between the need to see her again and the fear of doing so as it could reveal what she might now expect of him.

Except... he paced the drawing room... was the thought of a life together really that bad?

Yes, it was. He didn't deserve a woman like her — nor did she deserve to be brought down by a degenerate like him.

A knock brought him out of his reverie, and his valet's footsteps echoed from the corridor beyond as he went to answer the door, soon returning with a visitor behind him.

"Lord Donning," Hawkins said with a small bow before he left to continue with his work.

"Donning." Benjamin tried not to allow his dismay at the man's visit show as he crossed the room to greet him. He had enjoyed his past friendship with Donning, but his recent experiences with him had made him question the shallow relationship they had formed. "What brings you here this evening?"

"Don't sound too enthusiastic to greet me!" Donning said with a gruff chortle, crossing to the sideboard and helping himself to a drink without waiting for the offer. "I haven't seen you in a while."

"It can't have been more than a week," Benjamin said, deciding that if Donning was going to have a drink, he may as well join in, and he crossed over, sliding a glass for filling across the sideboard's wood top.

"That may be, but you used to practically be a fixture on

the wall at The Nomad and Chesterpeak's," Donning said with a laugh, and Benjamin nodded, unfortunately agreeing with him. "I'm on my way to The Nomad right now," Donning continued. "What do you say you come for the night — for old time's sake?"

"I don't know..." Benjamin hedged. "Does your wife not want you at home?"

Donning laughed.

"There is nothing to worry about regarding her," he said with a wave of his hand as he leaned his hip against the table. "Come now, a game of cards, and then you'll be back here to your lonely bed once more."

Never having been one to stand up to what others were pressuring him to do, Benjamin sighed and threw back his drink.

"Very well," he said. "Let me get dressed, and then lead on."

Donning smiled in satisfaction.

* * *

THE NOMAD HADN'T CHANGED. The same women lounged around the room or served drinks. Nearly the same patrons as ever fondled the women, played cards, or threw back drinks.

The tables of the billiard's room were still scarred. The cards were still falling apart. The walls were still bare but for the yellowing of the paint from cheroot smoke. The air still had that dirty scent of alcohol and smoke and bodily fluids.

How had he not noticed before how awful this place was? If he had to have chosen a club, there were plenty of others that would have, at the very least, been far more respectable.

Because, he reminded himself, this was where his father had frequented, and he had placed his father on something of a pedestal before — a status that had not been at all merited, yet was true nonetheless.

Benjamin sat and played a half-hearted game of faro before moving on to a hand of whist. He waved off a disappointed Jenny, and was then surprised when one of the other women appeared at his elbow.

"Lord Benjamin," she said, running her fingers up his arm, which he jerked away.

"Good evening," he said stiffly.

"I can make it a better one," she said, leaning down and whispering in his ear, but he shook his head.

"Thank you, but no," he said, and she pouted but then disappeared.

Only to be replaced by another.

"Lord Benjamin?"

"Please, just let me be," he said, raking his fingers through his hair in exasperation without looking up. When the air was filled with silence, he finally glanced over to the other young woman, who must have been new, for he didn't recognize her.

"Mr. Chesterpeak would like to see you."

"I'm in the middle of a card game," he said, sweeping his hand out in front of him, but when she looked at him with desperation, he realized that were he not to appear, she would likely face some retribution.

"Very well," he said, throwing down his cards and accepting the loss. "I know my way."

He wondered where Donning had gotten off to as the woman accompanied him to the office — likely to make sure that he didn't escape on the way, although what she would have done about it, Benjamin had no idea.

Chesterpeak was leaning back in his chair, his boots upon the table, one ankle crossed over the other. He waved a hand out in front of him, urging Benjamin to take one of the seats.

"Luxington, how are you? I've been losing money not having you around lately."

Benjamin chuckled nervously, wondering just what Chesterpeak had to speak to him about.

"Did you ask me in here to tell me when I can expect my investment to be returned?" he asked, crossing one leg over the other. He had to fight to keep himself from tapping his fingers upon his knee impatiently.

"I told you that it's coming very soon," Chesterpeak said with narrowed eyes, as though he didn't appreciate being asked. "But, since you seem so keen on making your money back, I have another thought for you."

"Very well," Benjamin said suspiciously, feeling that no good could come of this conversation.

"You've enjoyed the company of some of my... friends... in the past, have you not?"

"You mean the women you have introduced me to? Sure," Benjamin said uncomfortably, not wishing to dwell on some of his previous choices. He'd had his fun, but now he was beginning to wonder what Chesterpeak's agenda was.

"A few have been asking about you," Chesterpeak said. "They are wealthy widows, who are interested in a handsome face. I think if you played your cards right, you could land one of them, which would come with a fairly significant payday."

Benjamin was already pushing his chair back and standing up.

"I'm not interested in marrying for money."

"No?" Chesterpeak said. "Fine, then, if you don't want one of my women, what about that Cunningham girl?"

"What about her?" Benjamin asked, narrowing his gaze at the gambling establishment owner.

"I see that you have become rather friendly with her," he

said, his lips spreading into a slow smile. "What's her dowry like?"

"I don't see how that matters," Benjamin countered. "I'm not going to marry her."

"You should," Chesterpeak said, tapping his cheroot on the table. "If you need any help—"

"From you?" Benjamin raised his eyebrows. He was going to tell Chesterpeak exactly what he thought of the fact he was even broaching this subject, but suddenly he thought of Donning and of Alice's friend Madeline. Their match had been somewhat unlikely... did Chesterpeak have something to do with it? "Just how would you help?"

"Well," Chesterpeak said with a nonchalant-that-wasn't-truly-nonchalant shrug, "I could make an investment that would allow you to court her and to pay for a solicitor who can ensure you receive the very best terms."

An investment. Suddenly Benjamin had an idea just where his money had gone.

"How would you make that money back?"

"Through her dowry once you married," Chesterpeak said. "And then, since most men like you are rather averse to spending the rest of your life with one woman, or if she didn't suit your needs, then I would help you... move on from her."

Benjamin tried to keep his eyes from widening. Did Chesterpeak mean what he thought he might?

"I'm not sure I understand," he said, playing the fool.

Chesterpeak waved a hand in the air. "No need to speak more of it now. First, let's get you well and properly affianced. Tell me how much you think you might need."

"I—nothing, at the moment," Benjamin said, not wanting to commit himself to anything, for fear that he would then be forever tied to Chesterpeak and this investment of which he spoke.

"Well," Chesterpeak said, his expression closed off. "Why don't you think on it? Come back to me if you find yourself in need, and we can make ourselves a deal."

"And what about my initial investment?" Benjamin asked.

"Donning is working on it," Chesterpeak said, confirming Benjamin's suspicions. "He should come through any day now."

Benjamin's stomach sank. Alice had been right. Chesterpeak was arranging for gentlemen to marry women for their dowries. Benjamin didn't want to believe there was anything more to it than that, but he had the sinking sensation that he had — once again — found himself deeply involved in something he had been too naïve to question.

What he was supposed to do now, he had no idea.

But one thing was certain — he had to keep Alice far, far away from all of this.

He was supposed to call upon her tomorrow, to accompany her to the museum, of all things. She was to meet her friend, Madeline, which only further complicated the matter, for even if he did what he could to keep her out of it, she would always have that tie through Donning's wife.

He was in a pickle, that was for certain. But when was he not?

"Keep me apprised," he said with a forced smile, although he had the feeling it came across as one that more than conveyed the sick-to-his-stomach grimace he was trying to hide.

Chesterpeak, however, had already moved on from him, calling to someone beyond him in the doorway.

Benjamin took the opportunity to run.

CHAPTER 15

"You've never been to the museum?"

It was Alice's turn to be incredulous at what Benjamin had never experienced before.

"I haven't," he said, running a hand through his incredible, silky hair that she longed to touch once more herself. "Never had the interest, I suppose."

Alice could only stare at him with wide eyes.

"How could you not?" she asked. "It is one of the only ways one has to see the world. Well, unless you are willing to embark on a sea adventure that would take you around the globe, but I'm not sure many have the wealth nor the inclination."

"I'm happy on Britain's shores," Benjamin mused, although he cocked his head to the side as though he had never much thought of it before. "But I can't deny that it would be something to see the Americas, or perhaps India."

"I always wonder what the people there must be like," Alice said, warming to the subject now. "I've met people who have come *from* there, true, but the entire way of life must be different elsewhere, must it not?"

"I suppose so," Benjamin said with a shrug. "How much would their lives change with new rulers?"

"I couldn't say," Alice said, shaking her head. "But it would be sad if they did, wouldn't it? At the museum we find artifacts from their lands which impart information about them, but I suppose the fact that we now own them is akin to stealing, is it not?"

She rubbed her nose. She had never much thought on the subject before, but on talking it over with Benjamin, guilt nibbled at her, even though she hadn't done anything herself.

Benjamin seemed somewhat pained, but he quickly changed the topic, as she noticed he typically did when they began speaking about anything that caused him discomfort.

"Where are you supposed to meet Lady Donning?"

"Madeline said she would be waiting just within the front entrance of Montagu House, on the landing of the stairwells," Alice said, referencing the building where the numerous collections were housed. It was quite the imposing structure, the front façade covered in Doric columns.

After they had disembarked from the carriage — Ingrid following dutifully behind — Benjamin led them along the walkway through the gardens and up the massive stone steps through the front doors.

No Madeline.

"Are you sure this is where you were supposed to meet her?" Benjamin asked, and at the gruffness in his tone, she looked up in surprise. He was never this surly, but it seemed like something was off about him today. She couldn't say exactly what, but he was not his usual charming-the-skirts-off-every-woman self.

"Quite sure," Alice said, pursing her lips together at the fact he would call her memory into question. She had made certain of the location in their notes back and forth, for she was well aware of just how confusing the museum could be.

"We are only a few minutes beyond the time we arranged. Let's wait a little longer."

He nodded, and Alice was prepared for the minutes to pass by with the usual discourse of Benjamin's company. But not today.

Today he stood tall and stoic, his jaw firm and his gaze untrusting.

"Is everything all right?" she asked, and his aqua gaze swung toward her.

"Why would it not be?"

"I'm not sure," she said as gently as she could. "That's why I asked. You seem... unsettled."

"I'm fine," he responded. "I am just uncomfortable with us standing here in the open like this. If someone wanted to harm you, it would be much too easy."

"How ridiculous!" she said with a laugh. "I'm always out in the open."

"Exactly," he said satisfactorily. "You are far too trusting."

"I hardly think there is any cause for concern anymore," she said with a frown, wishing she knew what had caused this great change in behavior. "No one seems particularly interested in what I am doing anymore. I told Madeline that I wouldn't write her story, and at the moment I am stuck with no manuscript and no ideas."

"I didn't give you any ideas?" Benjamin asked, looking at her out of the corner of his eye with a raised brow and a curled lip that said far more than his words ever could in polite society.

Alice refused to allow him to see that he had affected her in any way. *Yes*, he had given her some ideas, but most of them could never actually be printed. At least, not with her name attached to them.

"I may have made some edits," she said, attempting nonchalance, "if you are interested in reading them."

His lips twitched as though he wanted to say more — or laugh — but he simply nodded. "I would love to."

"Madeline still isn't here," she said with some disappointment, for she had been looking forward to seeing her. "Why don't we take a quick tour of the museum ourselves and then return to see if she has arrived?"

"That is quite the walk to and from," Benjamin began to argue, but Alice looked up at him with her most imploring smile and it seemed to work, for he waved his hand forward.

"We don't have to go far," she said as they began down the first corridor. "At the front of the museum, there is a new display — one of a fossil found near Lyme. I have read that it is more akin to fish than any other animal ever found, and that the likes of it no longer seem to exist."

"I see," he said, although the way his brow was furrowed told Alice that he clearly hadn't read much — if anything — about it. In fact, she wondered if Benjamin read much at all. If he didn't, then the fact that he had taken time to read through her entire scribbled notes of a fictional tale told her something and it warmed her heart to think that he had actually spent such time on what many would consider to be frivolous work.

Alice had, of course, visited the British Museum many times before, but each time she was fascinated anew with all that it held. She hadn't yet seen the exhibition she had told Benjamin about, but was looking forward to it. When she turned the corner, she was slightly disappointed to find a large group gathered around the display case, but it didn't take long for them to move on and she and Benjamin approached.

"How... interesting," she said, turning her head to try to determine just how she was supposed to view the specimen. The head was long and narrow, while the body of it was a strange triangle shape. There were bits of bones scattered around it, like puzzle pieces waiting for the linking piece.

"How long do you suppose it is?" she murmured to Benjamin, but before he could say anything, another voice sounded from her left.

"Seventeen feet."

She turned to find a woman of about her own age, who stood back a few feet from the display case, apparently viewing the bones alone.

"Does it say that somewhere?" Alice asked, stretching her neck from one side to the other as she searched for the information, but the woman shook her head of thick, spiraled ebony hair.

"It doesn't," she said, her voice quiet yet full of confidence, as though she truly knew the subject of which she spoke. "I just know that it is."

Alice nodded, even though she didn't completely understand. Perhaps someone had told the other woman.

"There are quite a lot of vertebrae," she said, attempting to add to the conversation and hopefully sound like she knew what she was talking about as well.

"Sixty," came the response.

"Oh," Alice said, deciding to no longer feign intelligence but rather have her questions answered. "What do you suppose it is?"

"That, I am not entirely sure," the woman said, her deep brown eyes sparking as she warmed to her subject, seemingly pleased to have an interested audience. "It is obviously a marine animal, and yet it is not a fish. Unfortunately, many of the bones must have been destroyed by whatever crushed the fossil."

"Something crushed it?" Alice asked.

The woman nodded. "You can see by the way the lower jaw his been forced backward, the intermediate bone displaced. A portion of it is seen projecting beyond the base of the lower jaw. The vertebrae are twisted, while the ribs on one side of it have been squeezed into a mass, the pressure causing many of them to become fluted."

"How do you know all of this?" Alice asked, astonished at the woman, wondering if she was from England, or possibly another country where women were provided with much more education. Her skin was black, with a hint of an accent in the background of her words.

The woman shyly smiled, although when she bit her lip, Alice could tell that she was keeping her full story hidden behind her friendly, descriptive words. "I—"

Before she could fully respond, however, a tall man with a mustache seemingly sprinkled with sugar, so dusted it was, came up to Alice and Benjamin and began telling them all of the discovery made in Lyme.

"And you are…" Alice said, looking up at him.

"Ah! Sir Charles Gordon," he said with a slight bow. "I discovered the remains."

Alice couldn't help but steal a glance at the young woman, who, if she wasn't mistaken, snorted slightly as she turned her head away.

"I see you have been speaking with Miss Rose Ellis. She is from the Lyme area as well."

Miss Ellis smiled wryly at them, and Alice was overcome with the desire to learn more of her story.

Perhaps it was that she couldn't help her curiosity when she met new people. Perhaps it was because the woman had been so educated, so knowledgeable about the fossils. Or perhaps it was the fact it seemed there was a quiet strength of character lurking behind the polite exterior. Whatever it was, Alice sensed that there was a kindred spirit in there, one she longed to know more of.

"We are quite impressed," Alice said, taking a step backward. Sir Gordon, of course, had no desire to speak with her, however, choosing to converse with Benjamin instead. Alice took the opportunity to draw Miss Ellis aside.

"I am Alice Cunningham," she said in a low voice so that the gentlemen could not hear their conversation. "If you ever have the opportunity to do so, I would be pleased for you to visit me. I live with my brother in Mayfair. I would enjoy learning more about the fossil from you."

"Do you have an interest in fossils?" Rose asked, tilting her head in curiosity.

"No," Alice said with a smile. "I have an interest in people."

Benjamin returned to Alice and offered her his arm. Alice waved as they left, and Miss Ellis stared after her as though unsure what to make of her.

"You can't help it, can you?" Benjamin asked, and Alice would have been offended by his question had his tone not been laced with admiration rather than contempt.

"What do you mean?" she asked.

"Your interest in other people. Your propensity to ask questions."

"Some people like to discover new places or new things — like the fossil back there," Alice mused. "I find the most interesting creatures of all are people. It is fascinating to me how every person — every *single* person — has a story to tell."

"Do they, really?" Benjamin asked, wrinkling his nose. "I think some are best left unsaid."

Alice peeked up at him, wondering if he was thinking of his own life. He clearly was still of the opinion that he was not worthy of a full life of his own, but she had no idea how to encourage him to change his thinking on the subject.

They finally made it back to the front entrance, but once again, it was void of any sign of Madeline. Unease tugged at the back of Alice's mind, and she suddenly lost all interest in seeing more of the museum.

"I think we must go see what has kept Madeline," she said, surprised when Benjamin winced slightly at the thought.

"I don't think that is the best of ideas," he said, and Alice looked up at him with consternation.

"Why not?"

"I just..." He sighed. "If there is something keeping her away, then perhaps we should wait for her to tell you just exactly why."

"Benjamin!" she exclaimed, his attitude rankling her. "If something is amiss with my friend, then I think we should determine what it is. Something doesn't feel right — about her absence today, about her marriage, about Donning himself."

"Alice..." he said, losing all teasing and charm now, "is that really your business?"

"If it is not," she said hotly and resolutely, placing her hands on her hips, "then I am making it mine."

"Very well," he said, his Adam's apple bobbing as he swallowed hard. "Let's go visit."

CHAPTER 16

*S*o much for keeping Alice away from Lord Donning, Benjamin thought with a sigh as they climbed the steps to the eerie townhouse once more. He was torn between wanting to help Alice's friend and his primal instinct to keep Alice as far from harm as was possible.

Which, he was beginning to realize, meant keeping her away from both Donning and Chesterpeak.

Whether or not they were the ones who had threatened her life, he had no idea, but it was interesting that since she had let go of her endless questions into Donning's love story with Madeline, there had been no further attempts. He hoped the first two had simply been to scare her off, and that no harm would have actually come to her... he hoped. But something told him otherwise.

Alice was now knocking on the door — well, knocking might not be a strong enough word. She was banging on the door, her entire frame practically rigid with her determination to gain entrance.

When her summons was left unanswered, she leaned into the crack in the door. "Madeline!" she called. "Made*line*!"

"Alice," he said, stepping up next to her, "you're making a scene."

Even her maid looked embarrassed.

"I don't care," she said, and when she turned to him, her eyes were filled with such turmoil that he was immediately ashamed by his lack of care at Madeline's plight in favor of what passersby might think. "There is something wrong here, Benjamin. I can feel it in my very bones."

He didn't disagree with her.

"You and your maid return home," he said. "Take the carriage. I'll try to enter and determine what is happening within."

"I think not!" she exclaimed, her eyes wide as though she was horrified that he would ever think to send her home from a dangerous situation. "We wouldn't even be here if I hadn't insisted."

"Alice, I promise I will follow through on this," he said, closing his eyes for a moment in supplication as he ran his hand through his hair.

"And I will help you," she said, placing her hands on her hips and staring up at him, her feet firmly rooted on the step as though she would stand there long enough to become one with it.

He sighed. "Very well. Let's go down below."

The green wrought-iron gate creaked as Benjamin pushed it open, while Alice told her relieved maid that she could wait for them in the carriage. They took the steep spiral steps down, then crossed a small open area to the servants' entrance.

This time, a thin woman, her face red with heat likely from a stove, answered the door, her surprise evident by the way she gaped at them.

"My lord, my lady…" she said. "I believe you have the wrong entrance."

"No one answered the door above," Benjamin said, his smile strained but evident as he attempted charm. "If you would be so kind as to admit us, we will go in search of your employers."

"I'm not sure—" she said, shaking her head, but Alice stepped through the door with a smile of thanks and apology before taking off through the kitchen to find the stairs.

"To your left!" the cook called behind them, and it was all Benjamin could do to keep up with her.

Alice had been in the house but once before, but Benjamin had visited a fair number of times. He directed her to the ground floor, but, finding it empty, they continued up the stairs to the first floor.

Here, Alice finally hesitated, as though realizing that entering someone's home uninvited was more than likely to be frowned upon, but then her jaw set, telling Benjamin she had made up her mind. At this point he seemed to have lost all control to do anything but support her.

She opened one door after another, until she seemed to have found what she was looking for.

"Madeline!" she cried as she rushed into the bedroom, Benjamin following her, unable to remain behind. "Benjamin, something is wrong," she said, turning her head over her shoulder to look at him, her eyes swimming with tears of supplication. "We need help."

There was no way he was leaving her here in this house of horrors alone. Where all of the servants were — besides the cook — he had no idea, so he ran through the bedroom to the window that faced the front of the house. He opened up the sash window, stuck his head out, and called to the driver and maid who were, thankfully, still waiting in the front of the house, for they had not been sure how long they would remain within.

"Jenkins!" he called out to the driver. "Go find a physician! And hurry, man!"

He returned to Alice, who was holding Madeline's hand with one hand as she smoothed back her friend's blond hair, which had lost as much luster as her skin itself.

"What do you think is wrong with her?" Alice asked, while Benjamin wasn't sure how to answer, for he had an idea, but he didn't think now was the time to tell Alice what it was. For if he did, she might likely have the notion to take events into her own hands, and for that, he would like to wait until he could be assured that she was far from here.

"And where do you suppose Lord Donning is?"

That was a very good question.

Benjamin ran a hand through his hair, knowing what they had to do, even as he realized what the consequences would be.

"Alice, I think, when the carriage returns, we should take Madeline with us."

"What?" she turned an aghast face to him. "She doesn't seem to be in any condition to be moved."

"I know," he said, "but just trust me in this. I think it would be for the best to remove her from this house."

"Lord Donning will be irate."

"Yes," Benjamin said slowly, and a sudden knowing horror filled Alice's eyes.

"You don't think—"

"I don't know," Benjamin said, shaking his head, wondering if he was doing the right thing or if he was only adding to the potential dangers, "but I just don't want to leave her at risk."

"Very well," Alice said, her jaw setting in that way that told him she had made up her mind. "Let's get to it."

Madeline's breathing was shallow, but present, and once they saw the carriage returning from down the road,

Benjamin ripped away the blanket, wrapping Madeline in it before lifting her in his arms and carrying her down the stairs.

Alice went ahead of him, looking one way and then the next down each passage to ensure it was clear. When they exited the front door, Benjamin broke into a run, and as the physician opened the door of the carriage to disembark, the three of them surprised him so that he stepped backward and allowed them through.

"I say," he said, looking around at the lot of them as they joined him in the carriage while Benjamin told Jenkins to hurry back to the Cunningham residence, "what is this about?"

"My friend is very sick," Alice implored him, "we will be home in but moments, but perhaps you should start examining her now?"

"I'll do what I can," the man said, as he began to listen to her breathing and her pulse.

"It's weak," he confirmed, although they already knew that, but fortunately they were back in front of the expansive green beside the row of houses where Alice lived. Benjamin carried Madeline up the walk, entering the house and surprising Alice's mother and Lady Essex, who ran out to the entrance to see what all of the commotion was.

"What in the—" Alice's mother began, but they were already up the stairs, Alice pointing to a spare bedroom where Madeline could be laid down.

Benjamin followed, and in minutes the mad rush was over and he was outside of the room with Alice, Lady Essex, and Alice's mother, as the physician had asked to treat Madeline alone.

Lady Essex turned around and looked at the two of them.

"Well," she said, placing her hands on her hips, "what was that all about?"

They explained as best they could, but there were certainly pieces of the story which neither of them could properly explain, as Benjamin didn't quite see how he could share his conversation with Chesterpeak, for the man had never actually come out and said anything — it was merely Benjamin's intuition, which had never amounted to much in the past.

"What's going to happen when Donning knocks on the door, demanding to see his wife?" Alice's mother asked.

Without hesitation, Alice replied smartly, "He will never know she's here. It's why we didn't take her to her father. Now," she said, looking around, "I have some investigating to do. Please let me know what the physician says."

She began marching down the corridor, and Benjamin ran to catch up.

"Alice," he said, placing a hand on her arm, hoping that he hadn't become too familiar, "please reconsider. You're only going to put yourself in more danger."

"I shall be discreet," she said, but that hard look in her eyes told Benjamin otherwise. She was too bold, too brazen, too bent on discovering the truth.

Benjamin tried a different tactic. He placed his hands on her shoulders, turning her so that she was facing him. He tilted his head down to look deeply into her eyes, lowering his voice so only she could hear.

"Alice," he said, taking a breath, for he was about to reveal far more than he had ever planned to, but he didn't see any other way around it. "You cannot go searching out Donning or asking questions about him. There is far too much at stake, and if Madeline was in danger for the simple reason that she was married to Donning, think what could happen to you if you prove to be a threat to him. I..." he faltered for a moment, "I care too much about you for something to happen to you."

He dropped his eyes then, unable to look at her for fear of her reaction. For once in his life, he was fearing rejection from a woman — for this time, instead of offering a physical connection, he was displaying his vulnerability for her to see and use.

When he finally built up enough nerve to look at her again, he found he had nothing to fear. Her lashes were low on her face, her cheeks slightly pink, her bottom lip between her teeth.

"I care for you too, Benjamin. I'm sure you know that," she said softly. "But it's for that very reason that we need to see the end of this thing. We both know that there is no future to be had between the two of us. You are committed to never marry, and I will not give my heart to a man who has no intention of keeping it. It would be best for us to finish this and go our separate ways — the sooner, the better."

Benjamin tried not to allow her to see how the truth of her words hurt, but he nodded and stepped back, taking a breath to compose himself.

"We do this together, then," he said, firmly. "Do you promise me that you won't do anything alone?"

She hesitated for a moment, but finally agreed with, "I promise."

"Good," he said, before adding, "thank you."

Just then the physician let himself out of the room down the hall, and Alice hurried toward him, Benjamin following, noting with worry that the man looked awfully grim.

"Are you her family?" he asked, looking around at them with well-justified worried suspicion.

"I am her sister," Alice said boldly, stepping forward. "We were saving her from a harmful situation."

"Very well," the physician said slowly. "Well, I cannot be entirely sure, but I suspect she has been poisoned."

"Poisoned?" Alice exclaimed as the other women gasped and Benjamin's stomach dropped.

"Yes," the physician said, his countenance grim. "Arsenic, most likely. It seems to have been administered over time, gradually sickening her."

"I should have known," Alice said, shaking her head. "She was doing poorly for so long, but she always said everything was fine. I should have done something. I—"

Benjamin reached out a hand to still her words. "There is nothing else you could have done," he said. "Madeline is a grown woman and you could not have made any decisions for her."

"But—"

"Alice," Benjamin said, a hint of warning in his tone as he looked at the physician to remind her that now was not the time to speak of her suspicions. Fortunately, she heeded his warning and stopped.

"What can we do, Doctor? Will she recover?" Lady Essex asked, and they all turned to hear his diagnosis.

"It is good you found her when you did," the physician said, swinging his bag from one hand to the other. "If she had been exposed to any more, she likely would have died. As for what you can do... nothing much, I'm afraid. Just wait for it to be cleared from her system."

"That's all?" Alice asked, aghast.

"That's all." The doctor nodded, his lips set grimly together.

"I'll see you out," Benjamin said quietly, suddenly realizing what an interloper he was here in the first story near all of the bedrooms along with the Cunningham women. He escorted the physician downstairs, paid him, and then waited in the parlor for Alice.

She was quiet when he finally bid her goodbye, at the last minute shyly passing him her revised manuscript, and he asked her once again to promise to send for him when she wished to next go out.

She agreed, but her agreement was a bit too ready, a bit too sure.

He was going to have to keep an eye on her — and somehow, he didn't mind one bit.

CHAPTER 17

*A*lice sat at her desk for the rest of the day, staring at a blank sheet of parchment.

"Just write the words," she mumbled to herself. "Perfect it later."

With her mind in turmoil, however, it was difficult to add any thoughts to the page. She had a story to write, but at the moment, she had no idea how it was going to end.

The story was her own, of course, of a woman who falls in love with a verifiable rake. Not that Alice was in love with Benjamin — oh no, she had forbidden herself from doing so — but then, this was fiction, was it not?

It was simply that she was coming to the point where both the hero and heroine's objections now seemed ridiculous, and they should simply overcome their reservations and move forward — together.

But sometimes it was easier to say such a thing than to actually do it, as Alice knew all too well. Her eyes rose to the ceiling, where Madeline was currently resting and recovering. What was romance anyway? Alice questioned. Madeline had found the man of her dreams, and in all likelihood, he had been trying to poison her. One just never knew.

She sighed, throwing down her quill pen as she climbed the stairs to check on her friend. It had been a few hours now, and she cracked open the door, emitting just enough light for her to see.

She heard Madeline's steady, even breathing, and was about to return downstairs when she heard her name.

"Alice?" Madeline's voice was breathy, filled with air and not much strength, but it was better than the alternative.

"Madeline," Alice rushed in and over to the side of the bed, taking Madeline's hand as she sank into the side of the mattress. "I was so worried."

She was still worried, but didn't want to frighten her.

Madeline coughed, and Alice lifted a glass of water to her lips.

"Where am I?"

"In a bedroom at my house. Well," she amended, "at my brother's house."

"But why—"

"I, ah, well, I abducted you, I suppose you could say. Madeline... you've been poisoned."

Madeline said nothing for a moment until Alice heard her quiet response. "I figured as much."

"Madeline!" Alice exclaimed, aware she should be gentle with her friend, but unable to hide her alarm. "You knew? And you stayed?"

Madeline struggled to push herself up on her elbows, and Alice leaned in and re-arranged the pillows behind her so she was propped up.

"What was I supposed to do?" Madeline asked, clutching the blanket in her hands. "I am married."

"You were supposed to leave. You were supposed to tell

someone. You were supposed to not allow yourself to be killed!"

Madeline dropped her head back on the pillow, and Alice willed her to argue, to fight back, even if it was just against her. How could her friend have allowed herself to come to such harm? It was unimaginable. She felt a twinge of guilt at the thought that she was, ostensibly, doing the same by continuing to press and to ask questions when she would be better off to remain in her writing room, safe at her desk, but this was different. This was allowing herself to be taken advantage of — and why?

"What was I supposed to do?" Madeline asked weakly, and Alice shamefully remembered just how ill her friend was. She didn't need Alice pestering her. But she also needed her fighting spirit to be lit underneath her. "I couldn't return home as a married woman. No one would believe me if I told them my husband was trying to kill me. He wasn't home much, so I did what I could to stay out of his way."

"He must have had help," Alice said, beginning to pace the room with her hands on her hips. "How else would he have done it?"

"Perhaps the cook?" Madeline asked with a weary sigh. "They've all been in his employ since before our wedding."

"Hmm," Alice said, rubbing at her chin as she thought on it further. "But why? What reason could he have for wanting you dead? He would have received your entire dowry upon your marriage."

"Not quite."

"What's that?" Alice whirled around, her skirts nearly knocking over a side table in the process.

"He received my dowry, yes," Madeline said, her blue eyes tracking Alice as she moved. "But I have an inheritance left to me by a great-aunt who was convinced that women should be allowed to make a life for themselves if they so choose. She made it very clear that the money she left for me was for me alone, and included stipulations so that my husband could not control it. The only way he could do so—"

"Would be upon your death," Alice finished softly. "How horrible. And what a horrible man."

A sheen of moisture covered Madeline's eyes as she bit her lip, likely to hold in the tears, and Alice felt an ogre for causing her friend to relieve her pain.

"I thought he was a good man at first," she said. "So loving, so charming, so perfect. And then we married and he turned into a monster. Alice—"

She looked from one corner of the room to the other as though there could be someone listening to them, but then finally she fixed her gaze on her friend. "I don't think I was his first wife."

"What?" Alice asked, planting her feet now as she stared at her friend in alarm. This was getting worse as they went. "Why would you say that?"

"Mementos I found. His offhand comments. His entire attitude toward marriage. Is that ridiculous? Do you think I am losing my mind?"

"No," Alice said fiercely, crossing the room and taking Madeline's hands in hers. "Never think that. You were in an impossible situation and you shouldn't listen to me or allow me to make you feel bad. You did what you could, and what matters now is that you are here and he will not be a threat to you any longer. Not if I have anything to do with it."

"Please, Alice, don't put yourself in any danger," Madeline said, her eyes pleading, and Alice hesitated, not wanting to promise anything and yet understanding her concern.

"Very well," she said with a sigh. "I will ensure Benjamin is with me."

"Alice…" Madeline began, but stopped as though she was

unsure if she should say anything further, "I'm not sure if that is the best idea."

"To include Benjamin?" she looked at Madeline in surprise. "Why ever not?"

"When I tell you this, please know that I am not entirely sure what the connection is, but he and Stephen have been friends for some time. As far as I know they have been out together the whole night now and then. I just... I wonder if he is the type of man you can trust."

Alice's heart began to resonate in her chest with an odd bu-bum, and she rubbed her breastbone in an attempt to send it back to its usual rhythm. "Do you really think that Benjamin could be involved?"

"I honestly have no idea," Madeline said, wincing now, "I could be wrong. I wouldn't even have said anything except that I wanted to ensure you would be careful."

"I will," Alice promised, "not to worry."

She lifted the blankets to cover Madeline once more.

"Sleep," she said. "I'll return later to check on how you are feeling. I do apologize if I have caused you any distress, but I promise you that I will do my utmost to hold accountable those who are responsible. And yes—" she said, holding up a hand before Madeline could say anything, "I will be careful."

She left the room with a forced smile, which fled the moment she shut the door softly behind her. She squeezed her eyes tight as she considered all that Madeline revealed. Benjamin couldn't be involved in this — could he?

She thought she knew him well enough to understand his intentions. She knew his family, knew how much he cared for his brother. But then there was his father. He seemed to have abhorred the man, but... was it all an act?

No. She shook her head firmly. She would not suspect him of being involved in such a horrendous plot, and she could never ask him directly, for he was sure to be insulted.

But she wasn't completely naïve either. She would keep watch for any signs while she was surreptitiously investigating.

She would have to follow Lord Donning, she decided as she entered her bedchamber to change into a dress that was much less vibrant from the royal blue she was currently draped in.

Fortunately, her brother wasn't home, Celeste was napping, and her mother was out for tea with a friend when Alice tiptoed across the foyer to begin her surveillance. She was aware that going alone would be folly, so she asked Jenkins, the driver, and Adams, one of the footmen, to accompany her. They reluctantly agreed, although their suspicion was palpable.

She had just opened the door to meet them when she found that the step was occupied by a woman who had raised her hand to knock.

"Oh!" Rose Ellis said, her mouth rounding in shock. "Miss Cunningham. You are on your way out. I apologize. I should have sent round a note, but I found myself nearby and thought that I might call upon you."

"It's lovely to see you," said Alice with sincerity, but she wasn't sure if she could risk the timing of waiting to proceed on her mission, "however, I am about to go out."

"I could accompany you, if you'd like?" Miss Ellis asked, and Alice bit her lip. She sensed she would quite enjoy the young woman's company, and yet she feared placing another person in any risk.

She decided her best course of action would be to explain to Miss Ellis the conundrum. She sensed she was trustworthy, and besides, she was visiting from Lyme and likely wouldn't know anything about the players in this egregious game.

"Why don't we walk? I'll tell you what I'm about over the

first part of it," Alice said, "and then you can decide if you would like to continue on."

"That sounds... interesting," Miss Ellis said with the wing of an eyebrow, and Alice laughed.

"Perhaps a bit *too* interesting," she said, and, with Jenkins following in the carriage and Adams and Ingrid on foot, she proceeded to tell her new friend the story as they made their way toward Donning's townhouse.

"How utterly shocking," Miss Ellis said with wide eyes once Alice had finished. "It could be a work of fiction. You are quite the storyteller, Miss Cunningham."

"Please, call me Alice," she said, a sentiment which Miss Ellis — Rose — extended in return. "And while I thank you, I must say that I only wish it wasn't the story of one of my closest friends."

"This is where he lives?" Rose asked on a whisper when they came to a stop in front of Donning's house. Alice nodded.

"You should see it inside. It's the perfect setting for a murderous plot and villain," Alice said. "Let's go around the back. If his carriage and horse are still here, then we shall have to wait for him to emerge — which is the boring part and I completely understand if you would like to now return. In fact, I would encourage it. I don't want you drawn into any danger."

Rose looked at her with wide eyes.

"This is far too interesting for me to leave now," she said. "While I do have to return within an hour or two, I would love nothing more than to wait with you and hear more about the story and your friend."

"Wonderful," Alice said, pleased to have a partner. She desperately missed Benjamin's presence, and she hated this nagging suspicion that was following her around after her conversation with Madeline. "I am actually interested in hearing more about you," she said. "Have you always lived in Lyme?"

"Lyme has always been my home," Rose said softly. "Although I have found myself traveling to London more often than usual."

"What brings you here?" Alice asked.

"My work."

"You have work?" Alice asked excitedly. She was always intrigued by women who did more than search for a husband — not that she was trivializing such a thing, but there was so much more in life that one could find to make it fulfilling.

"I do," Rose said, smiling proudly. "I search for fossils."

"Oh! Like the fossil in the museum."

"Exactly," Rose said, her eyes glinting. "Exactly the one."

"It was *your* fossil?" Alice asked, incredulous. "But Sir Gordon said—"

"Sir Gordon bought the fossil from me, true," Rose said, and Alice didn't miss the glint in her eyes, though what it meant, she wasn't sure. "However, my brother and I have been searching for them for years. He now runs the shop where we include most of our discoveries, while I continue the search."

"How intriguing," Alice said. "I would love to know more. How do you find them? What do you use to dig? How do you ensure they remain intact? How—"

Just then, however, Lord Donning's carriage rounded to the front of the house from the mews, and Alice placed a hand on Rose's arm as they remained in their crouched position behind a tree in the green.

"There he is," Alice whispered.

"He looks an affable sort," Rose said back in a soft voice, "although I suppose that can also be seen as somewhat... distrustful."

"More than distrustful," she said. "Jenkins is around the corner. Come, we must enter the carriage before he leaves so that we don't lose him."

Jenkins seemed significantly unsure about the entire charade, but when Alice explained the extreme importance of following Lord Donning's carriage — though keeping far enough away that he wouldn't notice them — a spark lit his eyes at the assignment.

"Very well, miss," he said, turning around to face the horses as Adams climbed up top and Ingrid within, "although if your brother asks..."

"Then I forced you to do this, of course," Alice said, smiling impishly at him. "Here we go!"

As it turned out, her notion of the excitement a chase through London would bring about and the truth of the slow plod down the London streets were about as far apart as her dreams of a triumphant come-out and the actual event. They even had time to stop to allow Rose to disembark, as they passed close to where she was staying with an aunt.

"I envy you that no one ever questions your need for a chaperone," Alice said, which gave Rose pause.

"I have no one with me in London who would care so much about my need to be chaperoned, and in Lyme it's much different," she said, her smiling suddenly seeming forced, "although I suppose with one you must never be lonely."

"No," Alice shook her head, thoughts of her most recent "chaperone" invading, and despite seeing him just yesterday she missed him already. What would happen when he moved on completely? "That is true."

With promises to meet again soon, Rose departed and Alice ensured Jenkins still had Donning's carriage in sight before they resumed the slowest chase to ever take place in London, unless one counted the raindrops that had apparently been raced down one of the windows of White's Gentlemen's Club one boring day.

Alice was surprised when they turned down a road onto one of London's more prominent streets in Marylebone, just outside of Mayfair. She had been convinced that they would find themselves deep in the middle of St. Giles or the Seven Dials.

Perhaps she had been wrong. When Donning's carriage stopped in front of a nondescript red brick house, Alice rapped on the roof for Jenkins to stop as well. What she was going to do now, she had no idea — she had not exactly planned this out very well.

She disembarked, and the footman was there to help her down.

Both Adams and Jenkins looked slightly bewildered and most certainly unsure.

"Are you entering the house, Miss?" the footman asked, rocking back and forth from one foot to the other.

"I—I'm not really sure," she said. "I'm going to wait here. Jenkins, could you go round the back and see if you can determine who lives here?"

"No need," came a smooth, baritone voice from behind her — only, today the voice was filled with annoyance. "I can tell you everything you'd like to know."

CHAPTER 18

$\mathcal{W}$hy, for all that was holy, had Alice followed Donning to Chesterpeak's house? Benjamin didn't know how he was going to do it, but he had to convince her to leave before Chesterpeak found her here, which could only lead to disaster.

Benjamin was due to enter and meet with Donning and Chesterpeak, where he would play their game and hopefully learn more — but first, he had to get rid of Alice.

He cringed. Poor choice of words.

"Alice, you need to go," he said insistently. "Return home and I will come call on you afterward and tell you everything."

She winged up her eyebrows as she placed her hands on her hips. "Does this mean that you have been keeping things from me?"

"No," he said, but when she tipped her head to the side he knew that he had been less than convincing. "Although there are a couple of things that I have been waiting to confirm before telling you."

"Benjamin!" she exclaimed. "I thought we were in this together."

"We are," he insisted. "But I knew if I shared everything with you, then you would do exactly what you have done, although why I cannot fathom — chase Donning on some mission of retribution."

"He tried to kill my friend!" she exclaimed, and he then placed his hands on her shoulders in order to placate her, but all he achieved was tempting himself to pull her deeply into his embrace and hold her close, where he could ensure that no harm would come to her.

"I know," he said, softer now, "and I will make it right, I promise."

"*We* will make it right."

"Of course."

Noting that Alice's driver, footman, and maid were all looking off into the distance as though they would like to pretend that none of this was happening, Benjamin took the opportunity to steer Alice toward the other side of the carriage, where they would be hidden from view.

He couldn't help himself. He needed this. He needed her.

He took her heart-shaped face within his hands, marveling at the dimple that remained even when her expression was as solemn as it was now as she looked up at him. He saw her anger and arousal antagonizing one another, and he decided to give one side an unfair advantage.

Benjamin kissed her hard, with all of the strength and the passion of his frustration that she refused to remain out of danger, where nothing and no one could hurt her.

But, he reasoned, if she did so, then she wouldn't be the Alice that he had fallen in love with.

He wished he knew from where the thought had unexpectedly arisen so that he could push it back. But now that it had fixed itself into his brain, he didn't know how to be rid of it again. He groaned in agony, realizing that Alice's fear had come true — but in reverse. He had worked so hard not to hurt her, but in the process, he was the one who would be left in pain.

Alice took his groan to mean something else entirely, and she wrapped her arms around his hips, holding him close to her, and Benjamin wished they were in another time, another place, another life.

But he was Benjamin Luxington and she was Alice Cunningham, and this was all they would ever have — a passion the likes of which he had never known before and knew he never would again.

"Alice," he murmured, finally easing back from her. Her servants seemed loyal to her, but one could never be completely trusting — a fact he knew all too well. "We must go. You must go. I promise I will return to you and tell you all. Do you trust me?"

He looked searchingly into her eyes, and she seemed to be studying him with just as much question. Finally, she made her decision and nodded resolutely.

"I do."

"Good." He kissed her one last time, enough to hold him over until he saw her again. How he was going to store enough of these caresses, these kisses to last a lifetime, he had no idea. But he was going to try his best.

As he climbed the steps to Chesterpeak's residence, he desperately hoped that, for once in her life, Alice listened to what he said. She had to leave before Donning saw her. What she was doing running all over London without a chaperone he had no idea, but it wasn't her reputation he was most concerned about. It was her life.

He soon found himself within Chesterpeak's lavish drawing room, today occupied only by Chesterpeak himself and Donning. He nodded at the two of them, who seemed to be eyeing him with some suspicion — or perhaps that was his own wariness reflected upon them. He couldn't be certain.

"Lord Benjamin Luxington himself," Chesterpeak said from his place in his navy striped wingback chair, his lips spreading wide like a Venus fly trap about to catch its prey. "I wasn't sure if you would appear."

"Here I am," Benjamin said, spreading his arms out. "I have been busy."

"So we hear," Chesterpeak said before tilting his hands and lacing his fingers together in front of him. "We have a problem."

"We do?" Benjamin said, lifting a brow as he took a seat on the sofa. "Or you do?"

"If you would like your investment back, you share in this," Chesterpeak said, before leaning forward in his chair and placing his hands over his knee. "As a matter of fact, you involved yourself in this the moment you gave me your money."

"I still don't know what it was for," Benjamin said, feigning ignorance.

"Are you telling me you are truly so stupid that you gave your money over to a man without understanding anything at all about what it was for?" Chesterpeak said with a snort, and Benjamin had to fight to keep his head up.

For Chesterpeak was right. He had been naïve, blind to the fact that anyone could have such monstrous motives. "I have no problem in sharing with you our plan, since you cannot tell anyone, for you will then be as much to blame as the rest of us. We are awaiting Lord Donning's collection of his wife's fortune. What he didn't realize was that he would only receive it upon her death. As it happens, she is quite… sickly."

His grin matched his words, but then it disappeared as he continued.

"But the problem lies in the fact that Lord Donning," he looked over at the man, "has misplaced his wife."

"He what?" Benjamin said, widening his eyes to feign surprise.

"You wouldn't know anything about what has happened to her, would you?" Chesterpeak asked, eyeing him.

"Of course not!" Benjamin scoffed.

"Your Miss Cunningham is the best of friends with Lady Donning."

Benjamin shook his head.

"I know nothing."

"Very well, then," Chesterpeak said, leaning back, apparently resolved. He lit a cheroot before holding one out to Benjamin, but he shook his head. He had no interest at the moment. "You will receive your money after we can determine Lady Donning is no longer with us... in body or in spirit." He paused, lifting his smoke. "I am having guests this evening. Would you care to join? I am pleased to offer a fine selection of widows, all with a healthy sum attached to their names."

Benjamin's rejection was already on his tongue, but he then caught the look shared between Chesterpeak and Donning, who were clearly waiting for him to refuse. If he left now, would he only lead them right to Alice and Lady Donning? Did they suspect him of anything?

"Of course," he said weakly. "I would love to stay for some entertainment... but no women for me, Chesterpeak. Not tonight."

"That is not like you."

"Just tired."

"Very well," Chesterpeak said with a shrug, although his

eyes glinted in a way that rather scared Benjamin. "Let the fun begin."

Donning grinned, apparently not overly concerned about the whereabouts of his wife.

It was going to be a long night.

* * *

ALICE *WAS GOING* to go home.

Just not right away.

With Jenkins and Adams following along behind her to ensure that no one took the opportunity to put an end to her questions once and for all, she rounded the back of the house where the mews and the servants' entrance were located.

"Adams," she whispered to the good-looking footman. "Do you think you can find out some answers from the servants here?"

"Like what?" he asked, his expression pained.

"Like what is happening at the parties held here. Who is invited. Who the host is and what he does." She saw him hesitate, and she did her best impression of a coquettish debutante. "I would do it myself, truly I would, but I am not dressed at all like a servant and no one would trust me. Please?"

"My wife enjoys those stories of yours," he said gruffly, and Alice's eyes widened.

"You know they are mine?"

"Of course," he said. "I spend over half my life in that house, you know. Anyway, I should like a full copy in advance of your next work."

"Why, Adams, are you blackmailing me?" she asked with wide eyes.

"I—" His cheeks turned a bashful, endearing shade of red. "I didn't mean—oh, Miss, I—"

Alice laughed. "I love it. Yes, I would be happy to do so, as long as she understands that there might be edits later on."

"Thank you," he said with a whoosh of breath before knocking on the servant's entrance. Alice breathed a prayer of thankfulness when a pretty young maid opened the door, and Adams returned in a few minutes, his mouth twisted in a troubled grimace.

"What is it?" Alice asked.

"Let's get far from here," he said, "then we shall speak of it."

Was it really that bad? Alice wondered, her stomach in knots. What could Adams not want to immediately discuss?

They drove partway home before Jenkins finally stopped and, from a respectable distance at the bottom of the steps of the carriage, Adams shared all that he had found out. That while Chesterpeak owned The Nomad, a gaming hell, his home was also nothing more than a front for gambling and drinking and... his face pinked again, but Alice had already guessed before he said anything.

"Women."

Adams swallowed before nodding.

"Not just any women. Prostitutes are employed at his club, but women of good breeding attend his house parties. There are a group of men who frequent this place. Some come and go, living here for a time before moving out, and then back again."

"What in the..." Alice frowned as she tapped her fingers against the seat. "This is all preposterous."

And Benjamin was there. What had Benjamin been doing in there?

"I do not know much more," Adams said apologetically.

"You did wonderfully, Adams," Alice said resolutely, forcing a smile for him. "I so appreciate it."

He had given her much to think about on the drive home,

her stomach tight as she sat silently on the squabs, looking out the window while Ingrid said nothing, but allowed her to brood.

Oh Benjamin, what have you gotten yourself into? Alice wondered.

And what did she have to do with it?

CHAPTER 19

*B*enjamin left the house as soon as was possible without arousing any suspicion. The hour was late for most polite homes, but early for a night at Chesterpeak's.

It didn't matter what time it was. Despite the hour, despite the drops of rain that began to splatter on his forehead, he had a destination, and he refused to be deterred.

He had to see Alice. He couldn't explain it, but he was possessed with this need to have her in his arms, to soak in the goodness that would chase away all of the evil that surrounded him from all sides, the people he could never seem to be rid of no matter where he was in his life.

She was goodness, she was freshness, she was wholesomeness.

She was his, until she wouldn't be any longer. And he was going to take full advantage of the fact.

Perhaps if he hadn't seen her outside of Chesterpeak's, this dangerous desire wouldn't have followed him around all night. Perhaps if he hadn't had those few drinks — not too many but enough to remove the edge from his reason — he would have been more sensible, and known that this was a foolish idea. Perhaps if he was a man with more morals and less base instincts he would have just gone home.

But this was the truth of the matter. He needed to see Alice Cunningham and he was willing to go to any extent in order to do so.

Fortunately, his last visit to the Essex residence had imparted some extremely important information. As he had exited down the corridor after placing Madeline in the guest room, he had the opportunity to peek in through some of the open doorways.

Alice's room had been easy to spot, with its vibrant colors and bed canopies that likely made her feel like a princess.

The princess she was.

The princess she should be treated as. As he would treat her tonight, and then after that... well, her life would be out of his hands.

As the splatters of rain became a shower, Benjamin picked up one rock after another, creating a sizeable pile in one hand. He hoped he wouldn't need all of them.

It had been years since he had taken part in a game such as this, but he lifted one hand and tossed a rock up toward the window he hoped was hers.

Missed.

He tossed again.

But then the window next to it opened up and Alice peeked her head out, and suddenly it was all worth it.

"Benjamin?"

"I'm sorry," he said, wrinkling his nose as he looked up, "that bedroom next to yours isn't occupied, is it?"

"Not at the moment," she said. "What on earth are you doing? It's pouring rain out there."

"I'd like to come up."

"Absolutely not."

"Please?"

The one word apparently broke through her resolve as she sighed and leaned farther out the window.

"Can you scale a trellis?"

He couldn't remember when he had last done something of the sort, but he wasn't about to tell her that.

"Of course."

Thank goodness no one else could hear his empty boast.

"It climbs up the wall next to my window," she said with an interested smile and gleam to her eye.

He swallowed hard and nodded. Just one hand and foot in front of the other — and then he would have Alice in his arms.

His goal encouraging him on, he began to climb. His foot slipped on the slick wood once or twice, but he was strong enough to hold himself up, and with one final stretch, soon enough he was swinging one leg over the ledge and through Alice's window. The next thing he knew he was standing inside her chamber.

He had been in more than one woman's bedroom in the past, that was for certain. Every time before he had known exactly what to do.

Not tonight.

Tonight, he was adrift, lost at sea. Until his eyes found Alice, and she anchored him as she always did.

She was standing in the middle of the room, the moonlight highlighting her high cheekbones, the pout of her lips, and the near-golden flecks in her brown eyes that seemed, at this moment, rather... hesitant.

"I'm sorry," he said, anguish overcoming him as the recognition of what he should have realized earlier flooded him. She didn't want to be with him. Didn't want him here. What had he been thinking? She was not a woman who would welcome a known rake into her bedroom. He could not ruin her to soothe himself and his own demons. "This was a bad idea. I never should have come."

She took a step closer. Tilted her head.

"Why did you?"

"Because…"

He ran a hand through his wet hair, unsure of how to share all that he felt without scaring her.

"Because I couldn't stand the thought of another night without you. Because I went into Chesterpeak's house, gambled, was propositioned, was provided every vice in which I have ever indulged in the past and could ever want to again, and not one of them called to me. Because all I can think of is you. Every moment of every day. Because you make everything in my life better, Alice. You make *me* better."

He took a shaky breath, knowing that he was crossing over a boundary he had set quite firmly for himself, and that once he did so, there was no going back. But the alternative was no longer satisfactory. For he couldn't leave Alice.

Not tonight.

Or any night after that.

She clenched and unclenched the fists at her side, which held the white linen of her night-rail within them. Still, she simply looked at him, with open, asking eyes.

"What are you saying?" she said, her words husky, hot with emotion.

"I'm saying," he swallowed hard as he dripped a puddle onto the floor beneath him, "that I do not want this to be an empty engagement coordinated by your brother and I do not want to leave you once I know you are safe. I love you, Alice Cunningham, and I want to court you because I want to court you."

He paused, the words coming out before he even knew what he was saying. "Hell, I want to marry you."

Alice stared at him, her eyes wide, her jaw slack, her hands no longer relaxed at her side.

"Are you serious?"

"I jest about almost everything in my life, Alice," he said solemnly. "Except this."

She took another step toward him, and he remained rooted to the spot, waiting for her to come all the way.

"If you do not feel the same," he began slowly, as much as the words tore at him to do so, "I understand. This is not what you asked for. I am not a good man and likely not the right man for you. But I cannot help the way I feel."

She finally reached him, erasing all space remaining. Still, she didn't touch him...except with her eyes, which ran all over his face as she searched him, perhaps attempting to determine how much truth was in his words.

"I asked you before if this could be real," she said slowly. "You said no. Are you only trying to bed me?"

"Absolutely not," he said, shaking his head. "I will go, I promise I will. I just... I suppose I can no longer deny my own wishes... or deny you."

"If you mean it, if you truly mean it," she said, peering up at him with her wide, laughing brown eyes, "then I would like nothing more than to accept."

Joy began to bloom deep within his heart, before the stems sprouted and grew, overtaking all else like a weed, but one that held surprisingly beautiful flowers.

He released a low chuckle under his breath as he realized all that had happened within the past few minutes. He had entered this room a rake, attempting another conquest. He was leaving a man promised to one woman, and one woman alone.

As he stared at her open, honest, innocent face, a tiny seed of doubt planted itself within the shoots of happiness. She trusted him completely, and while he vowed he would never do anything to hurt her, people he loved always ended up hurt all the same. Was he being selfish, choosing his own happiness when it meant putting her at risk?

Before he could think on it any longer, however, she lifted her face to his, and he was lost in her kiss. It was soft, sweet sanity. She was the savior he never knew he needed.

She lifted her hands to his face, cupping his cheeks in their warm softness. He groaned as he leaned into her, his hands seeming so wide and his fingers so clumsy against the small of her back and the narrow of her waist. He slid them down, cupping her bottom before nudging her closer to him until she was right against him, wet clothes be damned.

"I should go," he said, breaking away from her, his breathing ragged. He had told her he would leave, and he would, though it would kill him to do so.

But it wasn't to be.

"Stay," she commanded, looking up at him imploringly, and he was powerless to do otherwise.

He claimed her lips again and again, unable to keep the urgency from them as he demanded more from her with all of the hungriness that had plagued him night after night as he thought of her. Her very presence in his arms changed everything for him, and he knew that no matter what happened — whether she would fulfill her promise and marry him or if she came to her senses beforehand — nothing would ever be the same for him again.

Benjamin had been searching for purpose, for home, his entire life.

He had finally found it in Alice's arms.

When he pushed against her tongue with his she moaned softly and he sought to pull her even closer, although he knew it wasn't humanly possible.

He had thought that he could make her his and that would make everything better, but what he was slowly realizing as he pressed his hands harder against her back so that she could feel every growing inch of him that longed for her, was that he didn't want to possess her — no, they were two people who were forming a new entity, one that included two souls, two hearts, that could never be properly parted again.

Desire coursed down through his body and right into hers.

Their kiss, their touch, their presence together in this bedroom created expectancy. Their hands, their heat, their finality in giving in to this tense desire that had been drawing them together for weeks now was their ecstasy.

This was no experiment. This was fulfillment.

Benjamin was torn between continuing the kiss that had fused them together and breaking away in order to remove all of the layers between them. His own desire finally forced him to choose the latter.

"Turn for me," he said, swiveling her hips around with his hands.

He tugged at the bottom of her plait, moving it to the side so that he could place a tender kiss on the nape of her neck, where the tiniest of hairs blew out of the way at his touch. She trembled against him as he nibbled at her earlobe and up the shell of her ear, even as he began to untie the plait that hung down behind her.

Her hair was silky, the tresses much heavier than he had imagined, and he curled them around his hand, gently tugging at them to expose more of her neck to his exploration.

"Do you remember the first time I kissed you?" he murmured, surprising himself even more so than her with the question. He hadn't meant to bring it up, but the memory was too present even now.

"Of course," she said, her voice husky, nearly broken

before she took a shuddering breath that seemed to pull the air into his own lungs, so deep it was. "I could never forget it."

"Ever since then, I have wanted nothing more than to have you like this, in my arms, again," he admitted.

"Then why didn't you sooner?"

"I didn't know if I could be the man for you — I still am not entirely sure. But I can't seem to fight against myself any longer."

She tilted her head back so that it rested on his chest, and he reached around her, encircling her in his arms while he found the tiny buttons at the top of her night-rail, now damp from his wet clothing. He began undoing the small clasps of the cotton garment until the top gaped open, just enough for his hand to slip through.

He teased her with a quick caress, one that was enough to cause her to gasp but not enough to bring her any real satisfaction. Instead, he turned her around, his blood pumping hot when he saw the glaze of desire over her eyes.

"I'm not sure I have ever seen anything quite as seductive as this night-rail soaked through," he teased, causing her to laugh, although her breath caught in her throat before she could quite finish.

He trailed his fingers down her arm until he reached the cuff of her sleeve, pulling it slowly over her wrist, her hands, her fingers, until her arm was lost in the garment. He did the same on the other side, taking his time, savoring every moment of his undressing.

He finally tugged it up over her head, until he had completely unwrapped his gift, and she stood in a chemise before him.

Now that he could see the soft outlines of each of her breasts, he couldn't wait any longer. He turned her around again, wrapping her in his arms as her bottom tortured his arousal. He nuzzled her neck as he reached around to cup her breasts, taking each nipple between a forefinger and thumb, rolling them even as he began to taste the hollow of her throat once more.

Alice seemed to enjoy it as she leaned her head back into his shoulder and he found himself taking more and more of her weight while her nipples peaked between his fingers. Her breathing became a pant, and Benjamin found that he soon forgot everything, including the fact that he wasn't worthy of her. Now, all he wanted was to give her this gift, the one thing that he could actually do for her.

She must have come to the edge of her own desire, for now it was Alice who was turning in his arms, Alice who was shoving his wet jacket off his shoulders, Alice who was unfastening his breeches. He could sense she knew what she wanted, but was not aware of the fastest way to get it.

He could help her with that.

Together, they removed his jacket, his waistcoat, his shirt.

They hadn't yet managed to remove his breeches when he was already drawing her close once more, pressing her hard against his arousal, closing his eyes when he thought of how it would feel to be inside her, the most amazing woman he had ever laid eyes on.

Her thoughts must have followed his as she pushed him away and reached for his waist, completely unfastening his breeches until the material opened wide enough that it was her turn to reach within and find what she was looking for.

Her grin was nearly as captivating as her touch, and Benjamin threw his head back when those inexperienced yet eager fingers found him, exploring him with all of the audacity and interest with which she approached everything else in her life.

He couldn't take it much longer.

He bent his head and kissed her again even as he lifted

her off her feet, somehow finding the bed nearly without looking. He laid her down upon it with all of the gentleness he could muster, all of the gentleness she deserved, before pushing his breeches down his legs, shucking them off as he gazed upon the feast before him with hunger so strong he wasn't sure how he was able to keep it at bay.

But first, Benjamin had work to do. He lay down beside her, kissing her as he pulled her close, skimming his hand down her side, feeling her own pulse jump along with his. He cupped her hip for a moment, holding her there against him, before continuing to trace his fingers over the soft, slim material of her chemise. He meandered over her pelvic bone, but avoided his final destination, to which she protested with a frustrated growl, before skimming over her thigh. He finally reached the hem of her chemise, and slid it up, higher and higher, revealing more of her skin as he went.

He thought of pausing for a taste when he reached the junction of her thighs, but first he broke the kiss just long enough to lift her chemise overhead, giving himself the most exquisite view before him. Now, *now* he allowed himself to take what he wanted, to give what she needed.

When Benjamin reached down and cupped her mound, her legs opened of their own accord, inviting him in. He didn't need any further invitation as he began to stroke her, his thumb finding her most tender nub, which he circled before reaching down with his fingers, starting slow and then increasing in intensity.

Alice began to move in time with his rhythm, her panting breaths quickening, and he caught her gaze, keeping it within his, though it seemed to be difficult for both of them to focus.

"Alice," he said, her name both harsh and soft on his lips, "you're the only one — the only woman — who has ever captured by heart."

She stared up at him through half-lidded eyes even as the firelight danced over her cheekbones, turning her soft skin dewy in the dim light.

"I can say the same," she said, her words just over a whisper, "although you're the first to have my body as well."

He nuzzled the curve of her neck until he moved lower, finding her hard nipples again although this time drawing them into his mouth, loving the heady feeling of her hand twining into his hair as she held him there.

She tried to reach down for him with the other hand, but he wouldn't let her — not yet.

He had things to do first.

He reluctantly left her breasts as he began to kiss his way down the soft center of her stomach, even as he lifted her hips up and moved his shoulders between her knees.

Alice seemed to still as she stared down at him in shock.

Benjamin grinned.

CHAPTER 20

*A*lice had thought she was fairly well educated when it came to manners of sex.

She had asked those in the know an appropriate amount of questions, even withstanding the laughter of the ladies of the night who had taken pity on her the time she had cornered them and fired her questions at them.

But they had not prepared her for this. They couldn't have.

Alice had thought that what Benjamin had done to her in the shadows of the Vauxhall Gardens was the most amazing, pleasurable act.

She was wrong on that.

Alice had also thought that when it came time to complete the act, it was primarily for the man's enjoyment.

That was most certainly not the case.

At least, not with Benjamin.

When he parted her with his thumbs and bent his head to touch his tongue against her, she nearly flew off the bed, so violently did she jump. Her hands flailed against the sheets until they finally found purchase, and she fisted the fabric in her hands as his mouth did things that could only be described as evilly carnal.

She moaned his name, which only seemed to urge him on. The more he stroked, the more a fire built within her, beginning where he touched her and slowly spreading out, the flames fanning wider with each incredible stroke.

When she didn't think the ache could burn any hotter, she unfurled her fists and released the sheet to try to push his head away, unable to withstand the sensation. But instead, she found herself holding his head against her, and when he began to swirl his tongue over her nub, the climax hit her with the full force of its flame, and waves began to undulate through her.

"Benjamin!" she cried out again, and even as she was in the throes of passion, she knew she was missing something, and reached out, finally finding him, long, hot and ready for her. She pulled him toward her and he came willingly. Her hips arched up toward him as though they already knew what they were doing, what they were waiting for, and soon he was there at her entrance, stretching her as he slowly filled her, inching into her too slowly for her liking.

She wrapped her arms around him and with a strength she didn't know she had, she pulled him close, causing him to thrust up deep within her, until he began to move, each pump more powerful than the one before it as their mouths met again, matching the intense rising frenzy of where they were joined.

His entire body finally went stiff above her, and he was surging into her one last time, pulsating within her. She could do nothing but match him, as her own release equaled his while they remained fused together — at the pelvis, mouth, and soul.

Alice never wanted him to leave her.

She had said yes to his proposal not entirely sure if he

actually meant it, or if he was acting on an instinct that would change as frequently as his usual vice.

But now... this had to mean something more than a usual pursuit of pleasure, did it not?

He finally lifted himself from her, lying beside her so that they faced one another. He reached out and tugged her close to him, fitting her head against the crook of his arm, even as he stroked the side of her body, his fingers hot against skin which she hadn't thought could grow any warmer than it already was.

Their bodies slowed and recovered, but Alice knew one thing was for certain.

She was forever changed.

And any notion that she would be able to move on from this if ever he left her was gone.

* * *

HE DIDN'T WANT to leave her — not now and not ever.

But soon enough, morning would come, and he would still keep her safe from whatever dangers awaited — which meant protecting her from a ruined reputation, even if he *was* going to marry her.

He reluctantly pulled his damp clothing back on, finishing with his boots, before crossing over to the window and staring down into the moonlit night below. It seemed much farther from this viewpoint than it had from the bottom.

"Are you rethinking this decision?" Alice asked, laughter in her voice.

While he knew she meant to tease him about the climb, he could tell that what she was truly asking was whether or not he was going to change his mind about his commitment to her.

"Of course not," he said with one last long, lingering kiss. "I shall see you very soon."

"I am counting on that," she said with a smile.

Benjamin told himself not to look down but did anyway, and then, summoning all of his courage, he boosted himself out the window.

Back down the trellis he went.

CHAPTER 21

*A*lice wrote more words the next morning than she had in the previous month. Her heart was singing as her pen flew across the page, unable to keep up with the thoughts that were racing through her mind.

Previously, she had written romance. Now she could write a love story. For she knew what it was, what it meant, and how utterly intoxicating it was to find it.

A tiny thrill travelled along her spine, and her heart fluttered. She was in love with Benjamin Luxington and he with her. For whatever reason, the known rake had learned that love was worth more than the rest of the vices he had lost himself in, and she was the one who had taught him so.

Memories rose... the feeling of his arms around her, of his breath skimming against the side of her throat, of his touch seemingly everywhere at once. She paused for a moment, hugging herself.

She should have said no, should have waited until she could speak to him further about what Adams had found out, about Chesterpeak and Donning and Madeline and what his connection was to all of it.

But she had been helpless to do anything save show him just how she felt in return.

"You were up early."

"Oliver!" she exclaimed, turning to find her brother in the doorway. "You startled me!"

"I'm sorry," he said. "I see you're writing. I shall leave you to it."

"It's fine," she said with a wave of her hand. "I am more interested in speaking to you."

She did have to get these words down, but she also needed to talk to her brother.

"Ollie—"

"Alice—"

They each began at the same time, then laughingly, ordered the other to go first.

"Very well, if you will not continue," Oliver said. "The ceasing of most of your questions and your 'fiction' seems to have worked, for there have been no further attempts on your life. We can tell Lord Benjamin that his services are no longer required. He can return to his life once more."

A tingling in Alice's chest as well as her core reminded her of his presence just a few hours ago.

"Ollie," she said slowly, unsure of how exactly to tell her brother this, "Benjamin and I have reached an understanding."

"Oh?" he asked with confusion.

"In this time we have been together, we have learned that we rather like each other," she said, obviously staying far from the full details of just *how* that understanding came about. "Our courtship will become a true one."

Oliver said nothing for a moment.

Then he laughed.

"You're not serious, Alice," he chuckled. "How could you be? Benjamin Luxington with a woman like you?"

"What is that supposed to mean?" she asked hotly.

"Nothing against you, Alice," Oliver said as Alice crossed her arms over her chest. "Just that Luxington appreciates anything in a skirt. You're one of the most amazing women I know, and I am not just saying that because you are my sister. But Benjamin Luxington would never make such a promise to a woman. He's never come close to it before, and I do not see him starting it for this pretense of an engagement."

"Think what you wish," Alice said primly, although Oliver's words hurt more than she cared to admit, and were causing her to throw everything in question — everything, that had seemed so promising in the dark of night.

Before she could think on it any further, however, Adams stepped into the room while a young woman lingered just outside the door.

"My apologies, Lord Keswick, Miss Cunningham. I must, however, speak rather urgently with Miss Cunningham."

Oliver's eyes went steely. "If you can say it in front of Miss Cunningham, you can say it in front of me."

Alice's eyes flicked over to her brother, but she knew she would never now convince him to leave, not when the footman spoke so cryptically.

"This is Miss Smith," he said, showing in the maid who Alice recognized from Chesterpeak's. "She sought me out to provide additional information. I'll have her tell most of it, but it's about Lord Benjamin, so I thought it is prudent you knew before anything further was promised to him."

Like my innocence?

"This sounds serious," Oliver said, and Alice perched herself on the edge of the couch to wait and listen, even as dread began to fill her stomach.

"You asked quite a few questions about Chesterpeak the other night, of course," the maid continued. "But you also spoke about Lord Benjamin Luxington. Well... he was much the focus of conversation tonight."

"Tell me more, please," Alice said quietly, although a part of her — the opposing side to that which willed the maid to continue — wanted to ask her to stop, to forget whatever she was going to say, and go back to where she came.

She had given herself completely to Benjamin — body and soul. It couldn't have been a betrayal. It couldn't have all been a set up. She would have known, would she not?

But the maid continued, unaware that her words were destroying the carefully built wall of hope that Alice had only just constructed.

"For some time now, Lord Benjamin has been visiting Mr. Chesterpeak's home, and there has been talk that he would be a logical addition to join Chesterpeak's group. Women love him, he could use the wealth it would provide, and he has the charming duplicity required. He's just like his father, Chesterpeak says."

But he *wasn't*. He was *nothing* like his father.

At least, Alice hadn't thought he was.

"I believe Lord Benjamin agreed last night. He came to Chesterpeak's, remained with him in his office for quite some time, and when he left, Chesterpeak seemed quite satisfied. I'm not sure who the woman is that he is going to take advantage of, but I do hope she can be warned."

Alice knew. Alice knew who the woman was.

She felt sick.

"What... what happens to these women?"

"The gentleman marries her. He takes all of her dowry and whatever fortunes she brings to the marriage. He shares part of it with Chesterpeak and his investors, and keeps the rest for himself. Then the man moves on."

"How so?" Alice croaked out, suddenly aware of Oliver's hand on her shoulder, and never was she more grateful that she had a brother who, despite how annoying he could be at times, would do anything to see to her safety and happiness.

"In most cases, he assumes another identity and marries again. Many of the men keep a wife in one town and have a second in another, or multiple families around London. Some…" she cleared her throat, her eyes shifting from one of them to the other, her next words a whisper, as though by saying them quietly they would lessen their meaning. "Sometimes the women must be taken care of. That's where Chesterpeak comes in. Not only does he provide the initial funds to ensure that the man can court the woman in proper style, but he will… get rid of them if necessary."

"Do you mean—?"

"Yes, that's exactly what she means."

They all turned to the doorway to find Madeline standing there. She was still dressed in her night-rail, but she held a wrapper tightly around her. She was still pale, her eyes still sunken, black circles around them, but there was a set to her chin and a determined glint in her eyes that hadn't been there before.

Her fight had returned. If nothing else, that was something to celebrate.

"Madeline." For a moment, Alice forgot her own plight and crossed the room to help her friend to a seat. "You shouldn't be out of bed."

"Oh, but I should," she said. "You shouldn't all be fighting my battles for me. I was foolish enough to be duped into this. Now I need to be smart enough to fight my way out."

"This isn't your fault," Alice said. "The man is a swindler."

"True," Madeline said, "but I have always prided myself on being smarter than that. I was prepared to take over my father's business, for goodness' sake. Then I allowed myself to be manipulated by a man like Stephen—"

"Lord Donning?" the maid rejoined the conversation. "He's a mean one, to be sure. Are you Lady Donning?"

"I am."

"You're his fourth wife."

Madeline's eyes grew the size of dinner plates.

"His what?"

"He's had four wives so far. I believe the first still lives, has a home somewhere. Children. She doesn't mind as he brings home a great deal of money."

"But he's an earl."

"He's not. Chesterpeak arranged it so that all would believe that he was the long-lost heir to the earldom, but it's not the truth."

Madeline sank her head into her hands, her legs giving out as she found a place next to Alice on the couch. Alice placed a hand on her back, rubbing small circles in an attempt to comfort her, although she could never understand the magnitude of what she must be feeling. Alice was sick at the thought of Benjamin potentially having taken her innocence and her heart as part of some grand scheme, whereas Madeline had been falsely married in front of half the *ton*.

And Alice had something else. She had hope. Hope that Benjamin had simply been playing a part, going along with the scheme in order to learn more about what Chesterpeak was involved with.

She would give him the benefit of the doubt. She owed him that. She owed it to herself as well.

"I can't believe Lord Benjamin would be part of such a thing," Oliver said, echoing her own thoughts.

"We can only ask him," Alice said, eyeing Madeline, more concerned about her at the moment.

But she couldn't get Benjamin out of the back of her mind. Of the way he had touched her last night. How he had kissed her with lips so tender, so sensuous, so all-consuming that she couldn't believe he was that good of an actor that it was all part of a greater scheme.

Not that she could provide her brother with that type of evidence. He would have an apoplexy.

Evidence — that was what they needed.

She wondered if Benjamin *had* managed to gather anything last night. That would be the first order of business, she decided, as her breath caught in her throat at the thought of seeing him again. No matter her suspicions, her body didn't seem to care what her mind knew, as every part of her vibrated with the remembrance of Benjamin in her bed.

Alice turned to the maid.

"Could you — would you — be able to gather anything from Mr. Chesterpeak's house that might provide us with proof as to what he has been doing?"

"Oh, I don't know…" the maid said, her face now shuttered. "If I was ever caught—"

"We would pay you handsomely," Alice said, although Oliver placed a hand on her arm.

"Alice, if she isn't comfortable, we should not force it," he murmured.

"What if…?" the maid said slowly, looking to Adams first as though requiring his approval to broach the idea. He nodded slightly. "If I was to find you information — would you provide me with a position in your household?"

"I would," Oliver said, and she brightened considerably.

"Thank you," she said. "I shall return with something. I'll look in his office tonight."

"Perfect," Alice said before Adams showed the maid out.

"I best be going to see Luxington," Oliver said, his brow furrowed with trouble.

"I'm coming with you," Alice said.

"No, you most certainly are not."

"But—"

Oliver rounded toward her, his jaw set in determination.

"You will stay here. For once in your life, Alice, stay out of this, please. Do not go begging for trouble. Do not get yourself hurt, or worse. Do you understand?"

She did not, but she wasn't about to tell her brother that.

"Very well." She sighed.

When just she and Madeline remained, Alice threw herself back on the chesterfield, attempting levity to help lift Madeline's spirits. "Here we are, two ruined, unmarried women. Who would have thought we would come to this?"

Madeline sighed and closed her eyes in pain, but then suddenly she sat bolt upright, her eyes on Alice.

"What do you mean... that we are both ruined?"

Alice proceeded to tell her of the entire affair, with Madeline affixed to her every word. When she finally finished, Madeline's mouth was round and her eyes wide.

"Oh, Alice," she said, shaking her head. "What are we to do?"

"Well," Alice said, "we are about to take matters into our own hands."

CHAPTER 22

*B*enjamin had never felt so utterly complete in his
life.

He had tried to fill all of the holes with a fair number of
vices, but all they did was distract him from what remained.

Now, Alice had done more in one evening than he had
done himself in a lifetime.

He could hardly wait to see her again, but first, he had to
extricate himself from the situation with Chesterpeak, and
hopefully help bring him down at the same time.

How many men had been caught in the same trap as he?
How many women had lost everything — some their very
lives? It sickened him. He contemplated going directly to the
Bow Street Runners with what he already knew, but first, he
needed proof. Proof that he had promised Alice and that he
had to determine for himself.

He hadn't quite made up his mind as to whether he
should speak with Alice first or return to Chesterpeak's as he
opened the door of his townhouse and started down the
stairs, stopping suddenly when he found that he had
company.

Donning and Chesterpeak were awaiting him at the bottom, taking the decision out of his hands.

"Gentlemen," he said, although they were anything but, "what can I do for you today?"

"You did not seem convinced of our scheme last night," Chesterpeak said easily. "Today we are here to convince you."

"Very well," Benjamin said, pleased that they would be providing him all of the evidence he needed. "What did you have in mind?"

"Come with us," Donning said, a smile on his face, "and we shall show you."

Benjamin reluctantly agreed.

They didn't get far down the street before a group of ladies caught his eye. Oh no, please don't let it be, he groaned inwardly. But sure enough, there was his sister-in-law Freddie, Alice's sister-in-law Celeste, and two of their friends, Mrs. Thompkins and the Duchess of Wyndham.

They were coming straight toward him.

"Ladies," he greeted them as they passed, but didn't stop to chat. In one quick glance, he caught Freddie's concerned stare and Celeste's suspicious one.

Damnit, he inwardly cursed. The last thing he needed was for Alice to hear any more of his dealings with Chesterpeak. She would understand one evening of sleuthing, but to be with him again today….

"I'm sorry, gentlemen, but I need to go," Benjamin said, beginning to back away, but Chesterpeak caught his wrist.

"Not quite yet," he said, raising a finger between them. "First, we need to ensure that you are doing your part of the plan."

"What plan?" Benjamin asked desperately. He really just wanted to go see Alice, to explain everything that had happened and ensure she didn't get any wrong ideas.

"To marry the Cunningham girl and bring us her dowry,"

Chesterpeak said. "Then it is up to you whether or not you'd like to stick with her."

He and Donning looked at one another with a smirk, and Benjamin stopped right there in the middle of the street and stared at them, his hands on his hips.

"You never told me any of this," he said through gritted teeth. "I thought I was just participating in some financial investment instead of something so... sinister."

"Sinister," Chesterpeak barked with a laugh. "Ha. Now, we have work to do."

"I'm not sure I have the... time to accompany you."

"We are looking for Donning's wife," Chesterpeak said, with a wave toward Donning. "We still haven't been able to locate her." He peered at Benjamin. "You wouldn't happen to know anything about that, now would you?"

"Me?" Benjamin blustered. "Of course not."

"Very well," Chesterpeak said. "We have a lead you can help us with."

Benjamin's heart raced. "Do you now?"

"We do. We believe she is being kept in an abandoned old house near the west end of the Strand. Come with us to check?"

Everything within Benjamin was screaming at him to say no and run the other way as fast as he could. But, he rationalized, if he was able to keep these men away from Madeline and the Cunningham residence in Mayfair, then would that not be more help than anything else?

"Very well," he said. "Lead on."

They took Chesterpeak's coach which, Benjamin belatedly realized, was a mistake. He should have ensured his own method of transportation, just in case he needed to have an easy escape.

But he was not exactly practiced in matters of investigation. Not like Alice. What did it say about him that he knew she would do far better than he at this, despite the fact it would be much too dangerous for her to do so?

As they were pulling away from his house, Benjamin sat up straight when he saw Essex through the window. He leaned back as far into the seat as he could, closing his eyes as though it would prevent Essex from seeing him.

He could only hope he had.

The ride there was fairly silent. Benjamin attempted one joke at Donning about losing his wife, but it was not met with a great deal of humor and so he resisted from making anymore. Soon enough the houses grew much closer together and the finishes were less and less polished. Finally, the carriage came to a stop in front of one particular run-down house.

"Are you sure this is it?" Benjamin said, peering out the window. "I don't see any light."

"This is what I was told," Chesterpeak said before opening the door and leading them out. "After you," he said, waving an arm inside the door, and a trickle of sweat leaked down Benjamin's spine as every nerve was on edge. He was very aware that he one, should never have come with these two men, and two, entering the house, especially first, was a very bad idea.

But he had joined them with full intentions of making them think he was in agreement with their entire scheme, and now he had no idea how to back out of it — especially here, where he was all alone with no escape.

He stepped gingerly through the door, turning back to ask Chesterpeak if he had a light of any sort or knew of how they could start the fireplace.

He turned just in time to see Donning's fist — a huge rock within it — coming straight toward his head.

* * *

ALICE WAS QUITE surprised to find that Chesterpeak's house was so quiet — she supposed that was the case during the daylight hours. She was only glad that she had convinced Madeline to stay behind. As much as her friend had insisted that she wanted to come along, Alice had shaken her head at the absolutely terrible idea.

"You can still hardly walk from your chamber to the dining room," she said, "and until you actually *eat* in said dining room, you will never have any energy to go anywhere else. Besides, what if Chesterpeak finds you there? You will be right back to the hell you left."

"What if he finds *you* there?" Madeline asked.

She had a point.

Alice sent Benjamin a note asking him to join her, but after an hour of waiting, pacing, and dreaming up far too many ideas of just where he could be, she asked Adams to accompany her instead.

He readily agreed, seemingly quite interested now in this entire mystery, as he asked her many more questions than would be usual as they walked to Chesterpeak's residence along with Ingrid.

Now here they were, no one answering the knock on the door. Alice stepped forward and bravely pushed it open.

"You're here!" It was Miss Smith, the maid, rushing toward them. She seemed particularly pleased to see Adams, nearly running into his arms, but he held her at arm's length. He had explained to Alice on the journey here that he was concerned Miss Smith may have the wrong impression of his intentions regarding her, and that he wasn't sure if she would continue if he told her that he had no interest.

"My apologies, Miss Smith, but—" he looked to Alice for help, seemingly unsure of just how to tell the maid that he was otherwise promised.

"Adams is married," Alice blurted out quickly, as they had no time to spare the maid's feelings.

"Oh," she said, stepping back, blinking rapidly as she looked at the pair of them. "I see. I had no idea. In fact, I—"

She stopped, twirling around a piece of paper she held in her hands. She looked at it, looked back at them, and then at the paper once more as though she was trying to make a decision.

"I have something for you," she said, and Alice reached out her hand for the paper, but she shook her head. "Not here. Come with me."

She led them through the house, telling them as she went that no one was currently home, the master out looking for Lord Donning's wife.

"Mr. Chesterpeak and Lord Donning suspect one of his business associates."

"Do they?" Alice asked, surprised. She thought the maid had been in agreement that Lord Donning was just as much behind this plot as anyone else.

The maid pushed open the office door, leading them in.

"I found his ledger," she said, striding toward the desk, where the black leather-bound book was conveniently placed in the center. "It was in his desk drawer. It notes who has provided him with funds and where they might have gone."

Alice and Adams exchanged a look. It sounded like the perfect evidence to tell them what they needed to know... but it seemed far too convenient.

"Thank you," Alice said, acknowledging the maid, who was awaiting their response. "Have you read any of it?"

"I took a quick look, but I didn't know much of what I was looking at," the maid said, waving a hand. "Although I did recognize some entries regarding Lord Benjamin Luxington, which may be of interest to you."

Did the maid have a self-satisfied gleam in her eye? Alice wasn't sure if she was reading too much into this, or fantasizing of the storyline she wanted to create.

For Benjamin couldn't have anything to do with this. He was *investigating* Chesterpeak and his friends. He was helping *her*.

"Thank you for finding it," Alice said, reaching out to take the book from her. She flipped through it quickly, seeing a practiced, even scrawl.

"Take it with you," the maid said, and Alice looked up at her, surprised.

"Won't Mr. Chesterpeak miss it?"

"He's preoccupied with helping Lord Donning find his wife right now," the maid said. "I'm sure if you have it back in a day or two, all would be fine."

A day or two. Enough time for Alice to use it as evidence against Donning and Chesterpeak if she worked fast.

"Thank you," Alice said earnestly, convinced that nothing within the pages she held would actually implicate Benjamin.

"There's one more thing," the maid said, looking up at Alice with wide, bright eyes. "Mr. Chesterpeak was leaving to see Lord Donning and Lord Benjamin once more. He said..." she looked down at the floor, rocking back and forth from her heels to her toes, "he said that Lord Benjamin was going to help lead them to Lady Donning, and that a portion of the funds they collected following Lord Donning's inheritance would go to ensuring that you married Lord Benjamin."

"Oh?" Alice attempted to hide her increasingly rapidly beating heart.

"Yes," the maid nodded sagely. "I am sorry, miss."

"Nothing to be sorry about," Alice said, forcing a smile. "Better to know earlier than later. Let's go Adams," she said, anxious to leave before she dissolved into tears on the spot. "We best go make sense out of all of this."

No sooner had they entered her home, when Celeste happened upon her. Alice hadn't even made it to her writing room when her sister-in-law was standing there, blocking the door with her belly, which Alice was certain had grown overnight.

"Alice!" she called as Alice walked down the hall. "I must speak with you."

"Of course," Alice said. "Come, let's go inside the room so that we can speak."

The second the door shut behind them, Celeste launched into a tirade about Lord Benjamin Luxington, and what she thought Alice should do about him.

"I know Freddie and Miles say he is a good man, and he has always been a great deal of help when we have needed him. But," she looked pointedly at Alice, "I don't think he is the type of man you should become involved with. He's handsome and charming, true, but how handsome and how charming? And why is he doing this with you?"

Alice's chest panged a bit. "Are you saying... that you don't think I would typically be the type of woman in whom he might be interested?"

"No," Celeste shook her head vehemently. "Any man would be lucky to have you in his life. You know that as do I. It's just..." She placed her hands on her hips, surrounding her protruding belly. "We just saw him."

"You did?" Alice's head snapped up at that. "Where? I was looking for him."

"He was..." Celeste cringed, "with Lord Donning and that Chesterpeak character."

"He was not."

"I wish I could say he wasn't," Celeste said. "From what I know and from what Freddie tells me, Benjamin is a good man. But..." she threw her hands up in the air, "it seems trouble finds him, or he finds trouble, I'm not sure. And I don't want you to get caught up in that."

Alice walked back over to her desk, looking down at the ledger. She didn't want to believe what she saw in front of her, but it was there in ink. Benjamin had given a good sum of money to Chesterpeak some time ago, and now it seemed he was the one benefiting from it, having received it back just days ago.

About the time their relationship had begun to change and deepen – or so she had thought.

She pressed the pads of her hands against her eyes.

No no no. This was all wrong. Benjamin was not devious, and she was not stupid. They were writing their ultimate love story, for goodness sake.

"I have to find him," she said, finally lowering her hands to look at Celeste, her face filled with pity that Alice did not desire, no matter from what good intentions it came.

"I need to know the truth."

CHAPTER 23

*B*enjamin opened his eyes with a groan.

A fair bit of light filtered in through a dirty window, but he was surprised to see Chesterpeak and Donning were still there, Chesterpeak sitting on a scarred hardback chair.

"Good," Chesterpeak said. "I was beginning to wonder how long it would take you to wake up. We didn't hit you *that* hard."

Benjamin rubbed the throbbing area on his head.

"What did you do that for?"

"We had to keep you here a while," Chesterpeak said, crossing one leg over the other nonchalantly as though he had not a care in the world. "A few things needed to happen while we were here."

"Like what?" Benjamin ground out, not wanting to ask but needing to anyway.

"Like for your beloved Miss Cunningham to realize that you are completely, entirely, to blame. For nearly everything."

Benjamin rose with a growl, advancing on the man despite the thudding in his head. "What are you talking about? I've done nothing."

"Maybe not," Chesterpeak said with a shrug, "but that's not what it will look like."

Benjamin narrowed his eyes at him. "What did you do?"

"Just set up a few pieces of evidence for your industrious Miss Cunningham to find. Oh, but she likes to ask questions, doesn't she?"

"You tried to have her killed," Benjamin said bitterly. "I knew it."

"I was only helping Donning here, who asked for the favor," he said, waving to the other man, who was standing with his shoulder resting against the doorjamb. "He was worried that if little Alice came snooping she might find something he didn't want her to learn, and he was right, wasn't he?"

He leaned over Benjamin now, so that they were nose to nose.

"Where is Lady Donning?"

"I don't know," Benjamin said, holding up all of his resolve. "But I hope that wherever she has run to, she is far from the two of you."

Chesterpeak snorted before looking back at Donning.

"We best return now. It should be enough time for Miss Cunningham to have found what she was looking for and for the maid to have provided all the answers."

"The maid?" Benjamin asked, looking back and forth between the two of them.

"Yes, one of my maids. A lovely little thing she is, and so devoted. She's quite looking forward to our marriage, which of course is never going to happen."

He threw his head back and laughed, sending a trickle of dread down Benjamin's spine.

What was he going to find when he returned to Mayfair?

"Come, let's go," Chesterpeak said to Donning before turning with a sneer to Benjamin. "Good luck finding your way home."

Then he closed the door, on Benjamin and all of his hopes for his future.

* * *

ALICE HAD SEARCHED EVERYWHERE for Benjamin.

He wasn't home. He wasn't at Lord Dorrington's manor, and no one there had seen him. She didn't even see signs of him at Chesterpeak's.

It had been a long, hard day, and when she flung herself into the folds of the sofa of her writing room, her eyes closed of their own accord and she nearly fell asleep.

She was physically tired, yes, but emotionally, all of her energy that had been funneled into believing the very best of Benjamin was beginning to seep through cracks that were appearing with every shred of evidence against him.

The ledger was clear. Benjamin apparently had not only invested in Chesterpeak's schemes, but had been one of the founders, and had been a beneficiary of those poor women's dowries.

The maid had also been quite forthright, although there was something off about her testimony. It was too practiced, too informed for what a maid would most likely know.

Then there had been Benjamin's own relationship with the men, and his continued presence among them. Was he truly trying to help her, or were they actually his friends?

And now he was nowhere to be found.

Suddenly the air in the room shifted, and she swung her feet over the side of the sofa before sitting up right.

"Benjamin," she breathed.

Was she dreaming him? For there he was, framed in the doorway, so tall, so handsome... so defeated.

As exhausted as she had thought herself to be, he looked a thousand times worse.

And yet, relief rushed through her.

Alice couldn't help herself. She knew that everything pointed to him being guilty, to being involved in the worst of crimes. But deep in her heart, she didn't believe it. She couldn't. In a few strides she was across the room and had jumped into his arms — arms that circled her, holding her fast. When she leaned back to look into his eyes, they were wide, incredulous.

"What's wrong?"

"Everything," she said, her words nearly a sob. "But you're here. The maid says you're part of it. The ledger shows your involvement. You spend far too much time with men I wouldn't dream of being close to. And yet somehow, I know you would never do any of the things you have been accused of."

"So," he growled out, "you don't suspect me of *anything*?"

"I should," she said, holding his face in her hands. "Benjamin, everything I have found implicates you in taking such a great part in Chesterpeak's schemes. But I know you. You couldn't have anything to do with it. Could you?"

The eyes that searched hers now closed for a moment, and he leaned his forehead into her chest.

"You're too good, Alice," he mumbled into her breasts. "No other woman would find it in her heart to believe in me so."

"Well then, no other woman is deserving of you," she said. "Not like I am."

He set her down on her feet, and she looked around him into the corridor. "Did no one follow you in?" she asked.

"The butler let me in and then I saw Lady Essex," he said,

referring to Celeste. "She showed me where you were and then allowed for us to have a moment alone — with the door open, she specifically added."

Alice let out a whoosh of breath, grateful to her sister-in-law for allowing them the time despite her misgivings about Benjamin.

She led Benjamin over to the sofa where she had previously been pining for him, and he sank into the corner, pulling her hand onto his lap and mashing it between both of his.

He told her what had happened to him over the afternoon, and she could hardly believe that Chesterpeak would go to such extremes.

"He is becoming desperate," Benjamin said. "He's gone too far and involved too many people — people who know better and who can do something about him. He and Donning were stupid to pick Madeline as a victim."

She told Benjamin about everything she had learned, how she had learned it, and who she had learned it from. He listened without interrupting, leaning his head back against the ledge of the sofa and closing his eyes while she did so.

When she came to the part about returning to Chesterpeak's, his eyes flew open and he raised his head, watching her carefully, although he allowed her to finish speaking.

She then waited for him to address everything that she had found about what Chesterpeak had likely framed him for. But instead, he surprised her by what had most bothered him.

"You went to Chesterpeak's alone?" he asked, fixing her with a hard glare most unlike him.

"I took Adams," she said defensively. "I tried to ask you to accompany me, but you were nowhere to be found."

"I was practically abducted!"

"Celeste saw you go with them willingly," she argued, "although I understand why you were doing so."

"I was getting information. Evidence, Alice," he said. "That is not for you to do."

He pushed himself up from the sofa, bringing a hand to his forehead as he began to pace the room.

"You are far too involved. You need to stay out of this. Away from here, away from Madeline, away from me."

Alice stood herself now, anger blossoming in her chest at his high-handed words, even though she knew they were coming from a place of care.

"You cannot tell me what to do or where to go. I would be a part of this whether you were or not. I *was* a part of this and would likely have been killed had you not been in the right place at the right time."

"You might have been warned off though, or better yet, had someone protect you who actually knew what he was doing. It seems that your footman kept you safe enough."

"I kept myself safe," she said, crossing her arms over her chest. "He was there just in case."

"I don't want to keep worrying about your 'just in case,'" Benjamin said. "I should speak to your brother. Perhaps he could take you away from Chesterpeak and London, out to the country, where you'll be safe."

"And what would I do?" she said, cocking her head. "Sit out there reading and writing and wondering what poor soul is going to be the next victim of Chesterpeak's schemes? I think not."

"And what happens if you stay?" he challenged her, the two of them now face to face, and Alice didn't know if she would prefer kissing him or throttling him. "We either get married and Chesterpeak takes your dowry, or he decides to do away with you instead. They already suspect you of helping Madeline escape. He could be here this very instant looking for her."

That caught her attention, and for the first time, Alice actually considered the thought of doing as Benjamin said, even if it was just to take Madeline away for a time, to ensure that she was safe.

Benjamin seemed to realize that she agreed, for relief flashed in his expression and he ran his hands through his hair.

"Her father has been here," Alice said finally, wandering away from their fighting stance to gaze out the window. "Do you think there is a chance he could come to harm — or that they might follow him?"

"I most assuredly do."

"Very well," she said. "I'll talk to Oliver in the morning about moving Madeline somewhere else. But what are you going to do?"

"I'm going to talk to the Bow Street Runners," he said, "to tell them everything. To try to find a way to make them believe me."

"There is one way," she said, turning back toward him. "We could pretend Madeline died, and then follow what Chesterpeak and Donning do with the money."

Benjamin's eyes lit up slightly at that. "That's actually not a bad idea."

"Why, thank you," Alice said wryly.

Benjamin stepped closer now. "Go with Madeline away from London. Stay there for just a few weeks, until I can ensure all is well here. Will you do that for me?"

Alice hesitated. She knew he was right, that it was the smartest way forward, but she couldn't help but notice how haunted his eyes were, how desperate his tone.

"And then what?" she asked, the coiling in her gut telling her that all would not be well.

"Then you can do as you please," he said slowly. "Stay in the country. Or return to London. Write your books. Publish them. Fall in love. Marry."

Alice stepped back a fraction, so that she could see the entirety of his face.

"I have already fallen in love," she said, her voice just above a whisper.

Benjamin closed his eyes, was shaking his head. "Not with me, Alice," he said, the lines around his eyes, normally lines of laughter, now harsh, angry.

"Don't be ridiculous," she snapped, lashing out at him to hide the pain that struck at her breast, and the desperation that ached deep within her soul. "You and I are going to see this through together."

"And then what?" he said, his words gutted. "We stay together, until the next catastrophe comes along? Nothing ever goes right in my life, Alice. Nothing."

"Your father created this world for you," she insisted. "What is happening now is the remnants of his hate and his fear. You don't have to live in that world any longer. Come with me into another."

She held her hand out, desperate for him to take it, but instead, he pushed it away, stepping in toward her and taking her face within his large, warm hands.

When his lips crashed down on hers it was rough, wild, tortured.

He kissed her again and again, taking and giving all of the memories she knew he was as desperate for as she.

Then he released her as quickly as he had kissed her, and, before she had any time to recover from his kiss or even to breathe, he was gone.

He hovered by the edge of the door, looking back at her with a grimace.

"Don't follow me, Alice," he said. "Don't come after me. Besides... I've come to realize that I could never commit my life to just one woman. It's not your fault. It's mine."

And with that final slamming of her heart against the wall, its pieces shattered across the floor, he left her.

CHAPTER 24

*B*enjamin had no idea how he made it home after speaking to Alice — for what he promised himself would be the last time.

She was everything that drink, women, darkness had once been to him before he had met her. He couldn't get enough, and just when he thought he had worked everything out, that he was through, he wanted more. Needed more.

He knew he had destroyed her, but he told himself she would recover. He had said what he knew he had to in order to convince her to leave him be and live her own life.

At least now she would go, and no longer be the temptation he was fighting so hard to resist.

But the crash downward was nearly more than he could bear.

He had been gone from her for less than an hour and already he missed her with a ferocity that struck pain in the center of his chest that seemed to now be spreading through him like an uncontained infection, poisoning each and every part of him.

This was for the best, he told himself.

She would be better off without him.

So why did it feel like such a bad decision?

He would put his plan into motion tomorrow, now that Madeline was leaving, away to the country. In the meantime, while he knew that he couldn't actually make himself feel better, he could, at the very least, numb the pain.

Benjamin stumbled into the house and up the stairs to the study he had taken over — the study that had been his father's — waving off his valet, telling him that he wouldn't be needing his services tonight.

He didn't wish to have any witnesses to what he was about to do to himself.

Benjamin had always enjoyed drinking, as part of his socializing, his nights out, his character that he played.

But he typically kept a fairly good control on his faculties. He had, at least, always managed to get himself home.

He was already home, however, and had nothing else to concern himself with.

Benjamin removed the lid of the bottle of whiskey, poured himself a tall glass, and drained it before pouring another.

* * *

ALICE FINALLY WOKE to an incessant knocking. She squeezed her eyes tight and placed her hands over her ears, trying to make it go away. For she was sure it was all in her own head, a mocking that would not allow her to sleep, but was incessantly nattering at her to get up, get over herself — and Benjamin — and see justice served.

But when it continued, only rising in volume, she finally realized that it was coming from the front door. Where was everyone? she grumbled to herself as she rose, rubbing her eyes, which refused to open.

They had a butler, a housekeeper, footmen and maids.

But alas, none seemed to be free to answer the front door.

She did so herself, squinting at the sun beaming through the door and stabbing into her eyes. She hadn't been able to sleep until the early hours and it must now be midday.

"Yes?" she asked the messenger who stood at the doorway, a box wrapped in brown paper in his hands.

"I've a package for Miss Alice Cunningham."

"That's me," she said, her curiosity overcoming her animosity at being disturbed from her melancholy. She took the package and rushed it into her writing room, free from the prying eyes of her family members, who were wont to appear the moment she had something she would prefer to keep to herself.

She tore open the paper, eyes widening when she pulled out a sheaf of papers. What in the...

"He's A Duke."

"My book," she whispered, flipping through the pages to find that every word she had written was inside of it, her first story, the one she had thought wasn't any good, but that she had revised after meeting Benjamin. It was published. By a publisher. Not a series, but a book, one that was all hers, all fiction, from her own thoughts. Her heart began a strange pattering in her chest at the idea of all of those people, people she didn't know, reading words and thoughts that had come from deep within her.

But with it came a thrill — it was everything she had ever wanted but had never thought possible.

Behind the book was hidden a sealed envelope. She opened it to find a letter, and when she pulled it out, a bank note fluttered to the floor.

Dear Miss Cunningham,

We were pleased to have received your submission of 'He's A Duke.' We hope you enjoy this advance copy as well as the advance funds for it. You will find that it is to be published by the end of the month. Please accept our sincerest congratulations. Should you have any additional manuscripts, we would be pleased to consider them for publication as well.

Harlow & Sons Publishing

The letter fluttered out of her fingers and to the floor as she took it in. Her books — published? By a publisher? How had it even happened? No one knew about the book, except the publishers who had rejected it — this was not one of them — and... Benjamin. Benjamin had the manuscript. Benjamin knew how much it would mean to her to have it printed.

Benjamin had done this. For her.

She didn't know whether to laugh or cry, as anger and elation warred within her.

Would a man do this if he was simply trying to have some fun with her for a time? Maybe. But it wasn't necessary. It was more than she would ever have expected, true, and meant that he actually listened and that he actually cared.

She sighed as she pressed her fingers against the backs of her eyelids. She had to go talk to him. She had to make him understand the truth.

The thought caused her stomach to twist as it seemed her heart had dropped right into it, but she had always followed her intuition, even when everything else was telling her that she was wrong.

She decided she had better go upstairs, get dressed, and check the mirror to see just how awful she looked.

She had a visit to prepare for.

* * *

UNFORTUNATELY, all came to naught.

Alice had spent the entire walk working herself up into a tither. Her palms were sweating, her heart was racing, her soul was searching.

And then Benjamin wasn't home.

She didn't want to think of where he might be, and she thought perhaps she could speak to Freddie, Benjamin's sister-in-law. She would pretend she simply wanted to visit, since she was here, but perhaps she could casually ask about Benjamin and determine if he had been anywhere near as distraught as she. Or distraught at all.

But Freddie was indisposed. Instead, another figure came down the hall and toward the door.

"Oh," she said with surprise, "Lord Dorrington. My apologies for disturbing you."

He was a rather intimidating figure, so silent yet observant. She always wondered what he was thinking.

"It's no bother," he said, a hint of what she thought just might be a smile on his lips. "Come in, will you?"

Seeing no other option yet wondering just what Miles Luxington might have to say to her, she followed him through the house and into the drawing room.

"I'm afraid I'm not much of a hostess," he said, surprising her with his jest as he waved for her to take a seat. She had thought Benjamin had stolen all of the family's wit. "I can, however, call for tea if you'd like."

"No, that's not necessary, but thank you," she said with a wave of her hand before she captured it with the other and held them both in her lap, wondering what she was supposed to talk to the marquess about. She could ask him about his love story — it was what she loved to talk most about — but she was well aware that that would not exactly be the thing to do, especially with the two of them here alone, but for her maid in the corner.

"Are you all right, Miss Cunningham?" he asked, tilting his head in concern, and Alice was horrified when her lip started to tremble and her eyes began to burn. She blinked rapidly as she bit down on her bottom lip to regain control.

"I'm fine," she said, before drawing a breath, somehow convinced to tell all of her truth when she saw his green gaze boring into her.

"Actually… I'm not fine," she amended, shaking her head fiercely. "Not at all."

Before she could stop the words, they came pouring out of her, as she told this man who she barely knew — Benjamin's brother of all people — all that had happened. The ruse so that Benjamin could protect her, the investigation into Chesterpeak, the evidence that continued to prove that Benjamin had been using her to further Chesterpeak's schemes, and finally his denial of her love.

She knew he had difficulties hearing, but he watched her closely and she was impressed when he seemed to understand all of her ramblings.

"I don't know what to do," she said, her voice breaking.

"I've learned recently," he began slowly, "that sometimes what we *think* to be true is not necessarily what we *know* to be true. Sometimes we must give those we love the benefit of the doubt."

He clasped his hands together in front of him before continuing.

"I know that Benjamin is not always the most steady, nor the most sure. But he is a man who loves more than any other person I've ever met. My father was not a good man. You know that. Benjamin always knew that. And yet, he still looked for the best in him because he *wanted* to believe the best. He didn't want to believe that his father could be as awful as he actually was. From what you say, he thought Chesterpeak was just a man to provide a bit of fun. He didn't want to believe someone could lower themselves to such schemes."

He sighed as Alice watched him with wide eyes. It was more than she had ever heard him speak before, so she knew how much importance to attach to each word from him.

"My brother may not always be the best judge of character," Lord Dorrington said, softly and stoically, "but one thing I know is that he loves you, Miss Cunningham, even if he doesn't know it himself yet. I can't say that it is particularly common for him to not only read a book but that he arranged for one to be published, well... I believe that says a lot. He knew what to say to push you away, and he used that against you. It likely hurt him more than it did you."

Alice was silent for a moment, registering all that this man said, the man who likely knew Benjamin better than anyone else in the world.

When she finally met his eyes again, she found that a lump had formed in her throat, one that was quite difficult to swallow.

"What do I say to make him see the truth – to believe in himself — and in me?" she asked, blinking back the tears that were attempting to resurface.

"I think," Lord Dorrington said slowly, "that if you truly love someone, anything is possible."

Alice nodded, standing, desperate to find Benjamin and tell him exactly that, to determine just whether there could still be a future for them.

"Thank you, Lord Dorrington," she said, and when he nodded at her, she realized that this was no ordinary conversation for him; that he had done more for her than he likely would for most.

Before she even realized what she was doing — for if she had, she would have known he would be well and properly embarrassed — she stepped in, gave him a quick hug of thanks, and then ran for the door before stopping to see his response.

She would forever be grateful to the man.

CHAPTER 25

"My lord?"

"Leave me be, Hawkins."

"My lord, you have a visitor."

"Tell her I am not home."

"It is not Miss Cunningham again, my lord."

Benjamin grunted. It had been another day of lying in bed.

He knew he should get moving on his plan. It was what he had promised, what he needed to do so that Alice wouldn't take it on herself. He had gotten himself into this mess. Now he had to do what he could to get himself out of it.

But not quite yet. He needed another day to just be miserable — if only his valet would leave him alone.

"Whoever it is," Benjamin ground out, "I am not in."

"Get up."

Benjamin jolted up in bed, bringing a hand to his head and as he did so a clanging began within it of its own accord.

"Miles," he exclaimed — or, meant to exclaim. The words

came out as more of a groan. "What in the hell are you doing here?"

"The better question is what in the hell *you* think you are doing," Miles said, arms crossed over his chest as he stared at Benjamin, his nose wrinkled in disgust. "Lying here, useless, after leaving Miss Cunningham in the throes of despair."

That got Benjamin's attention really quickly.

"What do you mean, the throes of despair?" he asked, pushing himself up and swinging his legs over the edge of the bed.

"She's been looking everywhere for you. Wanted to thank you for publishing her book."

"Oh, that," Benjamin said, running his hand through his hair, just as disgusted with himself as Miles was. "The process didn't take nearly as long as I thought it would."

"It was quite the gesture you made," Miles said, looking down his nose at Benjamin, who finally rose from the bed so that he was, at the very least, on even footing with his brother height-wise.

Benjamin grunted in response to his brother's words. "It was a good book and she deserved to see it in print. She just needed a little help in finding the right person to publish it."

"It's not like you to go out of your way to do such a thing," Miles commented.

"No," Benjamin said, "it's not."

"What are you going to do now?" Miles asked, running his eyes up and down Benjamin's naked torso and breeches from two days prior.

"I suppose now that Alice and Madeline are out of London, I'm going to follow through with the plan. Talk to the Bow Street Runners, and then set up Chesterpeak, telling him that Madeline has died so that they can follow where the money goes."

"A good plan," Miles said with a nod.

"It was mostly Alice's."

"You know she's still in London."

"What?" Benjamin's head snapped up at that. "She was supposed to go with Madeline to the country."

"She didn't," Miles said, shaking his head. "Madeline's father accompanied her, as well as Alice's mother. Alice was supposed to go, but apparently feigned a last-minute illness to remain behind. She said she needs to see things through. At least, that is what Celeste told Freddie."

"Damn it," Benjamin said, shaking his head.

"What are you going to do about her?"

"What do you mean, *do* about her? I'm going to tell her to get her ass to the country."

Miles raised one eyebrow.

"I'm sure that will be met with great acceptance."

"It doesn't matter anymore," Benjamin said. "It's just a matter of keeping her from Chesterpeak and Donning."

"Or maybe, you're trying to keep her away from you," Miles said, and Benjamin sighed.

"Let's go into the drawing room and have a drink."

"Make it a coffee."

Benjamin nodded, calling to Hawkins to find a maid.

Miles took a seat on the curved-back mustard-yellow sofa, his gaze running over Benjamin, who had thrown a clean shirt over his head.

"You've looked better," he said.

Benjamin couldn't help but laugh. "You've always been nothing but honest, brother."

"Which is why you must listen to me," Miles said, leaning forward with his elbows on his knees. "Why are you shielding your heart?"

"My heart?"

"From Alice," Miles said, taking a breath as though his patience was being tried — which, it likely was. "The two of you seem just as in love as Freddie and I, so why are you forcing her away?"

"It's for the best," he said, ignoring the odd flip-flopping of his heart at the thought that Alice might still love him.

"Is it, though?"

"It is," Benjamin said with a nod. "I'm not the man for her."

"No?" Miles answered. "Why? Because you will not watch over her, you will not love her, you do not want to spend the rest of your life with her?"

Benjamin couldn't look at his brother, and yet he had no choice, for if he looked away, Miles wouldn't be able to read his lips. "I would do all of those things," he mumbled.

"I'm sorry, what was that?" Miles asked, and Benjamin looked up at him with some contempt, as he had a feeling his brother might actually have heard him but just wanted him to repeat himself.

"I *said* that I would do all of those things," he said more clearly.

"So what's the problem?"

"The problem is that trouble follows me around. It always has. Unlike you, I am our father's son. His legacy seems to have become mine."

"Why?" Miles challenged him. "Because you made one wrong decision and trusted the wrong man?"

"I obviously have no intuition."

"You see the best in everyone."

"You sound like Alice."

"Well, she is right," Miles returned. "It's not the worst trait. But you don't have to allow our father's shadow to shade your path for the rest of your life. Just choose to walk in the other direction. You're already halfway there. You've been the man Alice deserves since you met her."

"But Chesterpeak—"

"Must be stopped. Yes, that is true," Miles said with a nod.

"Wait—how do you know all about him?" Benjamin asked, furrowing his brow.

"Alice told me," Miles said simply. "She came looking for you, and she and I had a discussion."

"Well," Benjamin said, falling back into the couch. "You two really did have quite the intimate conversation."

"She was very forthcoming," Miles said with a smile, "and she is perfect for you."

"Yes," Benjamin said, running his hands through his hair, "she really is."

He closed his eyes, rubbing his fingers against them. Was Miles right? Could he truly be the man Alice deserved? Could he decide himself to be rid of the trouble that followed him around? He would never have thought it to be true, and yet...

"You and Freddie..." he began, unsure of how to ask. Miles didn't help him by finishing the thought, though. He simply waited for him to sort out the question himself. "After everything that happened, how were you able to move forward?"

"By choosing love," Miles said, his green eyes wide and clear and imploring. "It's up to you, Benjamin."

"So it is," Benjamin said, inhaling a deep breath, his resolve hardening and, for the first time, the slightest flicker of hope begin to burn in his chest. "I best go. I have much to do."

Miles simply grinned.

* * *

BENJAMIN WOULD HAVE LIKED to have immediately gone to Alice and told her how wrong he had been, and implored her to reconsider and make a life with him. But first, he had to take care of Chesterpeak.

He paid a visit to Number 4 Bow Street. The detectives listened to his story somewhat incredulously, but agreed that, at the very least, they would look into it and follow where the money went.

One of them, who went by the name of Drake, agreed to accompany him on his visit to Chesterpeak's. Benjamin attempted to refuse, but Drake insisted.

"If you want us to believe you, despite the mounting evidence against you," Drake said, "then I suggest you allow us to come with you. We'll tell them that I am interested in investing, that I like the idea, and want in."

"I'm not sure..." Benjamin hesitated. "They are more than aware that I am against this entire scheme and might not take kindly to the fact that I have told anyone about it."

"Then I came upon the information by chance," Drake said, as Benjamin appreciated how quickly the man's mind worked. "I am your steward and stumbled across your ledgers when I was doing the books. I forced you to allow me to come."

"Works for me," Benjamin said pausing a beat. "There's something else."

Drake raised his eyebrows.

"I need someone to watch over Miss Alice Cunningham."

Drake nodded, spoke with a few of the other detectives, and then the two of them rose to begin their plan.

They were just exiting the building when a familiar figure rounded the corner.

"Alice?" Benjamin exclaimed, incredulous. He stopped and stared, taking her in. She was as beautiful as she had always been, and yet, now that he had resolved to make her his for the rest of their lives, she was all the more appealing.

Except... she seemed a bit paler than usual, and there

were dark circles under her eyes. Her dress was cream with blue piping, rather than her typical rich, bright shades.

"Benjamin," she said, his name on her lips a caress.

He longed to go to her, take her in his arms, and tell her that everything would be all right — that they would be together once they saw all of this through.

But before he could step forward, the dratted Drake did.

"Miss Cunningham, I presume?"

"Yes," she said, startled, looking at Benjamin for an explanation. "What are you doing here?"

"The same thing as you, likely," he said. "This is Drake. He works with the Bow Street Runners—"

"We prefer detectives," Drake interjected, to which Benjamin nodded.

"—and I've told him everything. He has agreed to help. But you, Alice, should be far away from here, with Madeline."

"I could not leave knowing that you were here," she said, lifting a hand helplessly. "I wanted to see this through, and it seems we have the same idea."

"So it seems."

Their gazes were still locked, and Benjamin nearly forgot about Drake once more.

"Shall we?" Drake finally said, stepping between them and waving his hand forward.

"I have a carriage," Alice said, and they all forged on ahead together.

CHAPTER 26

*a*lice was not at all pleased about remaining behind while the men went into the house.

But she was aware that it wouldn't make sense for her to go in with Benjamin and that it would be far more believable if he went alone, or with a man like Drake.

So she sat. And she waited.

She tapped her foot. She pulled back the curtain and looked out the window. She tried to dream up stories for her books, but she wasn't able to focus for more than a few seconds and ideas were as fleeting as a rake after a tryst.

Mostly, she thought about Benjamin.

Had she been fancifully imagining that he had looked at her with new intention, or was it merely that his longing for her remained but he was still refusing to do anything about it? For after speaking with Miles and her own careful consideration, she was sure that his parting words to her had been contrived to push her away.

They had worked — for a time.

Now, she knew that what she had to do was convince him

that he was worthy and deserving of his own happily-ever-after.

But how?

She was so deep within her own musings that she jolted upright in her seat when the carriage door swung open. Outside was Benjamin, his features tangled in a scowl, and Lord Donning, who also didn't seem to be particularly pleased.

"Hello," she said, freezing a polite smile on her face, at least until she determined just what had been revealed and what they were after. "How are you today, gentlemen?"

"Out," Donning said, ignoring her words and motioning behind him with his thumb. Despite her annoyance at his high-handedness, Alice was happy to comply, for she thought she might no longer be able to breathe if she remained in the stifling carriage for one more minute.

"Inside," he said now, one hand propelling her toward the house. Benjamin, however, mercifully stepped between them and led her in himself. The contact of *his* warm hand on her back had her quivering, but for altogether different reasons.

They said nothing, giving her no hint of why they had come for her or what they were after. It was only when they were seated in front of Chesterpeak's desk, with Chesterpeak on the other side, that she received any inclination. Drake remained standing on the outer edge of the room, apparently all but forgotten.

Chesterpeak didn't even greet her, but instead got right to his point.

"Luxington here tells us that Lady Donning is dead," he said, a smoothness to his tone that Donning's had been lacking. "Is this true?"

Alice heaved a sigh as she did her very best to look as distraught as she would have felt had it been the truth.

"Unfortunately, Mr. Chesterpeak, it is quite true," she

said, attempting to summon a tear. "Lady Donning passed just last evening."

"Where is her body?" Lord Donning demanded.

"It has been taken away already," Alice said, hanging her head. "Her father came for her."

"Why?"

"Because we were not certain what had caused her death and did not want to infect anyone else."

Benjamin lifted an eyebrow, likely a tad bit concerned at how quickly the lies were slipping off her tongue, but she had a defense — she was a storyteller, and these were the kinds of things she thought of.

"I see," Chesterpeak said, leaning back in his chair, a slow smile crossing his face.

"Would you like to tell us, Miss Cunningham, just why you felt the need to take my wife from my home and into yours?" Lord Donning demanded, and Alice waited a beat, unsure exactly how to answer that, determined not to contradict herself.

"Well…" she began, "I hadn't seen Lady Donning in some time. Nor had her father. We had… concerns."

"And now she's dead."

"Most unfortunately, yes," Alice said, dropping her head again so that they couldn't see her expression. Thank goodness they had rescued Madeline. The relief was flooding through her in such great waves that she knew it would be written upon her face.

"Very well," Chesterpeak said. "That's enough of that. I look forward to attending your nuptials, Miss Cunningham."

"My…" her head snapped up, and she looked toward Benjamin, who gave her a slight nod.

"Thank you," she said.

"That will be all," Chesterpeak said now, nodding to the door. "Perhaps Drake here can escort you home."

Alice's gaze swung toward Benjamin with question. He shook his head.

"Lord Benjamin will be remaining here with us for a time," Chesterpeak said, a sickly grin crossing his face. "He will be seeing you at your wedding very soon."

"Right," Alice managed, although her voice was strangled.

Drake stepped up and held his arm out to her. In an abstracted, faraway manner, she noticed how striking he was. But it didn't much matter. All that mattered was Benjamin.

But soon they were out the door and back in the carriage, Drake escorting her home.

"What happened?" Alice burst out once they were within and starting to move. "Why did you let Benjamin stay?"

"There wasn't much else I could do without arousing their suspicions," Drake said. "Now that they believe your friend is dead, we will follow the money and determine where it ends up. In the meantime, we are looking into the so-called Lord Donning to see if he is truly who he says he is."

"And Benjamin?" she prompted.

"Chesterpeak doesn't trust him," he said, shaking his head. "The man may be evil, but he is smart. He sees through him. He says he will keep him there until a special license can be secured and the two of you married."

"My brother will never agree to it!" Alice burst out. Besides that, she was not going to marry a man unless he actually wanted to be with her — forever. She would rather remain a ruined spinster than become a discarded married woman, and she had no idea just yet of what Benjamin's true intentions were.

"Chesterpeak doesn't want Benjamin telling anyone what he knows — including your brother," Drake said wryly. "You're of age. You don't need your brother's permission."

"But I would need him to agree to the dowry settlements," she said, desperately trying to find a way out.

"Benjamin told them they had been completed."

"What?" she looked up, shocked. "No, not at all. Benjamin has never even spoken to my brother about it. He must have just said it as he thought it was what Chesterpeak wanted to hear. Just what am I supposed to do now?" Alice asked helplessly.

"Go home," Drake said. "I will have a man watching over your house. We'll speak with your brother, inform him of all that has happened, and install our man as a footman. We will follow where the money goes and you will wait to be summoned."

"And then what?"

"Then we come with you, hopefully have enough evidence against Chesterpeak, and then take him away. You and Luxington can go back to your lives."

He didn't say it, but Alice knew the subtext. They could then choose whether or not they wanted to be together.

How long was she supposed to wait to find out her future?

* * *

As it turned out, it wasn't long.

By the next day, she had received a message that she was to come to a chapel just outside of London. A special license had been procured and she was apparently to be married that day.

She informed the detective, and soon enough, Drake was at her house.

She also finally told Oliver all that had occurred, seeing no other option. He was not at all pleased, but she knew she could never keep such secrets from him.

"Have you been able to determine anything?" she asked when Drake arrived, but he was already shaking his head.

"There hasn't been enough time."

"So what do we do?" Alice asked.

Oliver was standing in the corner of the room, arms crossed over his chest as he took them both in.

"You stay here, that's what," he said crossly, much surlier today than usual. "You never should have been involved in this in the first place."

"It's too late now," Alice implored. "We cannot leave Benjamin there."

"Luxington is a grown man who got himself into this mess," Oliver said. "Now he can get himself out of it."

"He did all he could by informing us," Drake said. "But they have worked faster than we could have. They must have some connections of a sort to secure a license so quickly."

"Alice will *not* be marrying Luxington under these circumstances," Oliver ground out.

"But did you put together documentation for Luxington to sign?"

"The dowry settlement?" If it was possible for Oliver's countenance to darken even more, than it did right now. "Yes. I don't understand, however — what does that have to do with Chesterpeak?"

"He thinks he has an arrangement with Luxington. Once Luxington has the funds secured, then a portion will go to Chesterpeak as per some agreement they have made."

"Why would Luxington agree to such a thing?"

"Because if he didn't, then Chesterpeak would ensure that all knew of his involvement, and he would continue to come after him time and again until he relented. He could even..." his gaze shifted over to Alice, "come after those he loves."

"So what do we do?" Alice asked again, looking back and forth between the men.

"I would suggest that you do come with us," Drake said, even as Oliver was shaking his head emphatically.

"Absolutely not."

Drake held up a hand.

"We will have men outside and will ensure that no harm will come to Miss Cunningham," he said. "If we can convince Chesterpeak to say something to incriminate himself, then perhaps we can move forward."

"And if not?"

Drake sighed.

"Then we will have to reveal ourselves and Chesterpeak will likely get away with all of his crimes."

They were all silent for a moment, until Alice stood.

"I have to do this, Oliver," she said determinately. "I have to do it for Madeline, and all the other woman that have and will be a victim to this man."

"Very well," Oliver said with resignation, "but I'm coming too."

"You can't!"

"I can," he said. "It's your wedding. That should be good enough reason for me to attend, should it not?"

"Very well," Drake said with a shrug. "On we go."

* * *

THIS HAD NOT GONE to plan whatsoever.

Benjamin could only hope that Drake and his men could move fast enough to incriminate Chesterpeak and Donning.

Instead, he was trapped here in Chesterpeak's home — if it could be called that instead of the house of sins that Benjamin was trying to distance himself from as fast as he was able.

He had spent most of it inside the bedchamber — or prison — he had been provided. Now he was being summoned to the front foyer, and he prayed to God that this meant he could return home.

He was to be disappointed.

"Our carriage awaits," Chesterpeak said, flourishing an arm to the front of the house. Sure enough, there was a carriage, not nearly as luxurious as anything Benjamin was used to, but one that would fit a few of them.

Donning, fortunately, was nowhere to be seen.

"We will pick up Donning and the vicar on the way."

Perfect.

"On the way to where?"

"Why, your wedding."

"My what?"

"Your wedding." Chesterpeak grinned. "And from there we will go to the solicitor's office to arrange the agreed-upon transfer of funds from both you and Donning to my account."

Which meant that Drake wouldn't have been able to collect any evidence just yet.

Benjamin knew this had been the plan, but had no idea it would be in motion so soon. He didn't see what he could do at the moment but go along with it and hope that, at some point, he would determine a way out.

"And if we don't?"

"Then you will never be able to rest, knowing that I am out there, a threat to you and your family."

He swallowed hard.

During the interminable carriage ride, he couldn't stop wondering about Alice. Would she come? Did he *want* her to come? How could he keep her safe, and what would her brother do if he heard about all this? He could only hope that Drake and his men could keep her from harm.

"Where are we?" he asked as the carriage finally slowed,

but there was nothing in sight but miles of field – and one tiny building.

"Not far from London," Chesterpeak said. "It's a bit of land that I purchased not long ago. Right now, it houses a chapel that I use for my own… purposes from time to time. One day I might build my estate out here."

His estate?

As they descended the carriage steps, it was not long before another carriage began rolling up the road that was barely worn in the grasses surrounding it.

Benjamin's heart began to beat fast at the thought of seeing Alice again, as well as what she might be thinking and expecting from today. What did she know? How was he going to explain it all to her?

The carriage rolled to a stop, and the first person Benjamin saw emerge was Drake. Good.

Secondly came Essex.

Benjamin cringed at his expression. This couldn't be good.

And finally, third came Alice. She looked around her before her gaze finally locked upon him, and he could only stare at her, longing to go to her, take her into his arms, and tell her that everything was going to be all right.

But he couldn't. Not now. Not yet.

"Our lovebirds!" Chesterpeak said, holding his arms out wide as he motioned Alice toward them. "Come, come."

Benjamin looked to the vicar, wondering what he thought of it all, but at the smug smile on his face, he realized that it likely wasn't the first of Chesterpeak's schemes he had been involved in.

They approached, and Essex seemed prepared to attack them all, but Benjamin gave him a slight shake of his head, to tell him that he would ensure everything would be fine.

Except that he had no idea how it would be so.

Alice's eyes were on him, glistening, and he wanted to believe that she was looking at him with love in her eyes, although he wasn't sure if it was possible after everything he had put her through.

"Ready for the wedding?" Chesterpeak asked, a gleaming smile on his face.

"May I have a moment with Miss Cunningham first?" Benjamin asked, not taking his eyes off her.

Chesterpeak seemed unsure for a moment, but then finally nodded his assent. Benjamin neared the trio.

"Alice," he said, nodding at her first before looking over to an uncertain Drake and a murderous Essex. He quickly repeated what Chesterpeak had told them on the way over. "I don't see any way out of this," he said with a sigh. "All we can do is leave."

Essex seemed relieved, and turned to go to the carriage, but then Alice's voice stopped him.

"Do you truly not want to marry me, then?" she asked.

"What?" Benjamin's head snapped over toward her.

"Is the thought of marrying me so terrible that you wouldn't do it, even to save all of those women victimized by Chesterpeak?"

"Alice," Benjamin said, his voice gutted as he said her name. Essex and Drake exchanged a glance and then through silent agreement took a step back to give them some space.

Benjamin moved toward her, risking placing his hands upon her arms, which were slightly trembling. He lifted a hand and grazed it over the side of her soft cheek.

"The truth is," he said gruffly. "I *do* want to marry you, if you'll have me. I want it more than anything. I want to marry you and spend the rest of my life devoted to you, doing all I can to ensure that you are the happiest woman in all of England."

"Benjamin," she said, her shimmering eyes finally dropping a tear. "You've changed your mind, then?"

"I was shown the error of my ways," he said, a smile coming to his face as he remembered the talk with his brother. "Someone — someone who knows me very well — finally convinced me that I do not have to be my father. And I won't. Especially if I have you. Alice, I love you more than I could ever express," he said, his words gruff, thick with emotion. "You are the most amazing woman I have ever met. You are intelligent, inquisitive, in love with love. I thought I could live without you, that I could let you go, that your life would be better without me in it... but I've come to realize that I need you, more than I've ever needed anything before. Is that selfish? Is that wrong? Possibly. But if it's what you want—"

Alice reached up and cupped his face in her hands.

"Oh, Benjamin," she whispered. "I love you too. You *are* a man worthy of love, of happiness, of a life full of the laughter that you bring to everyone else. Of course I will marry you."

He laughed then as he scooped her up and twirled her around in a circle.

"Are we ready then?" Chesterpeak called to them wryly.

"I think not!" Essex said, striding toward them. "You are not going to marry here as part of this ridiculous scheme."

"He's right," Benjamin said lowly. "We can't marry now. Not here. Not like this."

"I don't care where I marry you, Benjamin Luxington," Alice said, looking deeply into his eyes. "So we marry here, in front of Chesterpeak and his vicar and Donning. I don't really care. You and I are here and that is all that matters. And then we can save Madeline and all of those women."

"No," Benjamin shook his head, "not like this."

"Then we marry again in a proper church, in front of all of our family and friends and pretend it is the first time," she said with a shrug. "Why fight this when it can do such good and it doesn't make any difference?"

He supposed she had a point, but her brother was not so quick to agree.

Essex strode over, nearly pushing them apart as he came to stand between them.

"This is not happening," he said.

"It is, Oliver," Alice responded gently, looking up at him and then craned her neck around him to take in Benjamin. "All will be fine, not to worry."

"How do you know?" Essex insisted, looking toward Benjamin and then back to his sister. "How do you know that he isn't doing this to further Chesterpeak's scheme, that he actually means what he says? You could marry him, Alice, and then be out of your dowry, out of a marriage, and ruined for the rest of your life."

She stepped to the side then, and looked not at her brother, but right at Benjamin.

"Because," she said simply, her face glowing with its slow, steady, smile, "I trust him."

The words meant more than any other ever had, or ever would again.

CHAPTER 27

*A*nd so Alice married Benjamin in a small, dusty chapel in the middle of a field outside of London, surrounded by villains, a Bow Street Runner, and her scowling brother.

She had never been happier.

As she repeated the words that made them husband and wife, she couldn't stop smiling, thinking of the life to come, of all that Benjamin had promised her, of the fact that he was finally accepting that he was worthy of her love, and that of all others.

It was tempered only by the fact that following the wedding they had to pile into a carriage with Chesterpeak, for he didn't trust them not to abscond without him.

"Do as he says. Go to the solicitor's office," Alice heard Drake whisper in Benjamin's ear while shaking Benjamin's hand in congratulations. "We will ensure everything is in place."

Benjamin nodded while Oliver brooded.

He had reluctantly passed over the dowry settlement

papers before the wedding, which Benjamin had just as reluctantly signed.

Alice, who trusted both of them and didn't overly care what was in the dowry, had been the only one unaffected by the legal aspect. She ran over and hugged Oliver before they departed, ensuring him that all would be well. He still didn't look so sure, but she hoped she managed to convince him.

"Don't tell Mother," she hissed, "at least, not yet."

He nodded. "I will be right behind you," he said. "I still don't trust Luxington."

"You should," she said, and he gave her new husband — *husband!* — one final warning stare before climbing into the carriage.

Even though Chesterpeak was there with them, Alice was thrilled when Benjamin's strong, warm hand wrapped around hers, squeezing and holding on tight. She knew he would always look after her, no matter what came next.

The solicitor's office was on Bond Street, and Alice hoped it was the same office that Benjamin had told Drake about, and that everything was now in motion.

Benjamin helped her out of the carriage and into the office, where she was told to wait outside, but this time, she insisted that she accompany them.

She sat nervously in her chair, awaiting the man who greeted them. He was much younger than she would have assumed him to be, but was helpful nonetheless.

Donning took the lead regarding Madeline, his acting in sorrow at her death nearly convincing Alice — nearly. For he considerably brightened when the solicitor told him that Madeline's inheritance was now, finally, his.

They continued on to the transfer of Alice's dowry. It had all been arranged — including the agreement of what Chesterpeak had determined. All that remained was a visit to the bank. Oliver sat in stormy silence, although Alice assumed that he had been informed by Drake of all that was occurring.

Until Drake emerged from around the corner.

"We will not be going to the bank."

"Excuse me?" said Chesterpeak, his words not angry but rather wry, as though he knew something the rest of them didn't.

"I said that will not be happening. We now have enough evidence against you, Chesterpeak. Your schemes are finished."

He opened the door and two more Bow Street detectives entered the room. "As for you, Lord Donning — or should I say, Mr. Maxfeld — you will also be coming with us."

"Maxfeld?" Alice exclaimed, standing.

Drake nodded.

"We have determined that far from being the true heir to the Donning name, Kurt Maxfeld is nothing more than an imposter. An imposter who has been married multiple times, and has a wife waiting for him in a village near Oxford."

"And Madeline is not married," Alice breathed, feeling sorry for her friend at the confirmation, who, through no fault of her own, would now be ruined in the eyes of every person of the *ton*.

"No," Drake said, before fixing his gaze upon her, "although you are."

"We know," Alice said, smiling up at her husband, "and we are glad of it."

Benjamin nodded in agreement.

"While we will not transfer any money to Chesterpeak, obviously," Drake said, nodding toward him, "Luxington here will receive your entire dowry."

"Which Alice will have equal access to," Benjamin said resolutely, and Alice loved him all the more for it.

"Just wait a minute here," Chesterpeak said, standing

angrily. "We just signed all of the documentation to transfer funds. It is too late now!"

"You signed nothing," Drake said with a laugh. "Look closer at the documents. You'll find there are sections that render them completely null and void."

"This is ridiculous!" Chesterpeak raged. "I will *not* go willingly."

"Most don't," Drake said wryly, "but come you will. Let's go."

As they led them out the door, he turned around and looked at the two of them.

"Thank you for your assistance. I wish you my very best."

Left alone, Alice, Benjamin, and Oliver trickled out of the solicitor's office until they were on the street awaiting the carriage's return.

"Well," Oliver said, crossing his arms over his chest as he looked at the pair of them. "I hope you are happy."

"Oh, we are," Alice said, turning toward Benjamin, who wrapped his arms around her waist with a wide grin on his face, "very much so."

He began pulling her in toward him, until Oliver broke them apart.

"Enough of that. You are in the middle of the street."

"That's fitting," Alice said with a laugh, "since this is where it all began!"

"Well in the eyes of everyone else, you are not yet married," Oliver said. "We can never tell Mother that she missed the actual wedding."

"No," agreed Alice, "we most certainly cannot."

"The same with my mother," added Benjamin, "or Freddie and Miles."

"Or Celeste," Oliver said.

"Or Madeline," Alice realized.

"Our little secret, then," Benjamin said with a grin at the two of them, "along with Drake."

"Does this mean that we will not be… living as husband and wife for awhile?" Alice asked, biting her lip.

Oliver glowered once more. "Absolutely not."

Of course, they didn't let that stop them.

It may have taken them some time, but on the night of their engagement party, Alice was standing near the tray of lemonade, awaiting her drink, when suddenly she was nearly backed into the wall as a hand came and bracketed her against it.

"And just what is a such a beautiful woman like yourself doing here alone?"

His voice alone sent thrills up and down her spine. She had missed him.

She had seen him, of course — the odd walk or ride through the park, visits with their mothers present in the drawing room, but it wasn't the same. She craved his close-ness, his caresses.

Anytime he came close, even a whisper of fabric brushing against her skin sent tremors cascading through her body.

"I am waiting for a gentleman who might be interested in me," she sat, batting her eyelashes sarcastically seductively.

"Far be it from me to allow you to feel anything but want-ed," he said, leaning in toward her. "What do you say that we find a quiet corner somewhere in this house?"

Since it was his brother's house, she had a good idea that he knew exactly where such a quiet corner could be found.

He held out an elbow and escorted her from the large drawing room that had opened up to become a ballroom for the evening.

"I finished reading your new story," he whispered low in her ear, his voice full of suggestion. Alice turned quickly at his words.

"You did?" she asked, her heart beat increasing. "What did you think?"

"I think it was quite... inspired," he said with a wink, and the heat rose into her cheeks, which she was sure had turned very pink at the words.

She had finally finished her latest story. It was fiction, although it was based slightly on truth — this time that of her own story.

Only, she had added some embellishments to one copy that was for Benjamin's eyes alone.

"I do hope you are not planning on publishing the *entire* story," he murmured, and she laughed, shaking her head.

"I have another edit planned for my publisher. The publisher who is very interested, thanks to my first story. Thanks to you."

"I'm only glad that all of England will soon know just how talented you are," he said, his voice lowering as he led her up the stairs and then into what appeared to be an empty guest bedroom. When he shut the door behind them, the click of the latch sent a thrill jolting up through her. "Now, *wife*, what do you say we consummate this marriage?"

"I would say that it has been far too long, although we did somewhat get ahead of ourselves."

"That we did," he said, hanging his head for a moment. "Do you... do you regret it? I still haven't quite forgiven myself. I—"

She placed a finger over his lips.

"Not for a moment."

She replaced her finger with her lips, capturing his mouth with such possession that she felt him straighten completely at her touch.

She smiled before she slid her tongue along the seam of his mouth, to which he quickly parted his lips. She was trying to show him how much she truly wanted him — now and forever — and his own passion not only matched, but nearly overcame hers as he wrapped his hands around her back, gripping her against him with such possessiveness she nearly went limp in his arms.

Alice clutched the lapels of his jacket, both holding herself up and drawing him in close as sensations began to climb within her, the silky smoothness of his lips and tongue even better than writing with a perfect new quill pen.

He tasted like dark magic, and Alice could have continued to kiss him all night.

But they didn't have time for that — not yet. They may be married, but no one else was aware of the fact. If they were found out, her brother obviously wouldn't have to force them to be married — it was too late for that — but it would cause quite the talk if they both disappeared all night.

They both attacked, parried, and retreated, until finally Alice could hardly breathe anymore, so overcome was she by the need for Benjamin. As his fingers slid into her hair, dispersing a few pins, which dropped to the floor with a ping, he tilted her head, likely for a better angle. He kissed her with as much desperate need as she kissed him, and soon enough she found that her skirts were bunched up around her waist, held there by Benjamin, who had backed her up across the room to the bed.

"How did that happen?" she murmured, but Benjamin only laughed.

His laugh, however, was not humorous, but a low, dark chuckle, one that shot through her and caused a strange tingle to begin to hum at the juncture of her legs.

He picked her up as he shucked his own breeches, lowering them just enough. He held her up against the end of the bed, as he stroked her with his thumb, circling her where she needed it.

"Yes," she hissed. "Now, Benjamin. Please."

Slipping a finger into her, he was apparently satisfied, for he soon removed it and then was slowly sliding into her, inch by glorious inch. Alice threw back her head as she allowed the pleasure to radiate from where they were now joined throughout her entire body, as she welcomed him with all of her very being.

He began to move, slowly at first, but Alice ground herself against him as she did all she could to work to her own fulfillment.

"Alice." Benjamin groaned, "you are the devil, woman."

"I am?" she managed, letting out a short, rough laugh.

When his thumb found her again, however, she was no longer laughing but jolting over the precipice, exploding around him. He pumped just a few more times before he was moaning himself and then pouring everything he had into her.

He bent and placed a kiss on her forehead, before moving on to cover her cheeks, nose, and chin before settling a quick peck on her lips.

"You. Are. Everything." He pressed a hard kiss on her mouth. "Perfection."

She laughed a bit self-consciously.

"I don't know about that."

"Trust me," he said, as he finally broke away from her and they began setting themselves to rights.

"Consider this marriage consummated," he said with a wide grin and she swatted him.

"Already done."

"But now," he said, before drawing her close once more, "it is complete."

EPILOGUE

*T*heir wedding — their second wedding — was held at St. George Cathedral in Hanover Square, this time before a wide array of family and friends. Alice was as happy as she had been the first time she married Benjamin, although she appreciated not having Chesterpeak present — and the vicar was a good deal friendlier than the last.

But this time there was celebration. This time all knew that she and Benjamin were husband and wife, and no one would ever tear them apart.

"Ah, Lord and Lady Benjamin." Drake gave the two of them a short bow as they greeted all of the guests who were filing out of the church. While Drake was not a particularly close acquaintance and therefore was receiving a good deal of sideways glances from other attendees besides Oliver, he was the sole person of note who had been in attendance at their first wedding and they felt not only obliged to invite him, but privileged to have his presence there as well. "Congratulations."

His eyes sparkled with knowing.

"Thank you very much, Drake," Alice said, with a warm, true smile. "For everything."

"Yes," Benjamin said with a nod. "If it wasn't for you, I don't know where we would be right now."

"I'm glad everything was put to rights," Drake said. "That is what I strive for, for everything to be as it should be. Both Chesterpeak and Maxfeld are in Newgate with their crimes, and we have restored what we could to the young women who remain behind."

They had allowed the servants who had aided him to go free, so long as they confessed all that Chesterpeak had done. Even Miss Smith — who had been willing to help Adams, until she discovered he was married — had, in the end, imparted all that the detectives had needed.

"You did your job well," Alice said, smiling as Drake moved on and Madeline approached. She leaned in and embraced Alice.

"You are stunning," Madeline said, leaning back and looking Alice up and down. "I've never seen a more beautiful bride."

"Thank you," Alice said softly, looking over her friend. She still wasn't quite herself, but she was healthier at the very least. "How are you? You know you didn't have to come."

She hadn't wanted Madeline to be reminded of her own wedding — or non-wedding, as it were.

"Don't be silly," Madeline said. "I wouldn't have missed this for anything."

"Well, I do appreciate it," Alice said. "Oh, and here she comes. This is Rose, a new friend of mine."

Madeline and Rose greeted one another, soon enough chattering on as though they had been friends their entire lives, just as Alice had expected that they would.

It seemed a never-ending line of guests emerged from the

church, until finally they were able to leave for their wedding breakfast.

"And then on to our new home," Benjamin said with a grin, "well, so to speak."

They were living in his townhouse, but had completely changed the décor, so now it was their home with no remembrance of his father. Benjamin's mother had been more than happy to assist.

"I cannot wait," Alice said, snuggling up into him. She knew it was not at all proper, not with all of the people about, but she was having a difficult time holding herself away from him.

"That's enough of that until the wedding night," came a dry voice behind them, and they turned to see Freddie and Miles approaching. Freddie wore her typical wide grin, as she embraced Alice and welcomed her to the family. Alice paused a moment before stepping in and hugging Miles once more, and he stiffly patted her back.

"You look beautiful," Miles said, his words equally as rigid, but the smile on his face was warm and pleased.

"Thank you," she said, exchanging a look with Benjamin, "and thank you for setting us both on the right path forward."

"Miles, the matchmaker?" Freddie said, looking back and forth between her husband and the two of them. "Who would have thought it?"

They laughed before they continued on and greeted Oliver and Celeste quickly before Celeste hurried home to her new baby girl. Soon enough Alice and Benjamin were ensconced in the carriage, finally, blessedly, alone.

"Did you see my mother and Madeline's father?" Alice asked him, and Benjamin shook his head.

"I did not."

"They looked quite close," she said. "I wonder if I shall

have a stepfather. Interesting thought. I had assumed my mother would never marry again."

"I have thought the same of mine."

"It would be good for her," Alice said with a firm nod. "Strange for me, but good for her."

"Of course it would be," Benjamin said. "But this has been far too much talk about our mothers."

"Oh?" Alice raised an eyebrow. "What did you have in mind?"

"Well, we only have a few minutes until we arrive at the house," Benjamin said, smiling wickedly. "We should make them count."

"I am open to suggestions," Alice returned.

"How is it that all of your books end?" he asked, lifting her up and onto his lap.

She smiled into his lips as she tilted her head down toward him.

"Happily ever after."

"And so they did," Benjamin said.

And they sealed the words with a kiss.

THE END

* * *

Dear reader,

I so hope you enjoyed reading Alice and Benjamin's story in *Writing the Rake*! After all that happened to Madeline, you might be wondering if she could ever have her own happily ever after? You can find out in the next book, and start chapter one in the pages just after this, or you can download it right here.

If you have been following along, then you know that in most of my author's notes in this series, I tell you about my research, and what historical figure the story was based upon.

Well, this is not my first writer heroine, but Alice is my first novelist. She is based on a few historical figures, including Jane Austen, but also much of her work and inner dialogue regarding her craft comes from my own experience, which made this book extra special to write.

Don't forget to take a peek at Alice and Benjamin in the future in this extended epilogue.

If you haven't yet signed up for my newsletter, I would love to have you join us! You will receive Unmasking a Duke for free, as well as links to giveaways, sales, new releases, and stories about my coffee addiction, my struggle to keep my plants alive, and how much trouble one loveable wolf-lookalike dog can get into.

www.elliestclair.com/ellies-newsletter

Or you can join my Facebook group, Ellie St. Clair's Ever Afters, and stay in touch daily.

Until next time, happy reading!

* * *

Risking the Detective
The Bluestocking Scandals Book Six

She was swindled, ruined, and left for dead. She will take

back her life and her pride -- but she will never fall in love again.

Madeline Castleton was left a fool once, but she refuses to allow it to happen again. And so when she needs help, she reaches out to a man who has proven his trustworthiness -- Bow Street detective Drake.

Drake, however, does not have the time nor the inclination to look into the foolish imaginings of a woman who is just afraid of her shadow. Her father left the stone company in her hands, but perhaps they are simply less than capable. He has his own concerns -- namely, following a clue that just might help him solve his parents' murders.

But when one misfortune after another befall Madeline and Castleton Stone, Drake begins to realize that she just might be right, and he finds that he cannot say no -- to her offer of payment nor to the woman herself. The more time the two of them spend together, the harder it is for them to deny that "never' might not be as absolute as they thought.

AN EXCERPT FROM RISKING THE DETECTIVE

CHAPTER ONE

"*T*ake a seat, Miss Castleton."

Madeline straightened her spine as rigidly as she could.

She would not be cowed. Not today. Not anymore.

"As this is my office, Mr. Drake, I would invite *you* to sit."

He raised his eyebrows and she got the impression that he was passing some judgment upon her, although he didn't say anything that would belie what was lurking beyond those dark, expressionless eyes.

The silent battle of wills did not last long, for it seemed Mr. Drake soon realized that he would gain nothing by fighting her.

It was a new state of affairs for Madeline. A small step, but one that was immeasurably important.

He sat. As did she, across from, behind the desk that formed a barrier between them, one that she appreciated more than she wanted to admit.

"Now, then," he said, folding his hands in his lap over the notebook that sat upon those impossible hard, rigid thighs she was doing her very best to ignore.

"Tell me, where were you last night between two and five in the morning?"

Madeline's eyebrows shot up at the question.

"Pardon me?"

He didn't react – no sigh, no deep breath, no sign of annoyance whatsoever. He simply repeated himself.

Madeline narrowed her eyes when he did.

"Mr. Drake, why are you here?"

"To investigate the vandalism in your warehouse, Miss Castleton. It was why you requested my presence."

He may not have shown any emotion, but Madeline couldn't help her annoyance at his explanation, as though she was not intelligent enough to understand the situation.

"Clearly," she said dryly. "However, I ask, Mr. Drake—"

"Drake. Just Drake."

"Drake, then. I ask, because I am unsure as to why my whereabouts would be important."

"The whereabouts of everyone involved in this case are important."

"Mr. Dr—Drake, *I* asked you here."

"There have been many times that we detectives have been summoned by the very person who perpetrated the crime."

Madeline rubbed the crease between her eyes, unable to keep her expression as voided as the detective in front of her.

"Alice said you could help."

"I can."

"Then why—"

"Miss Castleton," he said, leaning forward, his eyes probing into her. "It is my turn to ask you – why did you call me here?"

"To determine who is trying to destroy my business, quite obviously."

"Your father's business."

She sighed quietly, not wanting him to detect her impatience.

"It is my father's business, yes, but he has entrusted it to me while he is away at Bath."

"With the mother of your friend, the lovely Mrs. Luxington."

She shot him a look as a streak of surprise sliced through her.

"Do you know everything?"

"I try to make it my business to," he replied, the slightest hint of smugness tightening his lips, the first bit of emotion she had seen from him throughout this encounter.

"Well. No matter who he is with," she said, drawing herself up and forcing what she hoped was some confidence to her face. "He always intended that I take over the business, anyway. This seemed to be a good time for a trial."

"Ah," he said, a dawning raining over his features which were far too dark and mysterious for his own good, "that is why this is of such great importance to you. Because it could cause your father to lose confidence in your ability to look after Castleton Stone."

"Mr. Drake," she began, taking a breath. If she was going to be the head of this business, she had to begin acting like it.

"Drake."

"*Drake*," she repeated, her frustration now clear. Why did he have to be so contrary? "Why I called you here does not matter. What matters is that I *did* call you here, and that it is your job to determine what has occurred. I can assure you that there is no reason whatsoever for me to have played any part in this. So could we please move on to finding the true culprit?"

"That is all well and good, Miss Castleton, but in order for me to solve this crime, I must be able to determine anything of importance that occurred at the time of the issue. Now, would you like me to do my *job*, as you say?"

"Of course," she said quietly, feeling somewhat foolish that she had challenged him so.

"You did not ask me here to pity you, did you?"

"*Pity* me?" she said, her exclaim harsher than she had intended.

She didn't have to ask just why he would pity her. She already knew. He knew. Everyone knew.

"Yes. Everyone else does, do they not?"

She dipped her head. Her stupidity, her naivety would follow her around for the rest of her life. This detective's opinion shouldn't matter, and yet she couldn't help the shame that washed over her at the awareness of what he likely thought of her.

He was intelligent enough to solve crimes that perplexed most, while she hadn't even been able to figure out that the man who claimed to be Lord Donning had actually conned her into marriage only to steal her dowry, before attempting to poison her to death to inherit all of her wealth.

"It was not your fault, Miss Castleton," Drake said now, his voice surprisingly gentle, causing her to snap her head back up to look at him. "You were not the first woman to be conned by Kurt Maxfeld – known to you as Lord Stephen Donning – but, fortunately, you will be the last."

"Thanks to Alice," Madeline murmured.

"You showed great bravery as well," Drake said, but Madeline couldn't meet his gaze. She knew he was just doing his job, playing the sympathetic detective. She had done nothing that denoted any bravery whatsoever. She had fled. She had hid. Meanwhile, her friend had caught the man who had ruined her life.

"We are not here to discuss Lord Donning – or Kurt Maxfeld or whatever his name is," Madeline said, not being able to bear the topic any longer. "We are here to discuss my business."

"Your father's business," he corrected her once more, and Madeline had to take a deep breath to keep herself from telling him exactly what she thought of his small barbed comments.

"Very well, Miss Castleton," he said, his knee bouncing ever so slightly as he crossed an ankle over the other knee, "will you tell me, then, where you were last night between two and five in the morning?"

She closed her eyes for but a moment to regain her focus.

"I was at home," she said. "Reading."

Finally it seemed that she had captured his attention. "Reading, you say? You were not sleeping?"

"I was not," she said, shaking her head. "I find it difficult to sleep after… last year."

"When you were nearly poisoned to death," he said, not seeming to understand the implication that she would prefer not to speak of it. "I suppose that would cause someone to be afraid to go to sleep."

"I am not afraid," she said softly. "I just… I dream when I sleep. Nightmares, I suppose you can say. It is much easier to stay awake all night."

"If only it were possible to live without sleep," he said, and she couldn't tell whether or not he was making fun of her. "Was anyone in the house with you?"

"I have an aunt who lives with us," she explained. "My father's older sister. She never married and came to live with us when my mother passed. She was home but was in bed by nine o'clock. I did not see her nor speak to her until morning. We also have a live-in maid who—" her cheeks flushed slightly as she was about to say that the maid helped her undress. "Who helped me prepare for the night to come before she retired herself."

"I see," he murmured, his eyebrows raising ever-so-slightly at the discussion of her nightly activities. "Very good, then. You were nowhere near Castleton Stone?"

"Not after five o'clock. Why are you continuing to question me about this?" she couldn't help but ask.

"We've discussed this. That is my job."

"I am not a suspect, Mr. Drake. This is my business."

"I never said you were a suspect."

"Then why are you treating me as one?"

He leaned forward in the chair toward her, and she wished that he didn't unnerve her. He was taller than her, his shoulders broad, but he was not an overly large man. There was just something about him... something that she couldn't quite describe but that was so mysterious, so intimidating, that it took everything within her to keep from shrinking back away from him and his dark, piercing stare that seemed to only ask questions without providing any answers in return.

"I just find it interesting, Miss Castleton, that the moment you take more control of this business, it is put into jeopardy."

She dropped her gaze.

"I would assume that my father's rivals are taking advantage of his absence."

"And the fact that he left a woman in charge."

Madeline eyed him again.

"Are you condemning him for doing so?"

He sat back now, assessing her as though her response held much interest for him.

"It is not for me to judge, Miss Castleton. Simply observe. And my observations tell me that most men would see a woman at the helm of a business to have weakened it."

Madeline nodded. "I am aware of the fact."

Drake opened his mouth, likely about to ask Madeline another question about motive this time perhaps, but was prevented from continuing by a new presence.

"I say, that is quite enough."

They both turned in unison to find her cousin standing at the doorway. His familiar presence caused relief to wash over her. She had hoped he would be here for this particular interview – if there was ever a rock in this family, it was Bennett.

"And you are…"

Drake was clearly not impressed, perhaps because he could no longer continue his bullying with another man, part of her family, in the room.

"Bennett Castleton," he said, his disdain for Drake apparent as his pinched nose somehow elongated as he stared down it at the detective. "Miss Castleton's cousin. It appears, sir, that you have upset her and I would ask you to leave."

Sensing the tension that immediately filled the air of the office, Madeline stood and crossed over to her cousin, placing a hand on his arm.

"It's all right, Bennett," she said quietly. "I called him here."

"*You* did?" he said, his voice registering shock as he stared at her, mouth agape. "But why?"

"Because half of our warehouse was *vandalized*," she said, wishing they were not having this argument, as slight as it was, in front of Drake. "We need to determine who did it and why, so that we can regain control of the business."

"And you think *he* can help us?" Bennett asked, tilting his head over toward Drake.

Madeline took a breath, suddenly wondering if Bennett's presence was so good after all.

"I hope he can. He is from the Bow Street detectives."

"The runners?" Bennett questioned.

"We prefer the term detectives," Drake responded from where he still sat, no hint of malice in his voice.

"Very well, then," Bennett said with a deep breath. "Find out who did this to our stone. But please do not cause my cousin to feel any further guilt for what happened. She has been working tireless since my uncle Ezra left for Bath."

"Why would she feel guilt, Mr. Castleton?" Drake asked, and Madeline had to restrain herself from rolling her eyes.

"I shall be fine, Bennett," she said softly. "We do not have much more to speak of." She looked over at Drake, who was watching her in turn. "At least not today."

Bennett looked back and forth between the two of them until finally, apparently satisfied, he pulled up a chair from the wood table and sat down upon it next to the wall.

Drake eyed him, until Bennett held up a hand.

"I shall say nothing. I am here to observe, and to offer my support when necessary."

"What type of support might you require, Miss Castleton?"

"I—"

Madeline was about to respond that she didn't actually need any, but Bennett interrupted once more.

"Well, now, Drake, you are aware of all that happened to Madeline a few months back, are you not?"

Madeline could only hope that her look toward him conveyed her wish that he not speak of it any longer. She and Drake had only just gotten past the topic of conversation.

Now Drake turned and stared at Madeline instead.

"Do you require assistance in regard to the actions of Maxfeld?"

"No," she said, unable to help the rush of gratefulness at being addressed directly. "I shall be fine. Although I thank you, Bennett, for your offer."

"Now, Madeline," Bennett began, but Drake quickly moved on, ignoring her cousin.

"Miss Castleton, if you are so convinced that Castleton Stone's rivals are at fault, why do you not tell me of them?" he asked, and Madeline sighed, relieved at the turn of the conversation to something that was not only focused on her, but could actually lead to a determination of the culprit.

"There is another stone company that has been a rival to ours for a number of years – Treacle Stone," she explained. "At the helm is a man named Jeremiah Treacle. He has recently inherited the business from his father, who now serves in an advisory role. While Mr. Treacle, the elder, and my father have always had a great deal of respect for one another, Mr. Jeremiah Treacle does not seem to have any qualms in putting his business's success over any relationship. I would suggest starting there."

"Absolutely," Bennett said, nodding his head in the corner. "Treacle. It has to be. Why, I would—"

"Thank you, Miss Castleton, Mr. Castleton," Drake said, straightening his black coat with its gold buttons as he rose. Madeline's fingers strangely itched to reach out and feel the gold buttons to see if they were as smooth as they looked from here. The sunlight through the window bounced in and glanced off of them, making her squint.

"When will you go?" she asked, standing herself, straightening her dress.

"When I am able to," he said cryptically, and she had the feeling that he was dismissing her. "Good day, Miss Castleton."

She had a feeling that he was dismissing her, that, to him, this tiny act of vandalism in her warehouse meant nothing, and that if he did follow up, it would not be with any true level of importance.

"May I accompany you when you do?" she forced herself

to call after him, and he stopped, turned around, and shook his head with a benevolent smile.

"I will come, as well!" Bennett added, holding a finger in the air.

"I am the detective here, Miss Castleton," Drake said, turning around and looking at her from over his shoulder. "You are a stone manufacturer. I will focus on my job. You should focus on yours."

And with that dismissal, he was out the door, leaving her with her fists at her side, her lips tight together, and shame in her heart.

Keep reading Risking the Detective here!

ALSO BY ELLIE ST. CLAIR

A Time to Love

A Time to Dream

Thieves of Desire

The Art of Stealing a Duke's Heart

A Jewel for the Taking

A Prize Worth Fighting For

Gambling for the Lost Lord's Love

Romance of a Robbery

Blooming Brides

A Duke for Daisy

A Marquess for Marigold

An Earl for Iris

A Viscount for Violet

The Blooming Brides Box Set: Books 1-4

Happily Ever After

The Duke She Wished For

Someday Her Duke Will Come

Once Upon a Duke's Dream

He's a Duke, But I Love Him

Loved by the Viscount

Because the Earl Loved Me

Happily Ever After Box Set Books 1-3

Happily Ever After Box Set Books 4-6

The Victorian Highlanders

Duncan's Christmas - (prequel)

Callum's Vow

Finlay's Duty

Adam's Call

Roderick's Purpose

Peggy's Love

The Victorian Highlanders Box Set Books 1-5

Searching Hearts

Duke of Christmas (prequel)

Quest of Honor

Clue of Affection

Hearts of Trust

Hope of Romance

Promise of Redemption

Searching Hearts Box Set (Books 1-5)

Standalones

Always Your Love

The Stormswept Stowaway

A Touch of Temptation

Christmastide with His Countess

Her Christmas Wish

Merry Misrule

A Match Made at Christmas

For a full list of all of Ellie's books, please see
www.elliestclair.com/books.

ABOUT THE AUTHOR

Ellie has always loved reading, writing, and history. For many years she has written short stories, non-fiction, and has worked on her true love and passion -- romance novels.

In every era there is the chance for romance, and Ellie enjoys exploring many different time periods, cultures, and geographic locations. No matter when or where, love can always prevail. She has a particular soft spot for the bad boys of history, and loves a strong heroine in her stories.

Ellie and her husband love nothing more than spending time at home with their children and Husky cross. Ellie can typically be found at the lake in the summer, pushing the stroller all year round, and, of course, with her computer in her lap or a book in hand.

She also loves corresponding with readers, so be sure to contact her!

www.elliestclair.com
ellie@elliestclair.com

Printed in Dunstable, United Kingdom